A BRIDGE HOME

A BRIDGE HOME

MONA ALVARADO FRAZIER

PIÑATA BOOKS
ARTE PÚBLICO PRESS
HOUSTON, TEXAS

A Bridge Home is funded in part by the Alice Kleberg Reynolds Foundation National Endowment for the Arts and the Texas Commission on the Arts. We are grateful for their support.

Piñata Books are full of surprises!

Piñata Books
An imprint of
Arte Público Press
University of Houston
4902 Gulf Fwy, Bldg 19, Rm 100
Houston, Texas 77204-2004

Cover design by Mora Des!gn
Cover photo by Javier Pardina/Stocksy

Versa Press, Inc., East Peoria, IL
February 2024–April 2024

24 25 26   4 3 2 1

Dedicated to the fearless advocates and champions of equality, both past and present, who fight tirelessly to dismantle barriers and build bridges of understanding and acceptance. Your enduring commitment to justice and fairness serves as a beacon of hope for future generations.

CONTENTS

CHAPTER 1
FEBRUARY 1972

The door swings open. Heads swivel right. The new principal of St. Bernadette High lumbers into senior history, stands at the head of the class and peers over her wire eyeglasses like an over-sized owl draped in a black tunic.

"Good afternoon, Sister Mary Grace," thirty voices say.

She nods, "Students."

Her bulk grows as she shuffles to the last row of seats, a grimace on her face. Sweat dampens my underarms.

Sister stares down at me. "Jacqueline Bravo, come to my office immediately after class."

The red brick administration building resembles a gothic cathedral more than a high school with its stained-glass windows, pillars and arches. Stone statues of saints and white rosebushes border the kneeling figure of St. Bernadette in the courtyard. The surrounding classrooms cast shadows over the area. The old place reeks of damp brick and wet dirt.

In grammar school, I learned St. Bernadette was the oldest in her family, the patron saint of poverty, and her middle name was Marie, like mine. All similarities end there unless I begin seeing visions of the Virgin Mary.

1

The closer I come to Sister Mary Grace's office, the tighter my shoulders shrink. There's nothing to be nervous about since I can't think of anything I've done wrong.

I brush off my burgundy blazer, straighten my pleated skirt and push open the heavy glass door to the school office. A small bell with a sign says, "Ring Once." I set my books on the long counter and tap the bell. Mrs. Jasper, the school secretary, jerks her head up. Her blonde flip hairdo doesn't budge. I guess that's why the students call her Helmet Head.

"Um. Sister Mary Grace said to come to see her?"

"You may go in, Jacqui." Mrs. Jasper waves her hand to the open door on her left.

The office is three times the size of my old elementary school. Better scent too. Lemon oil from the polished bookcases and mahogany desk lingers in the room. An enameled letter opener sits on one side of the desk, with immaculately labeled folders on the right.

Sister hangs up the shiny black telephone, motions to the chair. "Sit, Miss Bravo." Her cold voice is an order. She clasps her veiny hands on the desk and leans forward until the silver crucifix around her neck clanks against the edge.

I sink into the leather seat, grip the carved arms. A shudder runs through my chest.

"I understand your mother is a St. Bernadette alumnus and these are difficult times for your family, *but* we must have a payment on your tuition. February is the third month you're overdue. St. Bernadette has a *huge* waiting list."

Overdue? My teeth clench along with my shoulders, but I manage a tight smile. The transparent blueness of Sister's eyes focuses on me like she's trying to force me to explain.

I don't understand why my tuition isn't paid. Mom didn't say a word to me. "There must be a mistake."

"No. No error." Her thick finger thuds on the desk three times. "We called your mother two weeks ago, but no one answered. We mailed a reminder letter last week and haven't heard from her yet. The bill comes to one hundred and fifty dollars. When can we expect payment?"

The amount is a fist to my stomach. I fold into the chair, hoping to miraculously disappear. What happened to the hundred bucks Mom had in the cigar box in December? I just gave her fifty bucks last month—my entire pay. I shift my eyes to the carpeted floor, the ceiling, anywhere but Sister's piercing stare. My bottom lip quivers until I clamp my mouth shut.

"Miss Bravo, pay attention," her voice booms. "You are not taking this seriously. Perhaps a transfer to a public school is in order because of your circumstances."

"No way."

Her eyes blink a warning. I take a deep breath and fill my stomach with one of Dad's sayings: *Don't let them see you sweat.*

"Sister, I need to stay at St. Bernadette. This is the best school for me, and the UCLA alumnus scholarship is important. We'll come up with the money. I promise."

"College is expensive. A much more realistic avenue would be a vocational school. Someplace to learn secretarial or vocational skills until you are married."

Married? Vocational? St. Bernadette is a college prep school. Beads of perspiration make their way down my forehead.

"My mom started a new job. An office one. She'll pay the tuition soon."

Sister's lined face relaxes. "Good news. But if we don't have the bill paid by March first, you'll have to transfer."

That's twenty-eight days from now. I bite down on my lip. Hard. The sharp sensation travels across my face and stops the tears threatening to flood my eyes. Mom's first paycheck can't pay the entire bill *and* our rent.

Sister removes an envelope from a folder labeled *Jacqueline Bravo*. "Here's another letter. Hand deliver it to your mother."

The odor of wet wool from my sweaty blazer rises to my nose. Sister's thin-lipped smile makes me want to gag. Don't cry. Breathe. She stands, motions to the door without taking her hand out of her pocket like a giant bat spreading its wings.

I stumble into my sixth-period English class, my head full of questions about my late tuition. My future rides on that scholarship, and I'm not transferring out of here in my senior year.

All conversation stops as Ms. Fine, my favorite teacher, enters the room in super bell jeans and a yellow frilly blouse. Both are a huge no-no at St. Bernadette High, but I've noticed she's ditched her long black sweater and slacks for more colorful outfits in the past couple of months. But flares and a yellow blouse? She's living dangerously now.

She grabs a piece of chalk, writes *Ms.* on the blackboard. "Class, I'm changing how you can address me. Instead of Mrs., I'd like you to call me *Ms.* Fine." Her red lipstick grin stretches from one silver hoop earring to the other—another no-no.

Murmurs rise through the classroom. "Miz?" "Like Gloria Steinem?" "Radical."

We don't have a Ms. anybody at school. The lady lay teachers are Miss or Mrs. The male teachers are Mister. They wear old people's clothes. And Sister Mary Grace isn't going to like the new Ms. Fine. I bet Sister tells her she'll go to hell for calling herself Ms.

"Using my new prefix will take a bit, but times are changing," she says. "Take out your pens for a quiz. Jacqui, hand these out, please."

I'm Ms. Fine's helper, and I like that because she's always helping me out with stuff. She's talked to me about college and my future since I was a sophomore.

At the first desk, I slap a sheet of paper down. The kissing sounds from the back begin. "Smack," someone says. You'd think I'd be used to the juvenile comments about being a brown noser, but this is bearable because, in the last row, the middle chair is Petey Castro. The closer I move to his desk, the more I pray I don't trip on my big feet or drop the papers in my hand.

"Your quiz."

I slide the sheet on his desk while breathing in the strong scent of his Irish Spring soap. He must have showered after gym class because his thick hair is lined with comb marks and glistening with hair cream. I imagine moving one of those deep brown waves off his forehead. He raises his chin ever so slightly, but enough so my stomach flutters when he smiles. I tuck my trembling fingers under the hem of my blazer. Act cool.

"Hey, snap out of it," Larry says from the desk next to Petey.

Laughter surrounds me. My throat chokes up like I ate a jalapeño from Mom's salsa. *Damn that, Larry*. I slam the paper down on his desk and move on.

"Petey, don't you think Jacqui looks like Angela Cartwright from *Lost in Space*? She acts like she's lost in orbit."

His snorts are like a hail of rocks. I freeze. My cheeks flush hot. "Shut up, Lunkhead Larry, I'm amazed you're even cognizant of the word *orbit*. You dumb jock."

"Jacqui, it's just a joke. Lighten up," Petey says. "Why you gotta be so serious?"

"You're defending Larry? You wouldn't be here if it weren't for that sports scholarship, Pay-droh. And don't go acting like a rich guy. You live in the housing projects too."

"Jacqui, back to your seat and begin," Miss Fine says. "Margot Sanders and Jacqui, come see me when you turn in your quiz."

Ten minutes later, I finish and doodle inside my Pee Chee folder. I'm deep into daydreams about Petey until I catch Margot Sanders slink a long leg out of her seat. My cue. I hustle up to Ms. Fine's desk first. Margot rolls her eyes behind her John Lennon eyeglasses and flicks her wavy red hair behind her back.

"Good news. You both qualify for the scholarship." Ms. Fine waves two sheets of paper.

A wealthy alumnus sponsors the one-year scholarship to the University of California in Los Angeles. None of the public schools have anything like this award. UCLA is my number one college choice, and winning the prize is my chance to make it out of San Solano. I'll be able to live at college where cousin Bebe says, 'You're free to think as you want, to question authority and do your own thing.'

Margot reaches around my shoulder, takes the papers from Ms. Fine and hands me a sheet. *Autobiography and Scholarship Essay Questions are due March 30*th.

"Reference your college applications," Ms. Fine says. "Easy-peasy, right?"

"Sure, no prob. I keep all my records." Margot pivots and returns to her seat.

She's prepared, of course. I hear she has a private tutor. She probably has a secretary to copy and file all her schoolwork. If my parents owned the biggest department store in the city, we could afford all that too. I don't have a typewriter and need to figure out how to accomplish this before the deadline. I work after school, and I study when I'm not working. I'm taking care of my siblings when I'm not doing that.

"Uh. . . Ms. Fine, I don't have copies. I didn't know anyone with a copy machine."

She leaps to her feet, her shoes clacking on the floor to the filing cabinet. Bright red painted toenails peek out of her Candie slides. Ms. Fine doesn't care about fitting in.

"Here," she says and hands me the forms. "We'll go over your essay answers at the end of the week. I know you can do it."

Yeah, if I'm still at St. Bernie by the end of the week. I need to think of something quick to ensure that happens.

CHAPTER 2

Smack. The cold bedsheet and the stink of bleach sting my nose—a wet reminder of my little brother's problem. I drop the laundry basket beneath the clothesline and snap open the clothespins. The sheet flaps and brings me a memory. Dad holding up his arms, his shadow growing more prominent as he lumbered toward me like Frankenstein and growled. I'd pretend to scream until he scooped me up in his arms while Mom giggled and snapped a towel at him. The memory disappears into the plain white cloth.

The early morning chill cramps my fingers. I fasten the other clothespin on the corner of the sheet, which stands out like a big white sign that everything's changed.

"Your brother is a pee-pee boy." The neighbor kid appears at the chain-link fence and pinches his stubby nose.

"Da. . . ," I shout, until my mouth freezes. I can't call him. Not anymore. I swallow the rest of the word. The ache in my chest swells until my chin starts to tremble.

"He pees the bed, hahaha," the kid taunts, pointing at me through the fence.

"Shut up." I give him a rigid middle finger.

"Jacqueline Bravo, I saw that," Mom yells out the open kitchen window. "Is that what they teach you at Saint Bernadette?"

"But did you hear what he said?"

I trudge back into our kitchen and find Mom adjusting her pantyhose, like those are more important than the kid's remarks.

"He's seven, and you're seventeen." Her shoulders droop as low as her sigh and the corner of her eyes. "Go shower and finish making breakfast. *Ándale*."

Why can't she say thank you for washing the sheet? Or for speaking up for my brother? I run upstairs and slam the bathroom door. I can't believe I called for Dad, as if he was inside the house having breakfast. Like he was still here and today was a typical day. I click on the radio and shower. The pain in my chest sinks deeper until I can't breathe. Until I'm choking on my tears.

The radio announcer's voice bellows over the running water, "Still on the charts this February, What's Going On." Under the nozzle, I drench myself while Marvin Gaye sings out *War is not the answer*. The lyrics make me cry harder. Some days, I'm fine. On other days, I'm a mess.

"Hurry up. I gotta wash my hair." Caroline bangs on the door like a fire broke out.

"We need to use the toilet," John and Bobby, the twins, yell as they double knock.

One bathroom for five people is the pits. Two bedrooms for five is worse. Mom and the boys share the bigger room while me and Caroline barely have enough space for twin beds in our room. But we didn't get a choice.

"Mom, Jacqui won't let me wash my hair." Her whiny voice fills the hallway.

"Damn, not five minutes of peace around here. And forget your stupid-ass hair."

"Mom! Jacqui's cussing." Caroline hits the door again. "You think you're all that just because you're a senior now?"

I fling open the door, step out into the hallway. "Damn right. I should have certain privileges over an eighth grader like you, you big whiner."

Mom stands behind Caroline with her pink slipper in her hand and a wild look in her eye. The boys and Caroline swivel their heads between us. Mom's never hit me, but she can throw a *chancla* like a pro pitcher.

"You're getting on my last nerve, Jacqueline."

Well, everything's on my nerves, I want to say. Instead, I beat it to my room, yank on my school uniform, the wool skirt making my thighs itch.

Downstairs, I find that Caroline hasn't done her job. Eight pieces of white bread topped with limp bologna lay across the kitchen counter, waiting to be packed. I heat the *comal* for tortillas and mix water into the bowl of powdered eggs.

"Mom kicked me out of the bathroom." Caroline pokes her head over my shoulder, wet hair dripping on me as she plugs the hairdryer into the outlet near the stove. "She's super nervous about work."

The dryer roars into my ear while she moves the plastic nozzle over her long hair. Good thing I have a pixie cut. Shorter hair makes it faster to get ready, and I need every minute.

She pokes her nose in the bowl. "Needs more water. Keep stirring."

"I can mix these government eggs until kingdom comes, and they'll still taste like rubber. Now move away." I elbow her. "That's all we need, hair in the eggs. Mom will have a cow." I wrap the piping hot tortillas in a dish towel. "Everybody, come eat."

The twins clamber into the kitchen, stop short when they see the pile of pale-yellow scrambled eggs with a few beige cubes of Spam.

"Again? Those eggs taste like rubber. Yuck," John sticks out his tongue. "Why can't we ever have good cereal like Sugar Smacks?"

Bobby grabs the silver gallon container of peanut butter from the fridge, heaves it onto the table. Light glints off the USDA badge on the front of the can. Another reminder of change.

Homework in folders and house key in my pocket, I herd the boys like stray billy goats to the front door. After a last-minute comb through Bobby's thick unruly hair, I make sure their uniform shirts are tucked in and their black shoes shined.

Mom stops in the living room like she does every day. She makes the sign of the cross on herself beneath the grouped portraits of Jesus, the Pope, John F. Kennedy and Dad in his Army uniform. She wears a cute navy dress and shiny black pumps. All she needs is one of those silky neck scarves to look like Mary Tyler Moore on TV.

"Where'd you get that new outfit?" Caroline asks.

"*Segunda*," Mom says.

She twitches her shoulders. "Rich people's hand-me-downs."

We head to our rickety station wagon and pile inside. Caroline doesn't call shotgun anymore because she doesn't want to ride in the front seat of a car that looks like a brown hearse with faded wood trim.

"Jacqueline, give me my can." Mom adjusts the rearview mirror.

I unknot the shoestring that keeps the glove compartment closed and hand her the red can of Aqua Net. The hairspray spritzes out, dribbles on the side of the container. Empty. She tosses it aside and sticks the key in the ignition. Nothing. The engine moans. After the third try and a Hail Mary, it turns over with a kick.

The radio announcer blares as the motor warms. "For the third straight quarter, unemployment is up. Gasoline prices are climbing higher. We're headed for a recession, folks."

Mom clicks off the radio and steers the car onto the street. "Caroline, ask for Jacqueline's old babysitting job, now that she's working for Petra."

"The lady's husband's out of work. That's why Jacqui's not there anymore."

"Well, look for something."

The car stops with a jerk in front of St. Patrick's Church. The boys scramble out of the car, wave goodbye and run across the empty parking lot into the adjoining school grounds. Mom uses the time to brush mascara on her lashes. Caroline steps out of the car and uses the distraction to roll up her waist-band, making her skirt two inches shorter, like she's done since sixth grade.

We fly down the main street of our barrio, which isn't busy because most parents go to work super early like Mom used to until her big break. She steps on the gas to get over the railroad tracks before the train backs up the traffic. The red blinking lights of the railroad sign flash ahead. She jerks to a stop.

"Mom, don't forget to pay the water bill at lunchtime."

"I know." She glares at me when I hand her the bill, but we both know she'd be pissed if I didn't remind her.

I hate bringing up the letter from Sister Mary Grace. Mom will bite my head off. Maybe tomorrow when she's calmer.

"The city should do something about this train. Always holding up everyone."

Mom drums her fingers against the steering wheel while the train lurches on the tracks. The schedule is so unpredictable that we never know when to cross the tracks.

"Especially the ambulances. Cousin Bebe said a committee is asking the city council to make another street out of here or to build a bridge."

"Pfft," Mom rolls her eyes. "A group of her *Chicano* friends?"

Bebe and Chicanos are a sore spot for Mom. Uncle Mario, Mom's older brother, said Bebe changed from a sweet, responsible daughter to a radical when she joined a student group in college. My uncle's a nice guy, but so traditional. He allowed her to go to the community college, but after a year, Bebe left town to attend a university two hours away. He threw a fit. He doesn't like the idea of his only daughter living alone. People talk.

"She and her friends protested the war. *Desgraciados.* Those men died for their country, and those long-hairs protest?" She snorts.

"It's *because* people are dying. Bebe says the United States shouldn't be in. . ."

Mom's glassy eyes widen. "Are you saying your dad shouldn't have gone? That he died for nothing? Huh?"

I shake my head and murmur, "I didn't mean that."

"Those Brown Berets calling themselves 'Chicanos'. . . we're Mexican-American." She turns to me. "You know, with the dash in the middle."

"Hyphen, not dash."

"Don't be a smart-ass. You understand what I mean."

"Bebe doesn't feel like she's Mexican because she was born in LA, but she's not American either," I explain. "She's from both places. She says the hyphen splits her in two. Calling herself a Chicana keeps her whole."

Makes sense to me. Most of the time, I don't feel half of anything only pieces of many things. I'm the kid before Dad left for Vietnam, the kid when he was gone and the kid when he died. Now, after his death, the pieces aren't half of anything.

Mom sucks her teeth and guns the motor when the caboose clears the track. "That university put those communist ideas in her head. Marching. We're supposed to fit in, not stand out."

The tires bounce over the rails to the north side of town, the rich part and St. Bernadette High School. I've struggled to fit in since I began at that school.

"Not everyone wants to fit in, Mom. Sometimes, we need to challenge things, like my teacher, Miss Fine, told us. César Chávez and Martin Luther King Junior believed in non-violent protest to change things. They weren't Communists."

"Don't argue with me. Don't you dare become involved with Chicanos."

I don't want to make matters worse by pushing the argument. Mom has too much on her mind already. Bebe says we need to insist on change to make things better. I like improving the train situation, but I can't imagine demanding anything. No one ever listens to me.

Our station wagon jolts to a stop near my school. "Don't tell Bebe about your job with Petra. Your *tío* Mario can't find out."

If my uncle finds out I'm working as a cleaning lady at night, he'll make sure Mom takes me out of St. Bernadette before I get kicked out. If he had his way, we'd all attend public school so Mom could continue working part-time. He believes mothers must stay home, like Aunt Bernice and his mother. God rest their souls. That was fine for them but not for Mom, not for us.

"Don't worry. He won't find out our secret."

CHAPTER 3

The late tuition, scholarship questions and March dead-lines crowd my mind like buzzing flies while I ride the city bus. The bus lumbers toward the terminal, where I connect to another route that runs through my neighborhood.

A swarm of tired women, smelling of pine cleaner and wet sponges, board and drop down heavily onto the seats. One of the ladies is our neighbor, Petra. Mom's family grew up in San Solano, and her parents were friends with Petra. May they rest in peace. She returns home for a couple of hours before she and I head to our night job.

The bus driver revs the motor, shuts the door before everyone sits down. He's trying to beat the four o'clock train, which comes anywhere from three-thirty to four-fifteen. Petra's weary eyes droop like her loose black ponytail, while she jostles down the aisle carrying bulging bags in her red-spotted hands.

"Sit here." I scoop up my blazer and stack of books from the seat next to me.

She drops with a thud, sets her sack of cleaning supplies on the floor between her scuffed shoes. Her entire body sighs.

"Remember we start at five o'clock *mañana*, no more six." Petra's forehead scrunches, and her eyes turn down. "How's your *mamá* doing?"

"Good. She started that new county job."

Petra makes the sign of the cross and kisses her thumb. "*Gracias a Dios*. Your poor *mamá* has had such a hard time."

I sigh and nod my head. Our whole life changed when Dad died. Our house, friends, the food we eat, the clothes we buy, everything shifted like an earthquake tossed us up from one place to another, leaving us dizzy and scared. The only area unchanged is the schools we attend.

Most of our neighbors know Dad died in Vietnam two years ago, but they don't bring it up, and we don't talk about what happened. It makes me sad when I think how much Mom misses him. But I can't contemplate that right now.

We're in luck: no train delays. The bus jiggles over the rails and into our neighborhood. Graffiti covers the billboard advertising Marlboro cigarettes and the Marlboro cowboy.

San Solano is two places, like two towns. On the east side of the tracks sits our barrio, a maze of narrow, pot-holed streets, a few stores, tiny homes and government housing projects. On the other side of the tracks, the streets spread out with multi-story buildings and large houses with grassy front lawns. Those neighborhoods have their parks filled with leafy trees and working playground equipment.

The bus plods past the new Mini-Mart a couple of blocks after the train tracks. Even though it's February and sixty degrees outside, a couple of guys stand on the corner in white T-shirts and khaki pants, like it is an eighty-degree summer. At one end of the parking lot, older men in faded black leather jackets and tan polyester slacks crouch while they play craps. A couple of women in mini-skirts and furry jackets lean against the stucco wall of the liquor store. Their eyes dart up and down the street while they twirl bleached hair between their fingers.

"Jacqui, college is gonna help you do something good with your life, not like those *borrachas*." Petra points to the women.

"They don't look drunk. Maybe they're waiting for their boyfriends or husbands."

She shakes her head. "But you, you gonna help your *mamá* and do good things."

I hope so.

The bus rolls to a stop on the corner of Loli's Panadería. The door opens to the sugary scents of the yeasty sweet bread. *La señora* Loli is everyone's grandmother in our neighborhood. Every Friday, she bakes and gives away *pan dulce* to kids who show her a test with a B or better grade.

"You lucky you go to St. Bernadette and not that public school. They had a stabbing in the bathroom. *Imagínate.* And the *drogas, válgame Dios.* My *comadre's* grandkids, they told her."

Yeah, I can imagine that happening. The high school is over-crowded, and two rival gangs go there. Two reasons for me to stay at St. Bernie, and for my brothers and sister to stay at St. Patrick. We're safer there. Plus, I can't stand another change in my life.

The bus lurches past the Aztec warrior's mural on the side wall of Hermanos Market. The bright colors liven up the beige building with the image of jade mountains, a blazing golden sun and a black jaguar. Mr. Reyes and his brothers, who own the store, allowed a couple of guys to paint their walls. A few dads didn't like the image of the bare-chested muscled Aztec, so the artist added a big-busted Aztec woman, which pissed off the *abuelas.* But everyone likes the Hermanos. Mr. Reyes lets Mom run a tab up to five dollars.

"My stop." I pull on the bell cord.

"*Adiós*, Jacqui." Petra waves. "*Mañana.* Five o'clock, we start work."

The bus wobbles to a halt before the door hiccups open, letting in a murky cloud of noxious smoke. I skip down the steps. The wind picks up, sending dry eucalyptus leaves scurrying around my feet in circles. Smatterings of raindrops fall. The crush of leaves releases a pungent menthol stench as I sprint the last two blocks to my brothers' and sister's schools.

When I attended St. Patrick, Dad worked as a mechanic on the Air Force base nearby, and Mom helped out in the classrooms. She drove us home every day.

I never noticed how shabby St. Patrick Elementary looked until I attended St. Bernadette across town. The dingy white one-story building is surrounded by asphalt and patchy grass. First through eighth grade are contained in one long building resembling Army barracks. The place is the poor step-brother to my school.

Bobby waits under the covered patio. His thin arms wrap around his narrow chest. It makes me cold to watch him. His lips press together like Mom's when she's worried. Something's up. He waves at me. "The principal wants to talk to you." His eleven-year-old shoulders drown in his hand-me-down navy blazer. "I dunno why."

It could be that Sister George wants to ask how I'm doing. We always got along when I attended St. Patrick. She's the one who encouraged me to attend St. Bernadette High and aim for college.

"Go find the others and bring them to the office."

Bobby takes off running, yelling for John and Caroline. Inside the building, pictures of Pope Paul and a green-robed St. Patrick line the wall near the school office. These photos have been there for years.

"Hey," Caroline bumps my arm with her flowered tote bag. "Why do we need to go to the office?"

"Don't know. Bobby said the principal wants to talk to me."

We step into the cramped waiting room together. The stink of hairspray and heavy perfume fills the small space. Mrs. Candelaria, the secretary, still sports a sixties beehive hairdo, stiff as a rock. Her black-lined eyes narrow as her red lips purse.

"If it isn't the Mexican Kennedys." Her fleshy shoulders roll with her snicker as she points to the principal's door with one hand and continues typing with the other. "Just Jacqui."

"Oh, brother," Caroline says. "Come on, guys."

They split into the hallway. I knock at the slightly open door.

"Please, come inside." Sister George is polishing an empty bookcase and no longer wearing a nun's habit.

"Sister?"

"Oh, yes, I'm changing with the times." She sticks her hands in the pockets of her long blue cardigan, which matches her navy midi skirt and shoes. "What do you think?"

"I like the new outfit."

I don't tell her I'm surprised because only the new nuns wear regular clothes, and she's been around St. Patrick for ages. She does look younger, though.

"Have a seat. I'm redecorating my office."

A metal table stacked with books lines one wall, and silver filing cabinets are against the other. Dust motes float in the lemony air. Photos of graduating classes from 1945 to 1971 run across the wall next to me.

"There you are." Sister taps on the eighth-grade class of 1968 and one when I received the scholarship for the first year at St. Bernadette. "And there's your mother." She points at the 1950 graduation photo I've seen several times before. "Both of you, bright students."

She clears a space on her desk, moving worn brown folders aside. My pulse speeds up when she presses her fingertips against each other. She slides a manila envelope across the table. Her almond-colored eyes, usually soft and warm, have a twinge of embarrassment.

The heading on the front, *Monthly Tuition,* glares at me in thick black type. The January and February 1972 areas are blank. The last column stamped paid is November.

"Just an oversight, I'm sure," she says. "Perhaps Caroline forgot to give the payment envelope to your mother. Is everything okay at home?"

My headache creeps back, reaching the base of my neck with gnarled fingers digging into my skin. Why tell Sister that Mom's struggling? She and the church delivered Thanksgiving and Christmas boxes with chicken, canned corn and dried potato flakes to us. Mom filed the paperwork to request military aid over a year ago, but nothing except government commodities fill the pantry.

"When does your mother begin the new job Caroline told me about?" Sister's sing-song voice floats on top of the noise in my head like she's far away.

"Started Monday."

"Wonderful news. I'm sure the problem will be solved soon. Give her my best." A smile spreads across her face, but it's relief, not happiness.

"Thank you, Sister."

I grab the envelope, stuff it inside my Pee Chee folder and hurry past Mrs. Candelaria's scrutinizing eyes and tight lips. I take a deep breath to settle my nerves before I step out into the hallway.

Bobby jumps from the wooden bench outside the office. "What did Sister want?"

"Who's in trouble?" John gawks in Caroline's direction.

The twins flushed cheeks remind me they're still little kids, identical ones. It's hard to guess who's who in their uniforms. If it weren't for Bobby's perpetual cowlick, we couldn't tell them apart. . . until John opens his mouth.

No sense in telling them the truth and having them worry. I'm responsible for them and can't have them stressing out. The day Dad left for aircraft mechanic training in Texas, he told me to help Mom take care of the family. It's a huge responsibility, but it's a promise I need to keep.

"No one's in trouble. Sister asked me how I was doing at St. Bernadette. Let's go."

Caroline turns away from us and scans the playground. Next month, she turns fourteen but seems older because she's tall like Dad with curvy hips like Mom, while I'm the opposite.

The damp leaves gather around the fence in front of the school building. Their long finger shapes look like they're climbing over the chain-link fence. They want out of this city, too.

"Sister told you, huh?" Caroline says.

"Yeah. Mom must've forgotten. She'll take care of it."

Bobby tugs on my hand. "Can we get *pan dulce*? I got a B plus on my test, and I'm hungry."

"Loli's only does that on Fridays." I brush his hair away from his puppy dog eyes. "Let's see if Mrs. Washington's cats are in the window today."

His shy smile returns. He loves cats and dogs, but we can't have pets in the housing projects.

Pink hydrangea bushes, lilac vines and roses surround Mrs. Washington's wood-framed house. I only remember the names of her flowers because she's pointed them out to us before. The garden is her pride and joy, she says. The floral scents grow more potent the closer we move to the fence surrounding her home.

Bobby runs to the gate and gazes at the two fluffy orange cats sitting on the windowsill. Mrs. Washington lifts herself from her rocking chair on the front porch. She's as tall and slender as a sunflower, except for her hair, a short grey afro, which makes her look like a pretty dandelion.

"How are the Bravo children doing today?" She waves her floppy gardening hat.

Out of nowhere, a Doberman Pinscher runs toward us, barking. We back up from the fence.

"His name's Rider." She whistles to the dog. He turns his thick neck in her direction, wags his stubby tail.

"When did you get him?" Bobby asks.

"Last week he came from Texas, where my Jerome was stationed. His wife, Lorraine, and my grandchild, Jerome Junior, came to live with me." Her smile fades.

"Can I play with him and Junior?" Bobby asks.

"Anytime I'm here, honey, Junior's only two years old. Best run along home now. About to rain."

Mrs. Washington's son died in Vietnam a year after Dad. He was only nineteen.

We cross the street to where the housing projects begin. The two-story buildings all look the same with their faded yellow, drab green and white paint. The front yards all have a square cement porch with a skinny tree in the middle of the rectangle of grass. In the narrow strip of dirt against the wall, most people plant flowers, cacti or herbs like cilantro and *yerba buena*.

You can't do too much enhancement, or the housing authority people harass you like they did Petra. The altar she made to Our Lady of Guadalupe took up most of her front yard. She had to remove a few plaster angels but kept the bench for her husband to sit on and watch the people walking by.

Two guys, older than us, sit on their covered porch, lighting a cigarette. "Hey, baby doll," one calls out to us while the other lets out a long whistle when Caroline and I pass by.

"Keep walking," I say.

"If you don't want them whistling, why do you roll up your skirt?" John says.

Bobby nudges me. "She makes up her eyes in the school bathroom every morning."

"Shut up. I'll wear whatever the hell I want," Caroline shouts. "Nobody likes a snitch."

"You guys go on."

The boys run ahead. I turn to Caroline. "Why're you so pissed off?"

"Two weeks ago, I gave Mom the payment envelope. She said she'd take care of it. Why should I bust my butt studying when she can't afford our school bill?"

"True. I don't understand why she works so hard to keep all of us in Catholic school."

"It's because she graduated from there and St. Bernadette." Caroline stops walking. "Better if we all go to public school."

She may think so, but I don't. "I'll remind Mom later. I bet she pays the bill in a couple of weeks with her new job."

"Hey, Jacqui. Look," John says as he runs to our front porch and snatches a paper off the doorknob.

His smooth forehead wrinkles as he hands the red tag to me. *Notice of Water Shutoff.*

CHAPTER 4

How could Mom not pay the water bill after I reminded her yesterday? I glance at her hands tight on the steering wheel, focused on the road ahead.

"I'm going to ask Petra to give me an advance when I see her at the job later today," I offer. "Maybe that'll help out?"

"Don't. I'll pay the water bill at lunchtime," Mom says. "I need to drop you off here. We're running late."

The first school bell rings as I rush into the bathroom in the school's lower lot. Now I'm a sweaty mess. I throw my grocery bag under the sink, straighten my crooked skirt. A quick swipe with a few dampened paper towels across my face, and I'm good to go.

"Damn," Lucy Jáquez says, hitting the door open. "Did you take a bath in here?"

She brushes away her feathered bangs, stares at the wadded paper towels on the counter. The girl rarely talks to me, although we're both seniors and Mexican American. She hangs out with the cheerleaders and Margot Sanders. Mom says her parents work in real estate and live on the south side of town because they make lots of money. They'd live on the north side like Margot if they were wealthy.

24

I scoop the mess into the trash can while Lucy hoists herself onto the wide windowsill and struggles to open the window. It won't budge. She bangs the metal edge with the heel of her black and white Oxford. Still stuck.

"Ugh, don't you just hate this place?" she says.

"The windows are ancient because St. Bernadette was built in 1900. Romanesque Revival, you know." I mimic Sister Mary Grace's high-pitched voice and push open the window.

"Hey, you do a good imitation." She pulls a pack of Virginia Slims cigarettes from her suede-fringed purse. "Got a light?"

"What makes you think I smoke?"

"The quiet ones surprise you."

People who don't associate with me call me quiet. I prefer to say I'm a thinker and a planner. Traits I inherited from my dad.

"Check this out," Lucy says. "My mother's throwing me a coming out party like those Mexicans have, that *quince* thing." She flicks smoldering ashes out the open window.

"*Those Mexicans?* You're Mexican, or did you forget?"

Her mouth drops open as I stare at her.

"No, I'm born here. Anyways, you know what I mean." She blows a stream of cigarette smoke out the open window. "I'm having an eighteenth birthday bash like the girls from the Country Club's Debutante Ball. But you gotta belong to the country club. My parents are gonna rent a hall, band, even a limo."

I didn't have a party when I turned sixteen or seventeen. We had dinner at the Golden Chopsticks, and the fortune cookies were my cake. What did we have to celebrate anyway? Dad died a few weeks before my sixteenth birthday.

Like I said, the town is two places. One for the rich and one for the poor. St. Bernadette is like that too. Debutante balls, vacation trips, graduation cars. St. Bernie's world is too big for me, and my neighborhood is too small. I don't fit into either one.

The screech of the school bell sounds. I grab my paper sack of spare clothes and plastic gloves from under the sink and tuck it under my arm.

"What's in the bag?" Lucy says.

"P. E. stuff. You better split. Sister Mary makes her rounds after the first-period bell."

She blows out a stream of smoke. "So? I have a party to plan. Invites, dress, band. . ."

Watching Lucy sit there without a care except what kind of fancy dress to wear to her pretentious party while I work nights to help pay the bills pisses me off. I bang the bathroom door open and stash my bag of cleaning gloves and change of clothing in my locker.

Tuition and scholarship money. Both life and death situations. My only ticket out of this place. What did Mom do with the money in the cigar box under her bed? For months, I put most of the money I earned in the box every week. Before Christmas, we had a hundred bucks. She couldn't have spent it on presents because we all received stuff from Woolworths five and dime. Maybe it was the excitement of the new job that made her forget to send the tuition payments and pay the water bill. There has to be a reasonable explanation. There better be.

The city bus leaves me across the street from a boxy two-story building five minutes before five. Petra's new job assignment. The place has rows of windows in the front and grey concrete everywhere else. I rush to the back door before anyone recognizes me in my school uniform.

"Hola, Jacqui." Petra shuffles toward me, holding her tote bags of cleaning supplies.

I take the bags while she unlocks the door to an empty hallway, where I follow her to another room.

"They got it good here, huh? They only work until four-thirty," I say.

"And weekends off. *Imagínate*," Petra says. "We do the bathrooms first. You do the ladies. I do the men."

I change out of my clothes and into an old T-shirt and jeans, sticking my uniform into my grocery sack. I'm faced with four stalls, two sinks and one huge spotted mirror. The small trash bins in each stall overflow with used Kotex boxes and snotty tissue papers. Nasty. The stench of blood and piss gags me so bad that I hold my breath while emptying the mess.

"Okay, done?" Petra calls out.

"On my third toilet. Give me five minutes."

Petra pops the bathroom stall door on my butt. "*¡Ándale, con ganas!*" She barges into the next stall, where I hear the brush swishing. "You didn't put new towels in the thing."

"Sorry." I don't want her to think I'm a slacker or have her tell Mom I'm lazy.

My hands fly over the partitions with paper towels while Petra fills the liquid soap dispensers. We move into the office space, dragging another large trash can, broom and mop. The overhead lights illuminate rows of gray metal desks and about fifty chairs on the other side of a long, cluttered counter. A whiff of old smoke and dusty shoes hits my nose.

There must be twenty desks. Each one has those new electric typewriters, a telephone and three-tiered trays. Does Mom's new workplace resemble this one?

Two glass-enclosed offices with huge desks, swivel chairs and framed pictures on the walls are at the back. Those must be for the bosses, the brass, as Dad used to say. Must be cool to be away from all the typing and noise. Even better, to have a room of your own and have someone clean up after you, like Petra and I are doing.

Dad said there were bosses, foremen, skilled workers like him and the peons at most jobs. It seems like having a job is just like St. Bernie. There is the principal, the teachers, the rich kids and the poor ones.

I might be a peon today, but I'll be a big-time boss someday. I haven't decided what kind of career I want to have, but working in a place like this, with my own space inside a modern building, is something to think about. The room probably has air-conditioning too.

We clean windows, sweep, dust and mop before we take a break.

"My feet are screaming," I complain.

My T-shirt, wet with sweat, sticks to my back. I scratch at my damp scalp and plop into the nearest chair. "Nine o'clock, and we're almost done. I have a ton of homework to do and an application to work on."

"Done?" Petra points her crooked finger to the ceiling. "Those offices upstairs have carpets and more bathrooms. We lucky to be outta here by midnight."

CHAPTER 5

That's the last time I work on homework until one a.m. I couldn't keep my eyes open to fill out my scholarship application. The only thing keeping me from dozing off on the way to school is Mom's yakking. She talks a mile a minute as we bump over the railroad tracks to St. Bernadette on a foggy morning.

For the past few days, I've hidden the late tuition letters. If I can't come up with the unpaid balance, it's public school hell. I need to remind Mom today.

"Listen, *m'ija*. What about on payday we go to the second-hand store together? Find some outfits?"

"Buy clothes?" I suck my teeth at her ridiculous suggestion.

"What was that for?"

"Shopping? How can you think about that when Sister George said you're two months behind at St. Patrick, not to mention St. Bernadette?"

Mom brakes at the red light. Her hands grip the steering wheel so hard that her fingers turn white. "They'll have to wait until next month. I just paid the water, and rent's due this payday."

"Before Christmas, we had a hundred dollars to pay St. Patrick December and January tuition. What happened to the money? If Caroline loses out on the scholarship to St. Bernadette, she might not graduate. And what about the boys? You want them to fall in with the wrong crowd at public school?"

"Don't raise your voice at me. How do you think we were able to visit your grandparents? The five bus tickets, the food? Did you forget I stopped working at the packing house when the season ended before Thanksgiving? The pay there can't support a family, not without, um. . ."

Her hands slide off the steering wheel. She can't even say the words, "your dad."

My breath catches in my chest while my stomach twists. "Drop me off here. I'll walk the rest of the way." I grasp at the handle, fling the door open and stomp out to the curb.

The traffic from the boulevard blares in my ears, drowning out Mom's words. She's aware she's late with the tuition, but if I tell her about Sister Mary Grace's threat to transfer me, she'll have to decide which school to pay. What if she doesn't choose mine? There goes my chance for a full first-year college scholarship. If she doesn't choose St. Patrick, Caroline's the first to mess up. Someone loses either way.

It must be another mile before I get to St. Bernie. Each step reminds me of my cleaning job and the chicken feed I'm paid working nights. That money that won't make a damn bit of difference. Nothing to pay our debt except promises.

Seeing our stash of cash grow before the holidays made me happy because I thought, finally, we were catching up. When Mom said we'd visit our grandparents in Texas, I was for it because we hadn't seen them since Dad's funeral the year before.

During our school break, Mom took us on the Greyhound bus. We boarded with our dinner: burritos in foil. First, it was an adventure passing the towns decorated with Christmas lights and fake reindeer. I tried reading my book, but the boys squirmed in their seats, asking dozens of questions or whining.

Mom stared out the window most of the time, ignoring them until they fell asleep. I couldn't sleep because of the odor of greasy food and stinky socks. Caroline had her head down because she threw up at one of the stops. Mom gave her a washed out MJB coffee can in case she couldn't wait. She had to snatch it back when the twins got sick. We needed three cans. Disgusting.

After fifteen long hours, we arrived in El Paso, Texas. The rising sun over the Franklin Mountains and the colors in the sky gave the area some beauty. We stepped out into the cool morning, clutching our thin jackets against the wind. Once the bus pulled away, I saw my grandpa, his cowboy hat in his hand, standing near his old pickup truck. His lined, grim face brightened as soon as the boys ran to him, shouting, "Grandpa, we're here." His smile was my dad's smile. It was worth the visit.

⚜ ⚜ ⚜

The cars on the boulevard whiz by. One block left to go before I reach St. Bernie. Twenty-five days before my tuition deadline. I need to do something. Time's ticking. I need a second job. Quick.

My first period class is in the building up on the hill. I hustle up the flight of stairs and into the courtyard past the glass-encased bulletin board. My stomach drops into my feet. What the hell? *Reminder-Overdue Tuition*, the poster-sized paper says in bold black letters. *Bravo, Jacqueline* is right on top of the short list for everyone to see. Like I need another reason to be made fun of. If the board weren't locked, I'd pull the list down.

"Miss Bravo. Just the person I need to see." Sister exits the school office, plods to where I stand. "Did you give your mother the letter? She hasn't responded."

"Uh, she's really busy with her new job, Sister Mary Grace. She said she'd call you soon."

Sister rocks on her clunky black shoes while the school bell shrills. "Ensure she does."

Mom's never calling you, I want to say, but I turn and book it to my locker to put away my crumpled bag of janitor clothes. Oh crap! Petey Castro's headed my way. I spin my combination lock and keep my head down. Dang it, my fingers fumble over my lock.

"Those are tricky sometimes," Petey says.

"Yeah," I nod. *Slow down, Jacqui, breathe. Say something clever or funny or. . .*

"Sometimes it takes me three tries." He leans closer to me.

The bell screeches, I release the lock, and it opens. I turn my head a tiny bit to look up. He's smiling.

"Catch you later," Petey says.

Everything moves in slow motion. He said he'd catch me later. Petey's never said that before. I thought he'd be pissed off at me for calling him Pay-droh the other day. I throw my bag into the locker and run to first period.

While the teacher reads from the history book about the Napoleonic War, I have another battle going on in my head. I need to stay at St. Bernadette. How I manage that is another story.

The alumni scholarship application peeks out of my Pee Chee folder. First question: *Describe where you demonstrated leadership.*

I'm the leader of my brothers and sisters, and that must count for something. In my notebook, I write the jobs I've had since I was twelve: babysitting, strawberry fields and night janitor. I was the eighth-grade class president, but Margot Sanders is the Senior class secretary and volunteers as a Candy Striper. I need to come up with something better.

At lunchtime, I split to the school library. I spend my time there because after lunch is my free period. I have ninety minutes alone to think, plan and dream.

The familiar aroma of old books and Sister Agnes' odor greets me at the library door. She must have arthritis because she reeks of the menthol rub, Ben-Gay. Good old Sister sits behind her desk, pretending to snooze, as always. Poor thing must be eighty years old and still working. She and Sister Mary Graceless are the only ones who wear the nun's black habit while the two younger nuns wear long skirts and bulky sweaters.

The library has stayed the same in my four years here. Sister arranged the library's five tables in front of her desk. On purpose. The sly woman. I pull out a chair and rest my books on the table. Sister Agnes opens one beady eye. She nods when I sit and flip open my notebook and application.

Share a project you participate in to enhance your community. What? How am I supposed to answer that one? We don't have Girl Scouts in our barrio, although I did like that idea for a hot second when I saw them selling cookies uptown.

I'm sure Margot will list the hospital where she volunteers. Writing down that I clean offices so workers can have a clean area to mess up again won't cut it, but I jot it down anyway.

Next question, *What's the most difficult challenge you've faced?*

Easy. I jot down *Dad leaving for Vietnam to work on Army helicopters and then dying.* That's the honest answer, but I don't even want to think about that time, much less write about what happened. He told us he'd be safe. But he wasn't. My heart races like it usually does when I think of Dad gone. If I let go, I'll cry. Instead, I concentrate on breathing deeply, like Bebe once taught me. Once my heartbeat slows, I do something else.

I flip over to a blank page and write "Facing Sister Mary Graceless." Beneath the title, I draw a picture of her giant body standing over me in her office and give her bat wings and vampire teeth.

Someone nudges my shoulder. I cover the drawing of Sister Mary Grace with my arm.

"What're you doing?" Lucy reaches over me and grabs the paper from the table.

"Hey. Give it back." I grab at the sheet, but she holds it up higher.

"No talking in the library, girls." Sister Agnes shakes her bony finger at us.

Lucy shrieks out a laugh. "Oh, my god, that's so funny."

"Damn you, Lucy. What the hell?"

Sister springs from her chair like an Olympic hurdler and snatches the paper from my fingers and brings it close to her face. On the top of the sheet is my name.

"Miss Bravo." She shakes her head so hard that her eyeglasses veer sideways. "This is highly improper."

Lucy brushes back her bangs, hands her pass to Sister. "Mr. Laurent sent me for a book."

"I'll deal with you in a second, Miss Bravo."

Sister grabs the book and hands it to Lucy.

"Later." Lucy speed walks out of the library.

Sister Agnes pulls out her demerit pad from her deep pocket. "Detention, one hour."

"But I need to walk my brothers and sister home. Oh, and Ms. Fine, I mean Miss Fine, wants to speak to me after sixth period. Can you give me a warning instead? Please."

"I could give you three demerits. One for the disrespectful drawing, one for cursing and one for talking in the library, but I'll only give you one. Consider yourself a lucky young lady."

＊＊＊

Lucky girl, my butt. I'm the unluckiest person I know. Sister Agnes didn't fall for my lie about picking up the kids, but I couldn't tell her the truth about cleaning offices. I thought she liked me enough to let me slide once, but I guess not.

Ms. Fine's classroom is empty by the time I leave detention, so I sprint to the street corner to catch the 4:15 bus to work.

The city bus heaves itself to the terminal like a fat slug. If we go any slower, I'm going to be late for the connecting bus to the business center.

Finally, we stop at the terminal park. The door rolls open. I'm all shoulders and elbows as I push my way out to the sidewalk, hoofing it across the grassy center to the other side of the park where my bus waits. A few feet more, and I'm almost there. I quicken my pace, fall into a gopher hole. Damn it. My books scatter one way, my folder another. I jump to my feet and flick dirt off my knees. I'm within earshot of the rumbling motor. The door to the bus shuts. "Wait. Stop!" I wave my arm in the air, hoping someone sees me. The next bus is in twenty minutes. The office is about two miles away. I might arrive on time if I hustle. I tuck my bag of work clothes under my arm, jog up to the main street and turn right at the car lots.

Fifteen minutes later, I'm sweating in my uniform blouse. Even my socks are damp. Cars zoom by, spilling stinky exhaust into the air. The boulevard seems like it goes on forever. I have at least another mile to go.

I arrive at the office building late and find Petra in the first-floor bathrooms. "Sorry, bus problems."

She swivels her head to me, her gloved hand on a toilet brush. "Did you walk?"

I nod.

"*Ay, m'ija*. Go change, grab the vacuum and start upstairs."

A few minutes later, she steps into the office with an older man, who wears a blue jumpsuit, like a mechanic's.

"Here she is," Petra says. Her thin eyebrows arch high while her eyeballs move to the left where the man stands. "This is Jacqui, my helper."

"You were late." The man scratches at his brown mustache. "Saw you come in. You had on a school uniform. St. Bernadette? We require a work permit proving you're eighteen."

"But she's a good worker. Give her a chance," Petra says.

I'm nodding my head off, still vacuuming, when he moves closer to me.

"Sorry. This here's a state office, and I signed a contract. Can't lose it. You gotta go."

CHAPTER 6

Mom slams the skillet onto the stove. "He fired you for being underage? But Petra knew. I'll need to find a second job now."

I can't tell her I called attention to myself by being late, so I sit while she bangs pots and pans on the burners.

"Did you call St. Patrick's principal and tell them you'll pay next month?" I start the dreaded conversation.

"Too busy today. Stop worrying and peel those two potatoes."

Ever since Dad's been gone, my job, as the oldest, is to be manager for the family. The worrying part comes with that role, whether I like it or not.

"You're the one who asked me to remind you to pay the bills, what we need for groceries and the kid's homework assignments." I pause, waiting for her to say something, but she doesn't. "I need to go over to Bebe's this weekend so she can help me with the alumni application."

"Make sure all your chores are done first." Mom huffs. "And where's your sister?"

"Now, I got to keep up on where she's at all times, too? She doesn't do half the crap I do around here."

"Watch your mouth." Mom gives me the hairy eyeball until I wince and look away.

Caroline walks in the back door, snapping her pink bubble gum. The odor of Marlboro floats over my face as she passes where I sit dicing potatoes.

"Where were you?" Mom asks.

"Becky's house. We're doing a group project for school."

"Oh." Mom lowers the flame on the stove. "She comes from a good family. Better than that Matilda girl, the one they call Mousy. Too wild. No discipline at their house."

Caroline makes a face at me. "Going to my room."

After the potatoes and onions are diced, I run upstairs and find Caroline's smelly uniform jacket thrown on my bed. "Keep your shit off my bed." I throw her clothes on the floor. "And you're a big-ass liar. You've been smoking with Mousy, haven't you?"

"What the hell crawled up your butt?"

I throw a pillow at her, and she runs out of our bedroom, slams the bathroom door. My folder isn't anywhere in sight. The late tuition letter from Sister Mary Grace telling Mom I'll be transferred if she doesn't pay is still inside. I search under my blankets and bed. The bathroom door's locked.

"Caroline? Open up. Now." I kick at it so she can hear me over the radio. "Did you take my folder?"

She pokes her head out and waves my Pee Chee folder in front of her face before she hides it behind her back. "Looking for this?"

I could slap her, but I steady my voice. "That's mine. Give it to me."

"What's all the noise," Mom says, climbing the staircase.

"Caroline has my school folder, and I need to finish my homework."

Mom reaches inside the bathroom for it, but Caroline pulls her hand away, tries to close the door. Mom's no fool. She sticks her foot in the doorway, pushes it open with a bump of her hip, one two three, just like that, sending Caroline stumbling back into the toilet.

"A's don't fall out of the sky, Caroline. You need that scholarship to St. Bernadette. Go do your homework instead of teasing your sister," Mom says.

"Yeah!" I shout, snatching my folder back.

"I don't even want to go to a Catholic high school," Caroline says.

Mom gasps, steps back like someone slapped her face. The boys crowd at the top of the stairs taking in everything. Mom straightens herself up, pushes her hair behind her ears and leans into Caroline's flushed face.

"You're going to St. Bernadette, and that's that, little girl. Go to your room!"

We stare at each other for a second before Mom turns on her heel, stomps downstairs. Caroline comes out of the bathroom, flops on her bed.

"Stop making Mom mad," Bobby chastises as he runs down the stairs, following Mom, who I'm sure is praying in front of the altar she made in the nook beneath the staircase.

John stares at Caroline and shakes his head.

"Scram, John." I shut the door and jump on my bed. "Why don't you want to go to St. Bernie anymore?" I ask Caroline.

She examines the ceiling covered with her prized posters of Bobby Sherman and David Cassidy. "Don't act dumb."

"Mom's new job will get us out of this bind by next month. You watch." Now I'm the one with the phony voice trying to pretend my way into thinking everything will be okay.

"Better if we all go to public school. Mousy's going there for high school."

"Not better for me. I want that scholarship to UCLA. Don't you want to go to college?"

"I dunno." She turns on her side, props up her head with her hand. "What was in your folder? A letter from Petey? I thought after three years, you gave up on him."

"Nothing. Don't go telling Mousy. She's a *chismosa* like her sisters."

"Don't tell Mom I'm hanging around her, and I won't tell anyone about your crush. Mousy's oldest sister, Lena, is in love with him too. She'd do anything to crawl into his pants."

"Ew. That dropout is nineteen. She's too old for him."

"Guys don't care." Caroline jumps off the bed. "Let's go eat. I'm starving."

I open my folder and find the letter from Sister Mary Grace addressed to Mom. I can't give it to her now. If she reads it, she'll need to decide whose tuition to pay.

I need to find another job to keep us out of this mess. The sooner the better. I tear the letter into little pieces and throw them in the bathroom trash can.

CHAPTER 7

Bobby drops the Venetian blinds onto the windowsill. "Caroline's late. The streetlamp's out, and it's getting dark."

He drops into the chair at the kitchen table, where John and I play Uno. The twins love playing board games and cards. I bet they miss the times competing with Dad for pennies. I didn't even play back then, but now I miss hearing them whoop and laugh.

"Wait, she's here." Bobby flings open the door.

"Finally," John shouts. "Took long enough."

Caroline slams the door. "Oh, shut up."

"You shut up." John springs up from the table.

"Hey," I stand between them. "Knock it off. I gotta go to Bebe's. Caroline, you better take care of the kids, like Mom said."

"Why do I have to take care of the brats?" She twists her lip.

"We don't need her taking care of us. We're eleven," John says.

"But Mom said." Bobby gives me a lopsided smile, as he chews on his fingernails.

He follows me to the door with his forehead scrunched to his nose. I feel terrible that I'm leaving when he looks so scared. I realize I can't depend on Caroline, but she's all I have.

"Caroline? I'm calling here when I get to Bebe's. You better answer," I shout from the bottom of the staircase and brush the hair off Bobby's forehead. "She won't climb out the window again, okay? John, call me at Tío Mario's if there's a problem." I shut the door behind me and wave at Bobby, watching me through the window.

Uncle Mario's apartment is two blocks away. In the neighborhood, everyone calls where he lives the *viejo* projects because they were built fifteen years before the ones where we live. Faded colors of olive green, dingy yellow, with some blend that passes as brown paint, make them look like camouflaged cinder block buildings. He told me this was military housing back in the 1940s, and since he's a veteran, he can live here.

Bebe sits on a wooden stool on the tiny front porch. She looks like one of those American Indian women in a magazine I read at the library.

"*Prima*," she greets me, then licks her fingers and touches the cigarette tip to put it out. She sticks it in the pocket of her long turquoise sweater. "Let's go inside."

In her bedroom, she kicks off her brown suede moccasins. Only a twin bed and nightstand remain in her room, so we both sit on the mattress.

Once, Uncle Mario took me with him to San Fernando, to Bebe's apartment. The walls had posters of Emiliano Zapata, and Angela Davis and photos of César Chávez and Dolores Huerta. Hanging plants, bean bags and blue milk crates of albums filled the small living room. Uncle Mario frowned the whole time we were there, but I thought it was the coolest apartment I'd ever seen.

"Hope you decided on becoming a teacher. You could help the community, do really good stuff here," Bebe says.

"Mom and my grandparents want me to be a secretary, and you want me to be a teacher, but I'm not interested. Neither of

those jobs will make me big money so that I can live somewhere other than here."

"What?" Bebe springs off the mattress. "Are you ashamed
of coming from here?"

I gulp. "I mean, it's just I haven't decided on a career, and
I'm, uh, I'm frustrated with being poor. Everything changed
for us when Dad died." I pick at Bebe's bedsheet.

"Yeah, I hear you, *prima*." She takes the cigarette stub out
of her pocket, strikes a match and lights the cigarette. After a
couple of puffs, she touches the flame to an incense stick on
the end table. The tip glows in an ashtray filling the air with a
sweet but stinky odor.

"Hey, Solano High School is going to start a MEChA chapter. We met with their administration. Rudy, Javier and me."

If Mom catches me involved with MEChA, I'll never hear
the end of it.

"Your Brown Beret friends? I thought you were out of
business after the cops infiltrated you guys."

"We have so much more to do. We want to help improve education, call for the end of the war. So many issues. We need to
insist on change to make things better. It's important to educate
the youngsters about our culture, our history."

"But aren't we supposed to get along with everybody and
fit in?"

Bebe snuffs out her cigarette. "In our parents' day, they
wanted to assimilate into society. But the melting pot theory is
old fashioned, like from the forties and fifties. Assimilation
means a loss of our culture, language and traditions. Those are
parts of us to be proud of, but Chicano kids don't appreciate
that because they aren't educated. Informed students lead to a
better future, to positive change."

She already sounds like a teacher. I like the idea of changing and improving situations, but I can't imagine myself

demanding anything. Who'd listen to a Catholic high school girl? I'm too busy, anyway.

"So, can you help me with these application questions? They're super hard." I shake the paper at Bebe.

Her eyes scan the sheet. "'Share a project you participate in to enhance your community?' Damn good question. What do you have so far?"

"Uh, I was class president in eighth grade."

"No, too long ago. What about volunteering at the school and church fiestas?"

"Nothing in three years."

"See, if you'd started a MEChA club, there'd be something to put on this form. Tonight, we're going to show a film on the Chicano Moratorium. Actual footage. Come with me."

I want to find out what went on at the Moratorium besides what I saw on the news two years ago, which scared the crap out of me. I'm sure Mom won't let me go to the meeting, so I'll have to lie, again.

Javier, Bebe's boyfriend, parks his candy-apple-red '65 Galaxy at St. Patrick Church, next to St. Patrick Catholic Elementary. The school doesn't have parking lot lights like St. Bernie, so everything is dark and spooky looking, especially the lemon orchard across the street. I inhale the citrusy scent once I'm out of the car.

"Are we picking someone up here at the church?" I ask.

"We're going into the school. Hurry up, I don't want to be late for the *junta*," Bebe says.

"Does Sister George know you guys are here?"

"Of course. Step on it."

We hustle across the grass and blacktop to the eighth-grade classroom on the far side of the building. Javier has his guitar strapped to his back, as always. He knocks twice. The door cracks open. A pair of bushy black eyebrows and a mustache fill the space.

"We're here for the *junta*," Javier says.

The guy steps back and waves us inside. We squeeze through the area between him and the door. It shuts with a bang behind me. What's with all the secrecy?

"Hey, *carnal*," a few guys say to Javier.

All of them give each other the Chicano handshake. A few wear brown berets, the caps with a yellow patch and two crossed rifles. Pretty cool looking.

"Why are they still wearing the berets," I whisper to Bebe.

"The movement's not over. Lot of work to be done. You'll see."

There must be forty guys and girls in the classroom, all Bebe's age or older. Every desk is filled. A row of guys stands in the back against the wall.

"Bebe, over here." A girl wearing a brown fringe suede jacket leans against the far wall and points to an area in front of where she stands.

We sit cross-legged on the floor with two other girls. An older guy sits on a metal desk. Behind him, the chalkboard says, "Movimento Estudiantil Chicano de Aztlán. MEChA."

"Who's that man?" I ask Bebe.

"Rudy. He's almost a lawyer. Graduated from UCLA a couple of years ago."

The guy lets out a shrill whistle. "Everyone, listen up."

The place quiets. Everyone turns to face the front of the classroom.

"First, let me tell you that we can't show the news footage tonight," Rudy says.

A stir of voices arises from the crowd.

"Yeah, bummer. As soon as the Mortarium footage is edited, the MEChA chapter of UCLA will screen the film first. In a couple of weeks, I'll bring it here."

Everyone, except me, starts clapping, loud. Over and over, faster and faster until the noisy smack of their hand's thunders into my chest. Scary.

My eyes dart to Bebe. "What's happening?"

"The Chicano clap," she whispers back.

The clapping over, Rudy points to me. "Glad to see the youngsters here. You're our future."

Our future? That sounds like a lot of responsibility, and I have enough worries. I'm here for the community section of my application.

"Okay, let's get down to business." He takes a piece of chalk and writes in block letters on the chalkboard: *Empower, Educate, Equality.*

"We're organizing here in the barrio for three reasons. Number one, to empower the students and the community through political awareness." He makes a check on the chalkboard. "Two, to advocate for better education for our people by hiring more brown and black people in schools to promote higher education. And three, to take care of an immediate problem facing the neighborhood: the need for a street or bridge in and out of the barrio for emergency access."

He throws the chalk on the table and crosses his arms. "We need to help ourselves by making our voices heard."

"No one listens," a guy in an oversized green army jacket says.

"We're going to work hard to make them listen, *carnal.*" Rudy points to the girl in the fringe jacket. "Are you concerned about your barrio?"

"*Simón.* The city will think we don't care if we don't speak up, so why should they?"

"What does '*simón*' mean," I ask Bebe.

"That's Cholo slang for 'yes.'"

Another guy raises his hand. "My *abuelo* has bad asthma. He needs medical treatment quick, or he can suffocate. We can't wait for that damn train to clear the tracks for the ambulance."

I nudge Bebe and whisper, "Just like Petra's husband waited."

Rudy points to me. "This is your community, your *colonia*. Do you care, *carnalita*?"

All eyes turn to me. "Um, yeah, sure. My neighbor's husband might have survived his stroke if the ambulance had gotten to her place on time. My mom can't afford to be late to work, and the teacher will give me a demerit if I'm late to school."

Bebe stands up. "The kids at Solano say the teachers call them lazy every time they're late, but the train delays the bus. Teachers think the students don't care."

"Exactly. The stereotype of the lazy Mexican is reinforced," Rudy says. "For all the reasons everyone mentioned, we need to meet with the city council and collaborate with the school principals."

Collaborate? This guy speaks like he's so sure of himself, like Sister Mary Grace or one of our teachers. I wonder if a college education gave him the confidence to talk to politicians and principals.

Rudy jumps up and writes on the blackboard, *Chicanos for a Better Colonia CBC*.

Someone in the crowd yells out, "Chicano," and others shout, "Power!" The roars of "Chicano, Power" are followed by the Chicano clap. I hunch my shoulders. I want to clamp my hands over my ears, but at the same time, my body tenses. How can I be frightened and excited at the same time?

"See?" Bebe nudges me with her elbow. "That's why I said you need to go to college and be a teacher."

"Teacher? Nah, I want to be like that guy," I point to Rudy. "He's not afraid of anything."

"So, *carnalita*, what do you think?" he says. "Do you want to be part of the Chicanos for a Better Colonia?"

⁂

Bebe and Javier drop me off at the top of my block. Rudy's voice vibrates in my head. He sure has a lot of guts to talk to the city council and the principals of the schools. Part of the CBC? I nodded when he asked, but I'm only attending to fulfill my application requirements.

The street is darker than usual. Every other streetlamp is busted, but the neighborhood isn't scary to me. The soft sounds of Mexican ballads and Motown music travel through open windows. The faint smell of herbs from people's front yards slips by my nose. A few kids ride their StingRay bikes, shouting to each other over the tunes while they swing around parked cars and pop wheelies.

Bicycle brakes squeal behind me. I glance over my shoulder. My pulse speeds up.

"Hey, Jacqui," Petey says. "What're you doing out by yourself?"

Stay calm. I glance down at my wrinkled blouse and wonder how my hair appears.

"Coming from my cousin's house." I tuck stray hairs behind my ear. "Hey, sorry I made fun of your name in front of Larry."

"No biggie," he shrugs. "Pedro is my name, but only my dad calls me that. And I do live in government projects."

Huh? All this time, I thought he was embarrassed, like me. I chew on my bottom lip. What do I say now? The scent of wool and leather of his letterman jacket drifts through the still, night air. My head reaches his shoulders, which are wide enough for two of me. I can't help staring at him just to watch his lips move.

"Why are you out late?" I ask.

"Coming from baseball practice. Season's starting soon."

"Cool." The little puff of warm air from my mouth makes a light haze in front of me. I look at that instead of him.

"The streetlamp's out near your place," Petey says. "I'll walk you home."

"O-kay," squeaks out of my mouth.

My fingers tingle all the way to my shoulders. Why is he being nice to me? Maybe he wants to make up for Larry teasing me. We used to talk all the time until our freshman year. Before he started hanging out with the jocks.

My house comes way too soon. We stop, and he takes his baseball cap off, slides his fingers through his hair, then tugs the cap down tight.

"Hey, you like baseball, right?" He puts his feet on the bike pedals.

"Um, yeah?"

Petey rubs the back of his neck and glances away. My hands tremble while I wait under the flickering porch lamp, watching moths whiz around the bulb. Say something. Anything. "Uh, yeah, sure, I like baseball."

He turns back to me. Under the light, his eyes shine brighter when he smiles. "Come to one of our games next week, okay?"

"Uh-huh." I nod because I can't form any words in my dry mouth. He turns his bike around and disappears up the block.

Knocking sounds thud behind me. Louder. The faces of Caroline and my brothers at the front window staring back at me. John blows onto the window, making it steam up and draws a heart. The three of them giggle and point at me as soon as I open the front door. Dorks.

"I'm going to Bebe's house," Caroline imitates my voice.

I jog up the staircase. Footsteps run behind me. "I did go, nosey."

"Ooh, I'm telling Mom," John's voice sings.

"Tell me, tell me," Caroline says.

I beat her to our room and slam the door shut, grab one of her stuffed animals, wedge it under the door so she won't come in and tease me.

"Open up. I wanna hear all about it." She pushes on the door until it thumps open. "What the hell, Jacqui." She grabs her stuffed animal and reshapes its squashed body before kissing its head. "That's messed up. You smushed P Bear."

"Oh, damn, I'm sorry."

Dad won the teddy bear for Caroline at the county fair seven years ago. He called him Precioso the Oso, but Caroline named him P Bear. He's old and scruffy, but she still sews little shorts and vests to dress him up.

"I'm glad you have a boyfriend. Now, it'll be easier for me." She jumps on her bed with P Bear and shoos the boys out, but they stay in the doorway.

"You have a boyfriend?" Bobby brushes away his too short bangs, a casualty of Caroline's barbering skills.

"God, he's not my boyfriend. He came down the street at the same time as I did."

"Petey lives up the street from us," Caroline says. "Mousy said Petey told somebody who told somebody that you're cute, for a brainiac."

My eyes widen while my mouth drops open. "He did?" I grab my pillow, press it against my thumping heart. "He just asked if I like baseball. He's not interested like that."

"Oh, come on, Jacqui, why wouldn't he?"

"You're real nice, and pretty, and smart," Bobby says.

My cheeks flush while Caroline and Bobby nod like they are so sure.

"Sheesh," John says and tugs Bobby's arm. "Come on. Let's go finish that letter to Grandpa."

The door slams shut, leaving me and Caroline alone. "They're writing to him again?"

Caroline nods. "John writes, and Bobby draws pictures for him and Grandma."

"What if John tells them we're behind in St. Patrick's tuition, or that I'm working?"

"They'll give Mom shit for that," she says.

"Dang. What if they start that 'you should move to El Paso' speech again? Mom will be pissed."

"Don't worry about it." Caroline grabs a plastic baggie out of her purse. "Here, let me teach you how to draw eyeliner around your eyes, make them stand out even more. If you use green eye shadow, your hazel eyes will look more green than brown. I wish I had your color."

I push her aside on my way to find my brother. "Nope. I need to talk to John."

Caroline scrambles off the bed and follows me. "Come on, let me experiment. When I'm finished, Petey will ask you out to more than a baseball game."

"He will? Really?" I catch myself and take a breath. "Oh, who cares. I'll let you experiment, but don't pile it on."

I'll worry about my overdue tuition, John's letter and my scholarship questions tomorrow because now I have another reason to stay at St. Bernadette.

CHAPTER 8

The warm smell of flour tortillas hits my nose before I open my eyes. I wish we could have biscuits or pancakes on a Saturday instead of the same old, same old.

"Everybody up. Seven-thirty." Mom's voice penetrates the shut door of our bedroom.

Caroline moans, flips her pink blanket over her Medusa-looking head. I yank a sweatshirt over my pajama top and make my way downstairs.

Mom throws a dough circle on her cutting board, slaps the lump with her steel rolling pin. Even something as simple as Mom making tortillas reminds me of Dad. He cut a steel pipe for her to use a few years ago. I wonder if she thinks about that with every glide of the rolling pin. With quick up and down movements, the dough transforms into a perfect circle. She flips it on the black *comal* sitting on the stove. Bubbles rise in seconds. A skillet of diced *nopales* from Petra's yard and powdered scrambled eggs sit in the pan.

At the kitchen table, I reach for a hot tortilla from the stack resting inside a dish towel. From my seat, I notice a wet sheet hanging on the clothesline in our small backyard.

"Bobby had another accident?"

Mom exhales. "The doctor said he'll stop in time. He suggested counseling, but I can't afford that yet."

She throws me a glance that the conversation is over when footsteps pound the staircase. I want to tell her maybe we should talk about Dad more often with the family.

Caroline strides into the kitchen and grabs a tortilla. Smears of black ring her eyes.

"Are you using eyeliner?" Mom says.

Of course, Caroline throws me daggers as if I ratted her out. I shrug and eat my tortilla. The twins drag into the kitchen and look into the skillets on the stove.

"Yay, *nopales* and *huevo*," Bobby says. "Thanks, Mom."

"Caroline, look at me. Whose make-up do you have?"

"A friend gave me a couple of things. I'm old enough."

"None of my girls will wear make-up until they're seventeen. Only lip gloss. And no dating either."

"Oh my god." Caroline throws up her hands. "You'd think we're from a village in Mexico. This is 1972, Mother. Get with the times."

"*Malcriada*." Mom grabs the flyswatter, her face flushed. "Concentrate on school, not boys. You want to end up married at eighteen?"

"She said she's going to beautician school, not college," John says.

Caroline socks him on the arm. "You rat!"

He hits her back, and it's on, pushing and shoving until Mom slashes the air with the flyswatter.

"Gross. There's a smashed fly on it," yells Caroline as she ducks a swat.

Mom waves the swatter in the air, her face grimacing like she's daring us to open our mouths or move a muscle. "*Síguele*, see what happens. Don't be in a hurry to grow up. Concentrate on graduating from grammar school and then high school."

Everyone's quiet at the table.

"I tell you for your own good. You girls are smart and can go to college. Think about dating later." Her voice warms, and she fingers Caroline's hair. "I'm thinking of your future, okay?"

Mom pulls a list of chores out of her apron pocket and plants it up on the refrigerator door.

"Why do the boys only have to empty the trash and clean their room?" Caroline says. "Why do me and Jacqui gotta do the wash and everything else?"

Mom's jaw tightens. "Because I said so. If we had a lawn-mower, they'd mow the lawn."

"Well, they could clean our room while we're doing the wash," I say.

"No, they can't. They're little boys. Now hurry up."

Caroline and I know the real answer to her question. Boys hardly do anything while the girls cook, clean, shop and do the wash. That's the Mexican way, even if we live in California in 1972 and even if the boys are eleven or twenty-one.

"Dang, I hate the laundromat," Caroline says, dragging her feet behind me.

"Especially on Saturday morning when everyone in the *colonia* is there," I say yanking our old red wagon across the sidewalk. "Your turn to pull the wagon on the way back."

The odor of fermented strawberries, sweat and bleach saturates the air. The only redeeming feature of doing the wash is we're close to the new Mini-Mart and can hang out there while we wait for the clothes.

"Let's check out that new store," I tell Caroline. "They might have magazines."

We jam to the store, crouch before the tall rack in the back corner and flip through the pages of *Tiger Beat*. The photos of

David Cassidy and the rest of the Partridge Family are on the cover. Inside, there's a contest to kiss David, a poll of who's "foxier," David or Donny Osmond. Hands down, David Cassidy. But I can't enjoy the magazine knowing I don't have the extra fifty cents to buy one. I need to save every penny. I put it back. A loud sigh escapes my mouth.

"What's wrong with you?" Caroline says, putting down her *Teen Beat*.

"May as well tell you. The principal threatened to kick me out next month if Mom doesn't pay the tuition. She gave me a second letter to give to Mom, but I tore it up."

"You? Miss Goody-goody?" She bursts out laughing.

"Shut up. This is serious. We owe over a hundred bucks by next month."

Caroline sits on the floor next to me. "Where we gonna get that kind of money?"

"That evil nun put my name on the overdue list right up in the courtyard."

"Ugh, embarrassing."

"Humiliating. I oughta break that window and pull down the notice."

"Dang, you're really giving up being a good girl," Caroline says and laughs.

"I don't wanna transfer schools. I can't take another damn change."

A pair of legs in loose fitting pants appears. I glance up to see an old man wearing a white turban. "Excuse me. You buy?"

"No." Caroline jumps up and throws her *Teen Beat* into the rack. "Let's go."

The plastic name tag on the man's shirt says *Mr. Singh*. I straighten up the magazine and smooth the cover. This is the first time I've seen a man in a turban in our neighborhood. Even our barrio is changing.

"Mr. Singh, do you have any job openings? I'll work nights."

He shakes his head. "Too young, I think. My son, he owns the store. He hires."

"Maybe I'll come by tomorrow. . . if he's here. What's his name?"

"Ask for Mr. Singh. I'm Mr. Singh, too, but old Mr. Singh," he points to himself. His weathered brown face spreads into a broad smile.

"Okay, bye."

Caroline's already crossed the street and gone inside the laundromat by the time I arrive. We fold the wet clothes into the plastic baskets and heave them into the wagon. The wheels squeak over the sidewalk, causing every yard dog to run to the fence and bark at us when we pass their front lawns.

"Hey, I know. Mousy's oldest sister can pretend she's your mom and enroll you in the public school." Caroline scrunches up her lips. "What do you think?"

"Pfft. Blackboard jungle over there. Maybe I'd have a chance if I started there in ninth grade, but in the middle of my senior year? Forget it."

"It's a cool school, not much homework or rules. Have you seen the mini-skirts they can wear? So cool."

"Going there will mess up my plan for UCLA. Besides, public schools have slow, regular and college tracks. What happens if there's no room in the college prep classes?"

She shrugs and drags her feet behind me while I stop at the crosswalk.

"Hey, look." She points to a handwritten sign in the window of El Lobo's Bar and Café. "Evening Waitress Wanted-Must be 21."

"I'm seventeen, in case you forgot."

Her sullen face perks up as she bounces on the balls of her feet. "Ooh, I got an idea. Dress up in some of Mom's clothes, use make-up. I'll tease your hair."

I glance at my 34 As and shake my head. "Don't think so."

"Do you want to stay at St. Bernadette or not?"

"More than anything."

I peek through the window next to the sign. Two construction workers sit at the counter eating as they peer into a small television sporting a wire hanger for an antenna. Four booths fill the rest of the space. "Doesn't look too bad."

"I'll do your make-up and hair so you pass for twenty-one." Caroline grabs my arm.

<hr />

Wisps of talcum powder and hairspray stink up the inside of our small bathroom. Caroline elbows me aside. "Stand on the bathtub. Check out how you look now."

Teetering on the rim of the tub, I check myself out in the mirror over the sink. Caroline teased my short hair up so high it resembles a bubble about to burst. Mom's navy V-neck sweater emphasizes my fake boobs, courtesy of Caroline's idea to stuff my bra with the boy's tube socks. My year-old pair of flared jeans are tighter in my hips now, which is a good thing because I'm finally getting curves. I step off the tub and into Mom's red Candie slides.

"You look womanlier." Caroline adds water to the eyeliner bottle, shakes it. "Open."

My eyes are rounder with an uplift at the corners from the black eyeliner. She swoops green eyeshadow across my lids, brushes Mom's Mauve Glow blush across my cheeks.

"Caroline, take some off. I look like a *chola*."

"You're fine but okay." She dabs at both cheeks with a piece of toilet paper. "Let's get outta here before Mom comes back."

I snatch my jacket from the closet downstairs and catch a glimpse of our plaster statue of the Virgin Mary beneath the staircase. Her blue-robed outstretched hands appear to plead with me, "Why Jacqueline, why?"

"You know why," I whisper and run out the door.

If the Virgin wants me to have a Catholic school education and enter UCLA, then I have to do what I have to do.

CHAPTER 9

The *Waitress Wanted* sign is still stuck on the front window of El Lobo's Café and Bar. Caroline waits around the corner at the Mini-Mart, playing the lookout in case Mom drives by from her errands uptown.

The aroma of beef tacos, onions and cilantro hit my nose when I open the front door. My mouth waters and my stomach rumbles. A couple of people sit in the booths, munching on crunchy tortilla chips and red salsa. They shoot a glance at me and return to eating.

No waitress in sight. I check out the back of the place. At the end of the last booth, a double doorway is cut into the wall. The doors look like the ones in Western movies when the cowboys enter a saloon. They're upholstered in fake red velvet with black buttons in the middle. Cute in a tacky way.

I walk through to the other side. The room's dimmer and smokier than in the café. A woman about Mom's age sweeps the floor.

"Uh, excuse me?"

She straightens up, swings the broom to her other hand. "Hey, you can't be on this side."

"I'm here for the job posted out there." I motion with my thumb to the other room.

"Waitress? Oh no, no, no. Gotta be twenty-one." Her ginormous gold hoop earrings sway every which way when she shakes her head.

The dim light in here might work to my advantage. "I am."

The lady moves toward me, then around me. "Experience?"

I've waitressed since I was a little kid, bringing dishes to the kitchen table for the family. I use a calculator in math class. Plus, I only want to work for a month. Enough to catch up with my tuition. How difficult could this be?

"Yes, I have experience."

"Come with me."

She takes off her pink apron and tugs down her silky blouse. The scent of Jean Naté cologne entwined with cigarette smoke drifts off her clothes every time she moves.

"I'm Olga." She pushes the red doors open, grabs a sheet of paper behind the register. "Fill this out. I'll take it to the boss."

The application is one page. I write down Marie Monsivais, which is my middle name and my mom's maiden name. I'll squeeze a J in front of Marie and Bravo behind Monsivais, in case they pay me in a check. The Casa de Cambio cashes anything. I hand the paper back.

"Wait here." She turns down a narrow hallway on one side of the café.

A *telenovela* is on the black and white television on the counter. The café side has four stools at the counter. A couple of the red and green seats are covered with silver duct tape at the corners. Black and white tile crisscross the floor in a diamond pattern. The place is a little shabby but clean. A guy comes out of the kitchen with a dishpan and sets it on the counter.

Olga walks in, points to a stool. "Sit down. He'll be here in a minute. And you, Jerry, wipe down the counters. I don't have time."

The guy catches me staring at him. I knew it. He's a junior at St. Bernadette, too. I glance away. A man with shoulders as wide as a professional football player strides out of the hallway. A cushion of black hair makes up two inches of his height. Mascara flakes fall into my eyes. They start to water. I scrunch my toes in the Candie slides that are threatening to fall off my feet.

"I'm Henry. Marie Monsivais, huh?" His eyes scan my face to my feet. "You don't look twenty-one. Not even eighteen. Underage needs a work permit, and I don't want to deal with that."

I chew on my lip, taste the waxy lipstick. This is a long shot. "I got a baby face, but I am eighteen. That makes me old enough to work in the café part, right? I really need the job."

The boss' eyes match the color of his pompadour. He rubs his cheek. "Okay. An eighteen-year-old doesn't need a work permit. I could use someone waiting the tables. Part-time, four to nine o'clock. We're closed on Mondays. I pay cash, minimum wage. Olga will explain the tips."

My head bobs so fast I'm dizzy.

Henry points to Olga. "You work the bar because Marie can't serve liquor. Barbie can help you."

She screws up her hot pink lips but remains quiet. He extends his hand and shakes mine with a grip that men use with other men. "Don't steal, drink the liquor, come late or you're outta here." He glances over to Jerry. "Right?"

"You run a tight ship, Tío." He salutes his uncle.

"¿Entiendes?" Henry asks.

He scares the caca out of me. I wet my dry lips, nod. "Don't worry. I'm a good worker."

"One more thing. You can't be in the bar," He points to the back. "I get caught with minors, and I lose my license."

"Yeah, got it." I nod.

"Come back tomorrow, four o'clock, María," Olga says. "And don't be wearing those Candie's shoes. Wear tennies." She disappears through the red doors.

Jerry clears his throat. "Hey, don't you go to St. Bernadette?"

"Nah, you must have me confused," I say over my shoulder and tear out the front door.

The hard part is over. I got the job. How bad can thirty days be?

A tinny bell rings when I run into the Mini-Mart. Caroline sits on the gleaming linoleum floor reading *Seventeen*, a smiling blonde girl on the cover.

"Got the j-o-b," I shout.

She jumps up, hugs me. We twirl around right there in the aisle between the candy bars and the refrigerated section. We haven't done that since we were little kids.

"Start tomorrow. He didn't buy that I'm twenty-one, but I told him I'm eighteen. I can't serve liquor," I say, out of breath. "Two bucks an hour, plus I get tips. The owner, El Lobo, is a gigantor of a man. Scared the crap out of me."

Mr. Singh, the younger one, pokes his head in the aisle. "May I help you, ladies?"

"No, thanks." Caroline sets the magazine back on the top rack. "My sister has a j-o-b."

He smiles. "Congratulations."

"Yikes, Mom," Caroline says, pointing at the store window.

Our station wagon drives into the small parking lot of the Mini-Mart. A car horn blasts. After the first toot, the sound lowers into a whining moan like a dying cow.

"Oh, my god. She'll kill me if she finds me in her clothes." I squash my hairdo down and kick off the Candies.

"Run," Caroline says. "Quick, I'll stall her." She jogs outside and blocks Mom's view while I tear past our car.

"Jacqueline?" Mom's voice in the distance shrinks. "Jacqueline Marie?"

I run with my arms against my chest, hoping my boob socks don't fall out until I get inside the house.

My face burns after I scrub off the blush and red lipstick at the bathroom sink. The front door slams.

"Jacqueline, why did you run when I honked? I called you." Mom jogs up the stairs.

"Had to go pee really bad," I yell while running a wet comb through my teased-up hair.

The door flings open. Caroline pokes her head around Mom's shoulder. "Tell her the good news. About the Mini-Mart."

"Oh, yeah." Pushing Mom's red slides behind the door, I cross my fingers. "The owner, uh, Mr. Singh, gave me a job. I start tomorrow, from four to nine. Monday's off. I'll take my books with me, study when it's slow."

Mom's eyes narrow into a squint, her forehead splits into two lines. She leaves with a sigh gushing behind her departure.

"What's that about?" Caroline flops on her bed. "You'd think she'd be happy."

"Listen, I think the busboy Jerry recognized me. He's a junior at St. Bernie."

"Pretend you don't recognize him. Avoid him."

Bobby stumbles into our room, all in a panic. "Mom's praying the rosary. I think she's crying."

What happened now? Can she tell I'm lying?

Through the dim light in her bedroom, I make out the outline of the boys' bunk beds against one wall and the twin bed on the other. Mom's fingers work the crystal rosary her mother gave her before she died. The light in the hallway falls on the end table between the beds, illuminating the photos of Dad in front of a helicopter in Vietnam. My parents' wedding picture is next to that one. Mom's white veil surrounds her lacy bride's dress. Dad's looking sharp in his dark blue Air Force uniform. The grins on their faces and sparkling eyes make me think they were very happy to be married.

The boys and Caroline crowd behind me in the doorway. "Are you all right?" I ask Mom.

"I prayed for more money, but I didn't think it would come from my daughter," she says, sitting up. "You need time to study to get A's and get to college."

"Mom, I just want to help. We're behind in tuition at our schools. I can't attend public school in the middle of the year because I'll lose out on the scholarship."

Her chest lifts up and down like she's struggling to breathe. I can't bear to tell her there's a deadline of March first. She might snap.

Plum-colored lips press into a straight line across her smooth face. She stares at the framed photo of Dad as if asking him what to do. "You'll work just enough to help me catch up. Shut the door, please."

"We owe tuition money?" Bobby's big cinnamon eyes glisten.

"How much?" John asks.

Damn it. They're just little kids. They shouldn't have to worry about such things.

"Let's go into our room." I motion them to our bedroom.

Caroline closes the door. "Might as well tell them."

"We're behind a little bit, but it'll be fixed soon." I plaster on a smile so they don't get too scared. "With me working and Mom's new job, we'll be fine."

Bobby scratches his head. "We should write Grandpa for money."

"Good idea," John nods.

The twins take off downstairs. Caroline bites her lip. Mom will be so pissed if the boys ask our grandparents for money.

⚜ ⚜ ⚜

When we were at our grandparents after the funeral services for Dad, Grandpa and Mom had an argument.

Grandpa insisted Mom move us all out to live with them. When Mom said what was she going to do out in the boonies, the thud of a Coors beer can hit the kitchen table. Grandma flew from her chair like a little bird and shooed us into the living room. Caroline and I snuck back to the doorway and watched while Grandma entertained the boys with photo albums.

"I've already signed up back home for school," Mom explained.

"What do you mean, school?" Grandpa's penetrating voice was loud.

"I've signed up for night school to finish an accounting program." Her voice was quiet but strong. "Classes are four nights a week."

"Mothers take care of their kids. They stay home. Who's gonna watch them? Not strangers."

"I have a babysitter for us, our neighbor. I'll finish in six months, if I work hard."

"But you don't need a diploma to work in the meat packing house."

Her smile faded. She picked at her fingernails. Mom turned into a little girl before my eyes with her head dropped like a scolded child.

My bottom lip was sore from chewing on it. It was the only way to stop myself from barging in on them and telling Grandpa that Mom worked hard, she stood for eight to ten hours, sorting vegetables in a cold factory back home. Her plastic apron stunk like wet broccoli, even after she washed it late at night.

Mom must've prayed for strength because her head popped up. She stared Grandpa in the eyes. "I don't want to work in a factory or a slaughterhouse for the rest of my life. I can get a better job with an accounting certificate. Maybe go to community college."

His fist hit the table. "*Ay, sí*, college. What the hell are you thinking?"

Mom shrunk back into her chair, but she didn't stop looking at him. "It's for a better job."

"You don't even have a decent car," he said.

"If it breaks down, I'll take the bus," Mom's voice grew stronger. "Or walk."

"Easier if you and the kids moved here and lived with us. It's decided, *y ya*."

"Their lives are already upside down," Mom shouted. "I'm not changing their home or schools. I'll take care of them. That's *my* responsibility."

Caroline and I whispered, "Dang," which caused Mom to turn to see where the voices came from.

We scooted back into the living room.

Since then, Mom has been telling me we shouldn't ask anyone for anything because she can handle our family. When she first said that, I thought we'd be okay and everything would get better. But after we had to move from our house and sell Dad's truck, everything kept going downhill. Now it's overdue tuition.

The beginnings of a headache squeeze my eyes shut. I grab my pillow, clutch it against my stomach.

"Why did you tell the boys everything will be fixed soon?" Caroline asks. "How're you gonna handle this?"

Typical. I'm the one to solve the problem, but Caroline's right. I'm the oldest, and Dad said I had to look out for them.

"They're kids. They don't need to know the details. And I'm gonna stall Sister Mary by paying a little each week."

"Like a layaway plan? Please." Caroline rolls her eyes before she flops on her bed. "It won't work. I'd rather go to public school, anyways."

Her words say she wants to go, but she doesn't sound convincing. She's giving up, and I can't let her.

"Listen, I only need to make a hundred and fifty bucks, and then we're caught up until March. By that time, Mom will pay off St. Patrick's tuition and the other bills. Don't worry. I got it figured out. We'll be fine."

Now I'm trying to convince myself.

CHAPTER 10

No one says a word during the ride to school. Everyone is thinking about last night's scene when I told Mom about the new job. She drives into the large parking lot next to St. Patrick Church. The boys scramble out of the station wagon to deliver bookkeeping paperwork that Mom does for the rectory.

Caroline slides out of the car, leans next to my ear and whispers, "Maybe I'll stop by and check out your new job."

I hope Mom didn't catch her wink and smile, or she'll know something's fishy, and it's not our tuna sandwiches.

"Those boys are taking forever." Mom drums her fingers on the steering wheel. "Listen, I'm not telling your *abuelos* about your job at the Mini-Mart. Out at night in a place that sells liquor and cigarettes. Your *tío* Mario didn't like it either."

"You can tell him that Mr. Singh doesn't sell liquor. John wrote Grandpa a letter last night. He might have told him I'm working there."

"What?" Mom's neck swivels to me, her eyes saucers. "He's the last person I want finding about our business. I'm making a life for us here."

Barely, but I can't tell her that, she'll blow up. The boys return to the car and scramble inside for their books and lunches.

"Look, Father Armando gave us *pan dulce*," Bobby says, holding out a pink powdered piece of Mexican sweet bread. "Wanna piece?"

"Uh, John? You wrote your *abuelo* a letter?" Mom asks.

He nods, slips a piece of paper out of his folder, holds it up. "I need an envelope and stamp. And Bobby drew Abuela a picture of Mrs. Washington's new dog."

"So sweet of you, boys. Give the letter to me, and I'll mail it for you."

The boys pile out of the car with a quick wave. I wonder what Mom will do with the letter. I'm sure my grandparents won't find out about my job until she decides. The less they know, the better.

"I'll read the letter at break time," Mom says and pulls out of the parking lot.

I punch the radio dial. "In local news, an organization called Chicanos for a Better Colonia has called on the city council to build another exit out of a neighborhood citing emergency delays and medical mishaps."

"The what?" Mom turns to me.

"They said the Chicanos for . . ."

"I heard that, but *who* are they?"

The gulp in my throat grows as I debate whether I should tell her I'm involved. All I've done is attend one meeting. "What they're doing is a good thing. Isn't it?"

She smacks her lips and shrugs. "Troublemakers. Nothing will change."

I want to tell her that's not true. Her forehead smushes to her eyebrows, with a don't-push-me-scowl on her face. I could tell her that every day someone or something alters our life. The bus schedule, the train, the school and the city. Dad dying. At least if we're the ones deciding on the changes, things might become better. But I don't say a word. I don't want to add to her worries.

Mom parks the station wagon at the sidewalk a few blocks from St. Bernie and turns off the engine. "Be careful. Call me tonight when you're off work, I'll pick you up."

I give her a backhanded wave and watch the car swing back onto the road. I guess I'll need to keep my participation in the CBC undercover. Another thing to hide.

⚜ ⚜ ⚜

The whole school day, I dodge Jerry and Sister Mary Grace like I'm that guy from *The Fugitive* on TV. The sixth-period bell shrieks. Grabbing my books, I run to my locker and into the bathroom stall to change my clothes for my first shift at El Lobo's Bar and Grill.

If I had a compact mirror, I could put my make-up on in the stall or on the bus, but no such luck. I stick my uniform back into the wrinkled grocery bag and set my stuff down on the window ledge by the sink, where I cover my plastic sandwich bag of cosmetics with my books.

With no experience using an eyelash curler, I mimic Mom's routine. Staring straight into the mirror, I bring the steel thing close to my eyelashes, press down and count to ten. Now, the other eye. The thin brush inside the eyeliner bottle is goopy with black liquid. I skim some inky stuff off, when the bathroom door swings open.

"Give it here." Lucy snatches the bottle from my hand. "Sit up on the sink. Let me show you the right way."

While I try to balance myself on the sink ledge, she pulls my eyelid to the side. The cold, wet fluid slides above my lashes.

"Hey, that was pretty funny when you drew Sister and called her Sister Mary Graceless."

"Yeah, thanks for the demerit."

Lucy blows a long puff of air over my eyelid. "Sorry, but I couldn't help laughing. Hey, where you going that you're putting on make-up after school?"

The eyeliner frames my hazel eye, making them turn up in a cool almond shape.

"Tell me, or I'm not doing the other eye." She takes a step back, holding the eyeliner applicator hostage.

"Geez, I'm just experimenting. Hurry up. I gotta catch the bus." I grab the make-up, throw it inside my purse.

Her gaze follows the bag. "Let me show you how a pro does it."

In a minute, she has the other eye done, brushes on my mascara and finishes up with the blush. "No lipstick?"

I'm embarrassed to take my plastic baggie from my purse, so I shake my head no. She digs into her tooled leather bag until she brings out three colorful tubes of Yardley lipsticks. She dangles them in front of my eyes like expensive jewels. "Pinky, Tangerine or Berry-Licious? Pick."

One is Pepto Bismol pink. The other looks like Cheez Whiz. I point to the Cherry Jell-O color.

"Have it. I don't like that one. Too red for my skin tone." She drops the plastic tube in my hand.

"Thanks. Gotta go."

I jump off the sink, grab my brown bag and swing the strap of my purse over my shoulder. The bus is due in five minutes.

"See you on the flip side," she yells when I run out of the bathroom.

The doors to the city bus stutter open. The driver tugs on his thick mustache while I drop my dimes into the coin slot and take a seat behind him. I glance in the driver's rear-view mirror. The make-up does make me look older. That was nice of Lucy, but I wonder why she's so chummy with me all of a sudden.

A pendant with a huge Our Lady of Guadalupe image swings from the bottom of the mirror. It's probably sacrilegious to ask the Virgin to help me keep a job that I lied my way into, but I ask her anyway. *Virgencita, help me, just for a month.*

The pendant slaps the front window with a clack while we jolt forward. Was that a no? The bus heads down the boulevard, over the railroad tracks and toward the Mini-Mart. I pull on the cord. The bus jerks to a stop at Mela Street.

The Help Wanted sign is no longer in El Lobo's window. The Pabst Blue Ribbon clock over the counter shows three fifty-five. Made it. I swipe on a firm coat of Berry-Licious over my lips, fluff up my hair and stride inside.

CHAPTER 11

Olga twirls the black telephone cord between her stubby fingers, blabbing into the receiver. She hangs up the receiver and snaps her chewing gum. "Come, María."

Her voice sounds like the German Commandant on *Hogan's Heroes,* giving me an order. I follow her down the wood-paneled hallway where we pass a faded brown door with a white plastic Manager sign.

"Is that El Lobo's office?"

"Henry's the manager. El Lobo's the other one," she says smirking and unlocks the door to the small storage room. "María, you here to work, not be a nosey."

She throws me a few aprons from a stack on the top shelf. Paper goods, cans and cleaning supplies fill the other shelves. "Today, you bus the tables until Barbie gets here. Jerry's off."

"*Mah-ree*, not María," I correct her as I tie on my apron, then load up my arms with supplies and return to the counter.

Olga pushes the kitchen door open. I see a man around my grandpa's age, short and wiry, wearing a splattered apron and black hairnet.

"This is the cook, Pepe. He can help if you need him. But don't need him, *entiendes*?"

The man nods to me and continues chopping vegetables. Something boiling on the stove hisses. There's dozens of tortillas stacked nearby. Cans and spice containers crowd the counter behind Pepe. I wave to him.

"Okay, María, now fill the napkin containers, put out the bowls for salsa and give that table water cups."

The rapid-fire directions stop when she disappears through the swinging red doors to the bar side. Jerry's absence is the best news I've heard. One less thing to worry about.

Workmen trudge into the bar around four-thirty with their tired faces and cement splotches on faded jeans. The black lunch pails they carry remind me of Dad's. The twins would run to the door when he came home, fighting to see who carried it to the kitchen sink. For months, we all glanced at the front door around five o'clock. Sometimes, I catch the twins still watching.

Olga giggles while the men flirt with her. She attracts attention all right, swinging her hips in her snug yellow jeans and black low-cut top. She's nice-looking in a hard-girl way. Reminds me of Jayne Mansfield in those old movies Mom watches on Saturday nights.

After a while busing tables, sweeping, wiping down counters and giving orders to Pepe, my feet are walking bruises. I climb on a counter stool for a quick break and glance out the front window, where a lady paces back and forth. She clutches at her rabbit fur coat with one hand and a cigarette dangling in the other. The glow of the cigarette butt falls to the curb.

"Hey." The woman pushes in the front door and walks up to me. "You new here?"

The lady's sweeping fake eyelashes and ton of blue eyeshadow can't disguise that she's about Bebe's age, twenty. She runs her hand through her brunette hair while her eyes dart from me to the back of the restaurant and over to the hallway.

"Yeah, I'm Marie. Hired yesterday."

"I'm Barbie. How old are you?"

"Old enough. Olga said you're working today."

"Pfft." She pulls a light blue envelope out of the back pocket of her tight jeans. "Henry in his office?"

"Nope. Olga's in the bar, though. I'll go get her."

"No." Her hand flies up and stops at her shoulder. She twirls a strand of her hair. "Uh, I mean, don't bother. I'll just be a sec."

Barbie steps down the hall, but I can't follow her because another customer comes inside. By the time the guy sits at the counter and orders, she's back.

"I'll tell Olga you were here."

"Don't tell that *puta* anything. You didn't see nothing," she says. "And you're not eighteen, either."

Dang, I guess she doesn't like Olga, and she's not easily fooled. The front door swings closed behind her as she jogs across the street to the bus stop.

By seven o'clock, I want to lie down on top of the Formica counter. The pain in my arms from lifting the dishpan filled with dirty plates, utensils and glasses pulsates from my shoulder to my cramped fingers. Red chili sauce and blotches of refried beans decorate my apron.

The bar doors swing open. Olga enters with a tray of used glasses. "María, get these."

Before I make a move, a police officer stands at the front door. He glances left and right.

Olga perks up and gives him a toothy smile. "Officer Palermo. How you are today?"

The cop holds his motorcycle helmet in his hand and nods before he slides into a booth facing the door. By the time he puts his stuff down, Olga's ready with a menu. He glances over at me.

"She's the new girl. María," she says. "Part-time, started today."

The cop doesn't smile. I hope he's not one of those hard-asses who like to let everyone know they're in charge. I gulp at the thought that he might ask for my ID. I don't even have a driver's license. What would I show him? My school ID? Be calm, act older and stay out of his way.

He lowers his head to read the two-sided menu. Olga snaps her fingers at me, points to the water pitcher on the counter. I pour him a glass of water while she hovers over him, waiting. Against his fair skin, his dark eyes and black lashes look like a girl's eyes. They're so pretty.

He lifts his head slightly and smiles. "Thank you, María."

I let out a breath and back up to the counter. "My name's Marie. You're welcome."

"Your usual enchiladas?" Olga asks him.

"No. *Chile relleno*, no beans, just rice," he says. "And cof-fee. Black."

"Got it," Olga says before she wiggles her way into the kitchen.

Palermo adjusts his posture and glances over at me. "Marie's a nice name. My mother's name is Marie."

I nod and turn away. I don't want him staring at me for too long. The radio on his belt crackles with words I don't under-stand. He grabs it, says something and picks up his helmet.

"Box up my order. I'll be back later." In two long steps, he's out the front door.

Olga returns and scans the area. "He in the bathroom?"

"Had to leave, I guess. He said to tell you to box the order."

Olga smiles like I just told her he said, "Goodbye, *mi amor*."

"*Ay qué chulo.*" She gives a pretend shiver, pronouncing the word *chew-low*, like she's tasting the word and him. "He always leaves a good tip. Put extra tortillas and rice in his carryout."

"Is he Mexican?"

"*Ay, no. Italiano.*" She fingers her chin. "You heard what they say about the *italianos*?"

"Nope." I shrug, pick up his water glass and wipe the table.

"Ha, if you were eighteen, you'd know what I mean." She turns on her heel and heads to the bar.

She's weird.

The beer clock reads eight-fifty-five. "Hey, it's almost time for me to go."

Olga pivots and returns to flip the Open sign to Closed. She sticks a handwritten sign that says BAR Open in the window.

"Okay, we split the tips from this side, just you and me, since that *pinche* Barbie didn't show up." Olga reaches into her bra, throws dollar bills onto the counter, then wedges her hand into her front pocket and pulls out coins.

She moves the bills over in front of her. "This *dinero* is from the bar side."

I pull out my pockets, drop the coins I got for tips onto the counter. I'm counting the quarters and dimes in my head when she scoops up half of them and moves them to her pile. She's off by seventy-five cents. For half a second, I think I should let her have it, but I did more work than she did, especially all the heavy work. My dad always said not to let people take advantage of you, or they'll think you're a pushover.

"Hey, that was eleven dollars and fifty cents of coin, Olga. My half is five dollars and seventy-five cents." I reach for my portion.

"Give me a paper." She takes her ballpoint pen from behind her ear.

This time she counts the coins slowly and makes little hash marks on the paper. At a minute to nine o'clock, I grab a couple of napkins and dip them in a water glass to take with me. I'll need to take my make-up off on the run.

Olga scratches her head again and hands over the seventy-five cents. Damn, right I was correct.

"Thanks. I bet you're tired," I say instead.

"Three more hours in the bar." She lets out a long puff of air and adjusts the shiny clip in her hair. "*Cabrona*, Barbie. Wait till I see her."

Jogging to the end of the street, I run around the block to the Mini-Mart while swiping off my lipstick and eyeshadow with the cold napkins.

Mom's not even here.

A couple of older guys crouch by the side wall of the store, drinking from paper bags. I book it inside and make my way over to the candy aisle.

"You must be the owner, the young Mr. Singh." I unload my penny candy onto the counter. "The older Mr. Singh was here the other day."

His face widens with a smile of white teeth. The guy looks Mexican, except for the turban.

"Yes, my father." He counts each piece of candy before scooping them into a little bag. "Sweets so late at night?"

"I work around the corner. These are for my brothers."

"Very nice." He nods, hands me the bag.

The screeching sound of car tires fills the inside of the store. Mr. Singh and I go to the front window. A cop car, lights blinking, sits in the parking lot. Two guys take off running behind the store. Palermo drives his motorcycle onto the side-walk.

Our station wagon pulls up to the curb across the street. I beat it out of the store before Mom toots the dying cow of a car horn.

"What's going on? Was there a robbery?" Mom says when I jump into the front seat.

"Nothing happened in the store. The cops went after some guys drinking on the street."

"Your uncle said he stopped by the Mini-Mart to see you, but you weren't there."

He would check up on me. "Hmm," I shrug. "Probably stuck in the back unpacking supplies."

"He wants to make sure you're okay."

"Everything went fine."

If my uncle's keeping tabs on me, I'll need to come up with a few excuses ahead of time. There's no way I'm losing this job.

CHAPTER 12

The bell buzzes with a sharp blast releasing a crowd of kids into the narrow hallway. I dodge open locker doors, bob and weave around the circles of giggling cheerleaders who buzz near the jocks like flies. I've got to run to the girl's lavatory before I catch the bus to El Lobo's.

"Jacqui, hey, wait up." Petey touches the top of my shoulder. "You're not staying?"

His eyes scan mine as if we had a date after school. The blush on his cheeks reddens before he drops his chin and stares at his black high-top tennis shoes. This is twice in one week where Petey talks to me. I should have called him "Pay-droh" a long time ago, if that's what it took to get his attention. He scratches the back of his neck. What's he all tongue-tied about?

"I'm kinda in a hurry," I say.

"Oh. Yeah, well, I uh have a game and thought you'd stay to see me play."

A warm flush moves up my neck as each second ticks by. My cheeks must be flaming tomatoes and not from using blush, either. I press my palm against the side of my face to hide my embarrassment. "Can't, I gotta work today."

"Heard you work at the new Mini-Mart. I rode by last night on my way home, saw your mom's car."

"Uh, yeah, I work 'til nine."

He edges closer to me like he's going to tell me a secret. His deep brown eyes look into mine as I press up against my locker door, my arms tight against the grocery bag holding my clothes.

"On your day off, could we, uh, study together?"

My heart freezes, then starts pounding. My whole face is on fire. He doesn't budge. I check myself, trying to stay cool even though my legs quiver. "Okay, um, sure."

The spreading grin on his face makes me squeal inside, but I keep my body steady.

"Great. Okay, then."

"Later," I say as composed as I can be so the somersaults happening in my stomach don't betray me.

Bolting to the lavatory, I slap my hand on my mouth because I want to whoop and holler that Petey Castro asked me—the fumbling, brainiac Jacqui Bravo—to study with him.

"Saw that," Lucy says, popping the door open. "You got a thing going on with Petey?"

"No. He just wanted to study together."

"Probably needs help to pass a test."

My shoulders droop with the weight of her words. That's it. He wants me to help him study for an exam. Dang it. How could I think Petey's invitation was something more? I plunge my hand into my book bag, groping for my plastic baggie of make-up, find my comb and start teasing my hair.

"Aww, you got a boyfriend at another school, huh?" Lucy crowds behind me. "Oh my God, you do, and you don't want Petey to find out. I got it. Cool."

She's creating a *novela* about me in her head. What if she tells him?

"No boyfriend. I'm changing for work. So, if you'd leave me in peace."

Lucy's face scrunches up like someone just stunk up the bathroom. "Work? Don't your parents give you an allowance?"

This girl's never been poor. Next time, I'm using the bathroom on the other side of campus.

"Can you do my eyes again?" I ask.

"Sure." Lucy whips a bright floral cosmetic bag out of her cream macramé purse. With a few flicks, she's done. "You can have this make-up bag. If you want. I got lots."

People don't do stuff for someone else for nothing. Especially someone who hasn't talked to me in the past three years at St. Bernadette.

"No thanks."

⚜ ⚜ ⚜

Jerry lugs a tray full of clean glasses onto the back counter. "Grab more supplies out of the closet."

"Sure thing."

The less he can get a good look at me, the better. If he recognizes me as a senior at St. Bernadette and tells Olga I'm in school, she'll know I lied and tell Henry. He'll fire me because he doesn't like to mess with kids who need work permits.

I rush down the hall and bump into Olga coming from the boss' office. A smear of red lipstick coats the bottom of her mouth. She glances at me, turns the opposite way to the bathroom. Henry had a wedding ring on his finger when he interviewed me. None of my business, though. I grab supplies and hustle back.

"The napkin dispensers and salsa bowls need filling," Jerry orders, as he moves from booth to booth setting out water glasses.

He turns back to the counter, pauses and pushes his thick, black-framed glasses up his large nose. With a name like Jerry, he could have picked another type of frame. He looks like a pudgy Jerry Lewis from the *Nutty Professor*, except with good teeth.

"I'm a Junior at St. Bernadette," he says. "In the chess club. Used to be in audio-visual too, but I'm working here to buy a car."

I lower my head and concentrate on tying my apron. "Why isn't Olga helping us?"

"She'll be on the bar side most of our shift. I guess Barbie called in sick."

"On a Friday night? How are we going to handle everything?"

"Don't worry. I'll show you what to do."

A soccer team crowds through the door and takes up all the booths. I load their tables with baskets of chips, salsa and glasses of water.

"Hey, you're new. Come 'ere," an older scruffy guy says, patting his leg.

My nose scrunches before Jerry clears his throat. "Knock it off. This is Marie, my, uh, *prima* on my mom's side."

Whoa, who knew he could take charge? The group quiets down after that and moves over to the bar section.

"Thanks, Jerry."

He buses the soccer team's table. "Four more months, and I'll have enough money to buy my '68 Nova. Hey, how do you get to and from work? Wanna ride? My dad's coming for me at nine. Pops stays every weekend night, but I have my permit, so he lets me drive his car home."

"My mom's coming for me." He's nosy. "Eight o'clock, one more hour."

The front door swings open, bringing in the scent of powdery perfume and cigarette smoke. Olga's friends, wearing black mini-skirts and white knee-high boots, saunter inside. They wear identical clothes, but one is short and plump with auburn hair piled on her head, while the other is skinny, with a sleek pageboy and long bangs covering her brows.

"*Hola, chica. Hola,* Jerry." The redhead waves to us as she sways her full hips down to the last booth.

The other one follows. Her steps unsteady like she's already drunk.

"*M'ija,*" the red-head says. "Bring me a soda and chips. This one needs a coffee. Strong."

"The coffee's old, I'll make some fresh."

"No, no. She don't care." She glances over to Jerry and bats her false eyelashes at him. "*Ay* Jerry, when we gonna go on a date?"

A date? The lady is at least Olga's age. Jerry's chipmunk cheeks blush. He disappears down the hallway, saying he has to find the broom.

"*Chica,* what's your name?" the red-head asks.

"Marie. I'll bring some water and check the coffee."

"Mah-ree? I'm Socorro, but call me Coco. And this," she points to the other lady slouched in the booth, "is Cha Cha. Hey, wake up, *cabrona.*" Coco pushes at her thin arm.

I set the coffee cup down in front of Cha Cha, who inches her hand forward. Lady must be on downers or some kind of drug. She moves so slowly. Coco dumps four heaping teaspoons of sugar into the cup, stirs the coffee, then pushes it closer to Cha Cha.

"Drink it," she shouts.

An older skinny guy in a pressed Pendleton and creased khaki pants strolls out of the bar and sits with the ladies. He hikes up his pants before he sits, cocks his head at Cha Cha and moves his finger to her cup of coffee.

"*Trágalo,*" Coco says.

In slow motion, Cha Cha picks something off the table, places it on her tongue and gulps the coffee. All three disappear into the bar two minutes later.

Jerry shakes his head while he busses the table. "They come in after Palermo's gone."

I'm guessing they don't like cops, so I shrug. "Okay."

"You know, 'cause they're *putas*."

Jerry says this as easily as if he called them school teachers. The ladies are out there with their heavy make-up and tight clothes, but no different looking than Olga.

"Sorry," he says. "I should've said ladies of the night. Time to divide up the tips."

Jerry insists we divide them equally, although he did more work. Stuffing the tips into my pockets, I wave goodbye and jog over to the Mini-Mart. A huge new Buick LeMan's drives into the parking lot and honks. I don't know anyone in that kind of car, so I continue into the store.

"Hey, Mr. Young Singh."

He laughs, waves at me while I grab a big package of chocolate chip cookies for the kids.

"That was me honking." Jerry's voice behind me startles me. "You sure you don't want a ride?"

"No, thanks. My mom's outside waiting."

"Okay, see you later," he says, grabbing a bag of Granny Goose potato chips.

That was a close one. I take the brown bag from Mr. Young Singh and book it outside. Sliding into the front seat of the station wagon, I find the twins in the back seat.

"Got you a surprise." I hold up the cookies.

"Wow, chocolate chips," they shout and clamber over the seat.

"Where's Caroline?" I ask.

"That girl. I let her go to Becky's, and she's an hour late."
Mom guns the motor. "We're stopping by Matilda's place, and
Caroline better not be there."

We park in front of a dark little house with dirt for a front
yard. A bunch of old tires are stacked up at the corner of the
place. The porch light is out. The place seems deserted.

"Wait here." Mom keeps the car running and leaves the
headlights on.

She knocks several times and then bangs on the door.
Lights on the houses next to Matilda's light up, but no one
answers. Mom marches to the car, her jaw set. "That girl will
be the death of me."

We trail behind Mom, who unlocks our front door. Caroline's lounging on the sofa watching *The Flip Wilson Show*.
Bobby drops into the couch next to her and wrinkles his nose.

"Where were you?" Mom says and hangs up her sweater in
the hall closet. "You weren't at Becky's or Matilda's."

"I was at Becky's. I walk slow." She scrambles off the couch
and jogs upstairs. "I gotta shower."

I follow her to the bathroom. "Hey, I'm sure you're not
showering."

She pokes her head out, peers behind me. "Mom still downstairs?"

"Yeah, now, scram. My feet hurt, my back aches. I gotta
soak in the tub." I push open the door. "Where were you really?"

"We hung out with one of Mousy's friends. I met the cutest
guy there. He's sixteen. I think. They call him Sleepy 'cause of
his dreamy eyes."

She pulls her hair up in a ponytail to wash her face. A purple
bruise on her neck peeks out of her blouse.

"Ooh, you better hide that from Mom."

She pulls her collar up. "Oh, crap."

"Dang, you just met this guy, and you already have a hickey? You're not even fourteen."

"Almost." Her eyebrows tent. "How do I get rid of it?"

"Grab that pancake make-up Mom wears. It's thick. Use some of that."

While she searches for the make-up in the cabinet under the sink, I run hot water into the tub.

"Found it." Caroline flips open the compact and dabs the beige foundation on her neck with the sponge. "How does it look?"

The mark is now a greasy tan welt. Mom's skin tone is much darker than Caroline's. My eyes wince just looking at the spot.

"What?" She leans closer to the mirror over the sink. "Dang it. What am I going to do?"

"I overheard Bebe talk to her friends about hickeys. She said you can rub them out with a spoon."

"Really? Go bring me one." Caroline's voice rises and cracks. "Please?"

"Watch the water." I run downstairs, find a spoon.

Five minutes of spooning, and not one bit of difference, except the make-up rubbed off.

"I'm pooped, and my water's turning cold." I throw the spoon into the sink, step into the tub.

"Guess this stuff is better than nothing." Caroline dabs more foundation on her hickey. "How was work?"

I tell her about El Lobo, Olga and Jerry.

"Is Jerry cute?"

"Is that all you think about? He wears glasses, has a crew cut and is on the chess club."

She snorts a laugh. "Sounds like a dork."

"He's buying a '68 Nova soon and plans to go to USC. Sounds smart to me."

"Well, my guy is so cute, everyone wants to be with him. He has this wavy black hair, combed back, hazel eyes and oh, his lips, so. . ."

"Oh, brother, you sound like a cheap book."

"Okay, Miss Sophisticated-I work-at-El Lobo's. You probably see a bunch of old drunks all night."

"Mostly, but this cop came in, and he was movie-star handsome. Friendly too."

"Stop gossiping." Mom pounds the door. "I need to use the bathroom."

"Oh shit," Caroline whispers.

She unlocks the door and slips by Mom, who rushes into the bathroom, leaving the door open.

"Gawd, Mom. Do you have to pee while I'm in here?"

"When you gotta go, you gotta go, Miss Prissy. What were you girls gossiping about?"

"Work stuff." I slide the glass doors to the tub shut for privacy. "I told Caroline about the handsome motorcycle cop who comes by the Mini-Mart."

"Must be Palermo."

"How do you know a cop?"

"Never mind," Mom says and turns to shout to Caroline while she washes her hands. "I heard you calling someone cute. Remember the rules, Caroline. No dating 'til you're seventeen. At sixteen, you can go to school events. Start too early, by the time you're eighteen, and you think you know everything."

Mom has harped on dating ever since Dad died. I don't care about her rules, except if, by some miracle, Petey asks me out on a real date.

"You're so old-fashioned," Caroline yells back. "Lots of girls my age date already."

"Someone else's daughters, not mine. You go ahead and try behind my back, and you won't date until 1982."

CHAPTER 13

The switch from working a night shift to working this morning has me groggy. Olga asked me to help, since Barbie's still not answering her phone. The thought of extra money has me out the door in ten minutes.

The bright sunlight streaming in from the curtainless windows heats up the small café as much as the roasted red salsa we serve. Noisy babies with their mothers in church dresses and fathers in black slacks fill El Lobo's booths. The volume rises as I serve bowls of *menudo* to hungry families. The scent of spicy chile broth hangs in the air, along with the sharp smell of oregano, diced onions and lime wedges.

I hand Jerry four empty salsa bowls. "We could sure use more help."

"Barbie's missed so much work, my uncle fired her. He'll hire someone else."

"Your dad's car is out front. Where is he?"

"Back in the office with my uncle. Grab us more napkins while I fill these bowls."

The solitary bulb inside the supply closet casts a dim yellow light over the area, giving it an eerie look. A loud thwack, like a fist hitting a table, echoes through the hallway. Startled, I poke my head out of the pantry. A sliver of light peeks from under the boss' office door. Shadows crisscross through the space. Henry's voice climbs to a boom. Another thump.

"*Idiota*," a deep voice yells over and over. "How could you be so stupid?"

Damn, someone's in trouble. I hustle to the front of the restaurant and start filling napkin holders. Seconds later, a stocky man, older and shorter than Henry, strides into the restaurant from the hallway, reminding me of a bulldog with a thick mustache—the mean kind, not the cute cartoon ones. Beady eyes study me.

The man pivots to Jerry at the cash register. "*Ya me voy*," his voice rasps. "Tell your *tío* to bring you home when you're done."

"Sure, Dad."

Jerry's father slams the front door with his hand and disappears into his sleek LeMan's. Henry passes by, head down, hands in his pockets and shuffles to the bar doors, where Olga's suddenly appeared.

We return to work as if nothing has happened. Should I tell Jerry I overheard his dad yelling at Henry? Better not. It's none of my business.

"Your shift's almost over," Jerry says. "Your tips." He hands me several dollar bills. The money is way better than the other days.

"Thanks. See ya."

By my estimation, I'll have seventy-five dollars by payday on Tuesday, enough to take to the school office and stall them for a while. Hopefully, Sister Mary Graceless will take my name off that awful ding list.

Around the corner of Mela Street, Caroline and Mousy stand in the Mini-Mart parking lot with two guys dressed in starched khakis and white T-shirts. Caroline's wearing my flare jeans and Mom's red Candie slides. The nerve.

"Hey." I wave her over. "What're you doing with my jeans and Mom's heels?"

"You left early, so I couldn't ask you. Mom's at Uncle Mario's making Sunday dinner."

Thick black eyeliner outlines her lids. White eyeshadow streaks under her penciled black eyebrows, making her look like a scared girl ghost.

"Go home. Take off my jeans. And wash off that chola make-up."

She glances back at Mousy, who wears identical make-up. I don't want to embarrass her, but really, the flares are my favorite, and Caroline's stretching them out.

"Jacqui," she whines, bouncing on Mom's Candies, "I'm talking with that guy I told you about. Sleepy."

"Scram. Now."

She crosses her arms in front of her chest, staring at me with her chin lifted. "No. And if you tell Mom, I'm telling her you're working in a bar."

"Go on, tell her. Then I'm grabbing you by your hair and showing her your hickey," I say louder. "You got one minute." I stare her down, so she understands, I'm not messing around.

"Ufff." She turns, waves goodbye to her friends. "*Ahi los wacho*."

She never talks cholo slang but thinks she needs to make a show in front of her friends.

"We gotta hightail it to Uncle Mario's." I pull her along down the block. "Why're you hanging around with those losers, anyways?"

"They're not in any gang, if that's what you think. They just like to dress sharp. You know? Don't go telling Mom anything, either."

"She has enough to worry about. Don't make things worse."

"We were just talking. God." Caroline huffs. "You're the one who worries too much."

I stop walking. "Dang it, people always tell me I'm too much of something. Too serious, too much of a worry wart, too quiet, too smart." I put my hands on her shoulders. "I don't want you running with a bunch of people going nowhere."

"Damn, you sound like Mom. Lighten up."

We arrive at Uncle Mario's and stand on the porch for a few seconds. "Mom sees that hickey, and all hell will break loose," I warn Caroline. "Run home and use more make-up to cover it better."

Caroline steps out of Mom's Candies, pushing them into a corner of the tiny cement slab, and gathers her hair into a side ponytail to cover her hickey. "I'm staying five minutes, then leaving. She won't see anything."

"Be a knucklehead, then." I glare at her before I step into my uncle's apartment.

On Sundays, Mom visits Uncle Mario to make dinner. He buys the food, and she cooks up a feast for all of us. She's done this since he lost his wife, Aunt Bernice, three years ago. She died from lung cancer. Uncle Mario quit smoking after that and said no one could smoke in his house anymore. Aunt Bernice didn't smoke. Go figure.

Hamburger meat, tomato sauce and the scent of onions frying fill the living room that adjoins the kitchen. Must be meatloaf. I flop on the couch to watch the football game with Uncle Mario, while he cracks sunflower seeds in his mouth. He passes the bag and the ceramic ashtray to me. Caroline perches on the edge of the other sofa.

"Where are your shoes?" Uncle Mario asks her.

"Outside. Got mud on them."

"Caroline, come help me with the biscuits. The dough's ready. You just need to cut them out," Mom calls out from the kitchen.

"Ask Jacqui. I'm not staying. I, uh, have cramps."

Caroline stands up. One false move, and Uncle Mario will see the hickey on her neck.

"She just got off work. And you had cramps last week." Mom walks into the living room, wiping her hands on her checkered apron. "Or did you forget? *Mentirosa.*"

Caroline sighs but doesn't budge. Uncle Mario throws a sofa pillow and pops Caroline in the face so hard she jumps, her side ponytail bouncing back away from her neck. He rises out of his seat quicker than a flea jumping on a dog.

"Caroline," his voice booms throughout the apartment. "What the hell?"

Mom's eyes grow wide. "*¿Qué paso?*"

The purple hickey on Caroline's neck looks enormous when her ponytail flaps away from her neck. Thankfully, Mom can't see it from where she stands.

Caroline darts out to the front door and runs out, leaving Mom's shoes on the porch. Uncle Mario follows her with Mom right behind him. They both stop on the sidewalk facing each other. His arms gesture wildly in the air before he points to his neck. Mom puts both her hands on her head, starts running in Caroline's direction, like a comic book scene. I stand on the porch and pop a sunflower seed into my mouth.

CHAPTER 14

The portable television on the restaurant counter blares Olga's favorite soap opera, *All My Children*, to an empty restaurant. Not many people come in on Tuesdays at four. Which is fine with me. I could use the slow period to work on my application.

"Olga, I'm here." No answer. "Olga?"

The further I move into the hallway, the louder the grunting noises sound. I stop at the supply closet, and the sounds begin again. They're further down the hall, at Henry's office. Olga's high-pitched voice utters, "*Ay, Dios, mi amor, ay Dios*," in rapid succession. Grabbing packages of napkins, I beat it to the front of the restaurant before I'm discovered. Nasty.

The coffee pot perks while I roll the utensils in individual napkins, fill water glasses and set them on a tray. Heels clatter down the hall toward the bathroom while Olga hums, and a door shuts. Through the front window I watch a cop cruise to the curb on his motorcycle and remove his helmet. Officer Palermo. Earlier than usual. He strolls in, slides into a booth facing the door.

"Just coffee, please."

"Cream?"

"No, but I'll have a slice of apple pie." He winks and takes off his black gloves.

He realizes El Lobo's doesn't have pie or cake. Not even *empanadas*.

"Where's Olga today?" he asks as I set his coffee cup down in front of him.

She's been in the bathroom for five minutes, but I don't tell him that. "Busy in the back."

"And the other girl? Haven't seen her around here."

"Beats me."

Palermo tilts his head and rubs his chin but doesn't ask any more questions. Olga prances down the hallway in jeans so tight, the seams must be screaming. Her fuchsia blouse hugs the bulges at the sides of her waist.

"Hola, Officer Palermo."

Lemony Jean Naté cologne hits my nose as her big butt brushes by me.

"Your usual?" she asks him.

The hallway door squeaks open. Henry walks by, glances at Olga and Palermo before disappearing into the bar section.

The radio on Palermo crackles. "No, got to run." He gulps his coffee, strides out the door.

In two seconds, Olga slides over to the cash register and elbows me. "How long he here before I come out?"

"Five, ten minutes." I book it to the table to wipe it down before she catches my hand trembling. Palermo's left a dollar for a fifty-cent cup of coffee.

"And you?" she asks.

"Couple of minutes before him." Dang, stop asking me questions already. "Hey, I finished my first week, so today's payday."

"Oh, yeah. Later." Olga places the back of her hand against her forehead. "I'm not feeling so good. Had to go to the bathroom for a long time." She pours herself a glass of water.

"Did you guys hire someone in Barbie's place? There's a lot to do."

"You and the cook can take care of the food. Jerry's busy today. I'll be in the bar." She turns on her heel and disappears past the swinging red doors.

For the next couple of hours, only a few people come in for a quick bowl of *albóndigas* or *caldo de res*. I wouldn't mind having beef soup on this chilly evening myself.

At eight o'clock, more customers come in, but they bypass the booths and head straight for the bar. For a Tuesday night, the bar is as busy as Saturday. Even Olga's friends, Coco and Cha Cha, skip their tortilla chips. Both of them wear bright silky crop tops tied under their black bras. Coco waves at me as Cha Cha makes a beeline to the bar.

My shift's finished, but Olga hasn't come out yet. I peer inside the swinging red doors of the bar entrance. Although the light is dimmer, I make out Olga against the bar, her back to me, smoking a cigarette. Henry sits at a table with the skinny guy from the other day. He was also with Caroline's guy, Sleepy, yesterday.

"Psst, Olga. Psst." I whisper. "Olga."

Cha Cha strolls over with crooked steps to where I stand. "Whaz up?"

"Time for me to leave. Can you tell Olga to come here?"

Cha Cha bobs her head. I shoo her away, so she knows what to do.

"Sure, sure, Ma-ree-a." She slurs her words as she wobbles to the bar on her platform heels and thumps Olga on the back. Olga pivots. Cha Cha puts up her thumb, motioning behind her.

The grimace on Olga's face is clear. She rushes toward me. "You can't be on this side."

"Yeah, but today is payday, and I need my money before I leave."

She waves her arm. "Go in the restaurant. I be there soon."

Dang, she acts like the bar section is a secret hangout. I back up and slide into a booth to wait.

"María," Olga pushes on the swinging doors with Henry following her. "Come on."

We wait outside Henry's office as he unlocks the door and flicks on the overhead light. A lamp illuminates the messy desk piled with invoices and receipts. An ashtray is blackened with use. Cigar smoke, whiskey and wet dog odor hang in the air. I try not to wrinkle my nose when he plops into a swivel chair behind the desk.

"Okay, María, you worked twenty hours."

"Twenty-five hours last week, five tonight." I glance back at Olga so she can back me up.

He shakes his head. "Olga, next time, write down her hours. Give them to me before the end of her shift. And you," he points to me, "remind Olga at the beginning of your shift, not the end, when she's busy."

Olga nods. "Yeah, we're busy here."

You'd think I asked for a handout instead of my pay. "Sixty dollars is what I calculated," I say.

Henry scribbles down some numbers. "You're right."

At least he can count correctly. He slides open the top drawer of his metal desk and pulls out several keys.

"Did Palermo come back tonight?" he asks while he flips through the ring.

They sure do wonder about him a lot. What are they worried about? Couldn't be his one order of *chiles rellenos*.

"Nope."

"Here." He counts out ten- and twenty-dollar bills. "Good money for a waitress, especially since you get tips. If you're here as long as Olga, you'll make real money. If you're as good as she is."

Olga's face turns into a toothy grin. She gazes at him like he's the best-looking man on earth.

"Okay, María, go home now." He slams the drawer shut making me jump.

He doesn't need to tell me twice. I run down the hall and out to the Mini-Mart, wiping my face and combing my hair. Mom's station wagon is parked by the sidewalk with the twins inside. Mom isn't there. John knocks on the inside of the window and points to the store. I run inside.

"There you are," she says, standing in one of the narrow aisles. "I came to look for you."

"Dumping the trash in the back." I rush out of the entrance ahead of her, and slide into the front seat of the car.

Mom starts the station wagon. "Were you paid tonight?"

"Yep. A whole week."

She sighs and pulls out into the street. "Good, because I need to talk to you at home."

CHAPTER 15

Could Mom have seen me leave El Lobo's? Maybe Uncle Mario saw me serving tables through the front window of the café and telephoned her at home.

"Boys, up to Caroline's room," Mom says, pointing upstairs. "Jacqueline, we need to talk. In private. In my room."

Next to Mom is the statue of the Virgin Mary under our stairwell. You can only lie so long, she seems to tell me. I follow her into her bedroom and stand by the door. "Am I in trouble or something?"

The bedroom door closes quietly. She grabs her rosary beads from the dresser. Everything in the bedroom, from the votive candles in front of her Lady of Guadalupe statue to a crucifix over her bed and talcum powder canister on her dresser, is the same as usual. Her fingers work the beads over and under her hand.

What's so serious we need to talk in private? Is she going to pull me out of St. Bernadette? Did she decide that all of us will transfer to public school?

Mom inhales, raises her chin with flushed cheeks. "I need twenty-five dollars."

"What? I need this money to keep myself in St. Bernie."

Doesn't she realize that the UCLA scholarship is the stepping stone to my future out of this mess? Asking me for money is like pushing me out of St. Bernadette.

"I'm behind on the rent. The housing authority is demanding a partial payment. The twenty-five dollars will help us keep our place."

My mouth dries up like I sucked in all the air in the bedroom. We're always behind with something. The light from the novena candle flickers over the Virgin's tawny face, illuminating her downcast eyes and clasped hands. She seems as sad as I am.

"I need the money." Mom's voice is firm, quiet, but strong. "I hate to ask, and I hate things this way, too. That's why I went to night school for accounting. I'm trying to get ahead. For all of you. This is no way to live, struggling every day, worrying about tomorrow."

Her voice is far away, but when I look up, her moist eyes stare right through me. Don't I know the feeling? That familiar twist in my chest returns. My throat shrinks. I can't cry in front of her. That'll make her as miserable as I am, and I don't want to see her like that again.

I run to my room and slam the door. "Damn it."

"What's happening?" Caroline bolts upright in her bed, clasping her *Teen Beat* magazine.

The boys turn to me. There's no way I'm telling the kids about Mom's request. "Nothing, but I don't want to talk to Mom."

"All right with me," Caroline says. "You guys, out."

The twins trudge out the door, staring at me. Ten minutes ago, my dreams were within reach. Sixty dollars and my tip money made eighty-seven bucks.

I'm taking my money to the school office first thing tomorrow morning and getting my name off the ding list. I'll win that scholarship and move the hell out of these projects, this town and this life.

"Poor David Cassidy. There's so much pressure on him." Caroline points to an article in *Teen Beat*.

"Whatever trouble he has is trivial. He's a movie star. Stupid rich people don't have serious problems."

"What's wrong with you?"

"Nothing. And where'd you get the magazine, anyway?"

"Don't worry about it. Mousy lent it to me."

"More like she stole it." I grab my sweater. "I'm outta here."

I tiptoe downstairs, crack open the front door and step onto the porch. The cold night air cools my seething anger. With the busted streetlamp and the neighbor's porch lights off, the stars shine brighter, white and sparkly, not the usual yellow dots in the sky.

From here, I see a bulb casting a weak glow on the porch down the street. The apartment belongs to the Castro's, Petey's place. His family leaves the light on for their father, who works two jobs and comes home at midnight.

Why did my dad have to leave for Vietnam? Why couldn't he stick to working at the military base over here? We had a rental house and no worries. Why did he have to die?

We just never seem to catch a break. Chilled air settles in my throat. I duck back inside the house. Bebe would have an idea. I'm calling her, even if it's long distance. By the time the bill arrives, I'll give Mom two dollars.

On my way to the telephone, I pass the altar under the staircase. A novena candle with a picture of a green-robed St. Jude sits next to the Virgin Mary. He's the saint of desperate causes. I touch the pedestal. "Do something for us, please," I whisper.

My lips touch the lower part of the phone cupped in my hand. "Hello, Bebe?"

"Jacqui? It's ten o'clock. What's wrong?"

"Mom asked me for money for rent. Twenty-five bucks. Can you believe that?"

"Yeah. She wouldn't ask unless she was desperate. If you have it, give it to her."

"What about my tuition?"

"She won't receive a full paycheck until next month. Even with her job, your mom can't make it yet. It'll take a few more months. Understand?"

I get it, but I'm pissed off. "But, we're behind on school payments. The principal's threatening to transfer me if we don't pay by mid-March."

"Give your mom fifteen, and my dad can lend her ten. The rest of what you have can go to your tuition. Stall the principal somehow."

For this, I spent a couple of bucks on a phone call. "I thought you were on my side. You know how important it is to win the alumni scholarship. My dream is to attend UCLA."

"Your grades are good enough for any college, and you applied for financial aid. Something else will come through. You can always count on me, but your mom needs the money now."

The stabbing pain in my throat builds up. "Sorry to bother you. Bye." I slam the phone down and crush my wish to attend UCLA.

Why is everything so complicated, so life and death? I pass Mom's open bedroom door and find her kneeling at her bed, head bowed, clutching her rosary beads. She struggles to stand and glances at me with her María Félix eyes, the Mexican movie star whose eyes are sad and wistful one minute, brave and challenging the next.

"My knees locked up." Her grimace turns into a weak smile as she rubs her leg.

"How long have you been kneeling?"

"I hope long enough. It's late." She points to the bunk beds where the boys are now sleeping and moves to where I stand. Her eyes are bloodshot and puffy. Dang it. She wouldn't ask me for money unless she's super worried. I pull twenty-five dollars from my jeans pocket and hand it to her.

"Thank you, Jacqueline. I'm sorry I had to ask you. I applied for a second job. Weekends. I don't know if I got it yet, but if I do, I'll catch up with the kid's tuition."

"Even with my paycheck, I'll be short with my school bill," I say.

"I'm juggling the utilities, the rent, food."

It's now or never, and I pick now, even though it's like socking Mom with another punch. I can't hide Sister Mary Graceless' late tuition letter any longer. "The principal said you didn't call her, so she gave me another letter."

She rubs her cheek with the palm of her hand. "I'll pull Caroline and the boys out of St. Patrick. With that money, I'll pay St. Bernadette's tuition."

That would make Caroline happy, but the way she acts, she'll spend her time slacking off, hanging out with Mousy. Instead of preparing for college, she might end up pregnant. Mom will have a heart attack, and Grandpa and Uncle Mario will tell Mom that's what happens when you're not home to take care of your kids.

"No. Caroline needs to go to St. Bernadette. The boys need to stay in St. Patrick. Pay their bill first. Uh, I'll make enough by the deadline to pay the tuition."

"I'll meet with Sister George, explain our situation and ask for a payment plan," Mom says. "Sister's very understanding."

"Yeah, a payment plan. Everything will be okay."

Mom gives me a weak smile and nods. "Things will get better."

"Yeah," I nod. "Goodnight."

What else is there to say? I need to hang on for a few more days, even if I feel like throwing up. Giving Mom money for rent instead of school makes me want to scream, but I clamp my mouth shut and bolt to my room. If I could change the past, I'd return to three years ago and beg Dad not to volunteer to go to Vietnam and work at the helicopter base. I don't care if he said it was his duty. His first responsibility was to us, his family.

Caroline murmurs in her sleep across from my bed. The bruise of the hickey on her neck has faded to a smudge of a circle. Thin lines crease over her eyebrows. Her head jerks, and I can tell she's about to have another nightmare. I pick up P Bear from the carpet and edge it close to her arm. She settles down as she hugs it close.

CHAPTER 16

Mrs. Jasper, the school secretary, pulls out a huge three-ring navy binder, plops it on the school office counter with a thud.

"A payment? Let's see. Bravo, Jacqueline." She flips through the pages, stops and runs a freckled index finger down the column of the page. Adjusting her goofy eyeglasses, she clears her throat. "Ah, here you are."

Her floral muumuu sways as she walks to the principal's office. My heart beats faster. Doesn't she want my money?

She knocks on the principal's door. Sister Mary Graceless steps out and peers at me. Mrs. Jasper whispers something in her ear. Sister's pale pink lips quirk to the side like she's had enough of me and my late tuition. Mrs. Jasper trots back to the counter. My stomach somersaults while my chest squeezes. Is it too late?

"Sister said a partial payment is acceptable. For now." She opens the book of receipts and takes my money. "We need one hundred and twenty dollars by the end of the month. And Jacqueline, we haven't heard from your mother. Sister says your mother needs to call her by tomorrow."

I don't know what calling about a bill Mom already knows about is going to do. "Okay, thank you, Mrs. Jasper."

The thought of transferring to public school and losing out on my chance for UCLA makes me want to puke. I duck into the bathroom instead of going to Ms. Fine's sixth-period class.

The icy cold toilet seat in the stall chills me right through my skirt. Those twenty-five dollars I gave Mom was a mistake. Even if I make another sixty dollars at El Lobo's by next week, I'll still be short on what I owe. My tips won't cover the difference, and by that time, next month's tuition will be due. I chew on my ragged thumbnail while I think of a plan.

"Jacqui, you in here?" Lucy pounds on the three stall doors before she hits my stall. "Saw you run in. What's wrong?"

My lungs ache from holding my breath. "What the hell do you think a person does in the bathroom?" I shout. "I started my period, okay?"

"Need a tampon?"

Dang, she uses tampons? Mom said virgins couldn't use tampons. That's why she buys me and Caroline sanitary napkins. I hate those thick Kotex pads. They may as well be surfboards.

"I have the slender kind. They go in easier."

"Dang it, Lucy, I don't need a tampon. Can you give me some privacy?"

"Geez, Louise. You ducked in here so quick. I thought you were gonna throw up. Excuse me for worrying about you."

Concerned about me? I swing the door open and step out. "I do feel sick because of my period. You know?"

"Ditch class, stay here with me."

Yeah, why should I work on my essay with my uncertain future at St. Bernie?

"Guess what? My invitations are ready," Lucy says. "I want you to come. There'll be lots of food, and a band. My brother's bringing some liquor to spike the punch."

Is she messing with me? Inviting the poor girl to the rich girl's party? "I work weekends."

"Can't you ask for the night off? Please." She presses her hands like she's praying.

"Too funny. You don't even pray at first Friday Mass."

"I know, huh?" Lucy burrows into her purse and pulls out a midnight blue cosmetic bag with gold stars. "Brought this for you. My aunt and mom got me the same one last Christmas. You can have it."

She tosses the cool bag to me and lights up a cigarette.

"Lucy, this is too pretty to give away."

"Take it. I don't need two of the same. I threw in an eye shadow and a blush. I already have those colors."

She's lying. I'm not anyone's charity case. "Nah, don't need the stuff. Thanks, anyway."

"Do you have a sister? Give it to her, or I can throw it away, I guess. There's only me and my brother. He's up north in college."

"Which one?"

"Crazy Berkeley. He's all long hair now, calling himself a Chicano. Pisses my parents off." Lucy laughs.

"I thought you said you were French and Spanish."

"Maybe two hundred years ago. My brother told me the French invaded Mexico way back, and that's how we got our surname. But we're Mexican American."

I need to ask Bebe about that or look it up in the *Encyclopedia Britannica* at the library. You'd think if we learned about the Napoleonic War in History, the French invading Mexico would be important too.

"Geez, I can't wait to be on my own at college, like my brother," Lucy says. "So, tell me about your job."

"One of those convenience stores in my neighborhood. I gotta run. I need to meet with Ms. Fine before sixth period ends."

"Thought you might want to know I invited Petey Castro to my party, too."

"Uh, cool." I try to keep my voice steady, play it off. If he's going to be at the party, I'll need make-up. I grab the cosmetic bag. "Thanks for the stuff."

Ms. Fine glances up from her desk when I slide into my seat late. Everyone has their head down, scribbling on paper. The shuffling sound of her Birkenstocks approaches my desk. I heard Sister Mary got on her case for wearing heels and hoop earrings, so now she wears hippie shoes and stud earrings. She drops a half sheet of paper on my desk. *Let's review your alumni package after the quiz.*

I hadn't done any work on the questions since last week when Sister Agnes busted me with the vampire drawing of Sister Mary Graceless. Flipping through my Pee Chee, I find the application and compose a few more sentences.

Ms. Fine calls time. I furiously check off the answers on the multiple-choice quiz.

"Jacqui?" She crouches by my desk. "Bring your application up after class."

Her eyes scan the essay when I take the desk closest to her. "Margot Sanders outlined her answers. Use that technique to help you hit the important points. Let's start from the beginning. *What is your biggest challenge?* Tell me the first thing that comes to your mind."

My chin drops to my chest. I shrug.

"I'm not saying this to embarrass you, but is your father's death challenging for you and your family?"

My head jerks up. The muscles beneath my neck coil into knots. Everything after his death is a challenge.

"Jacqui? Am I wrong?"

"Um, no." I bite my teeth together so I won't tear up in front of Ms. Fine.

"How do you feel about that?"

A jumble of emotions takes flight in my stomach and lets loose in my twitching legs. The sound of my shoe tapping against the linoleum and the ticking of the wall clock fill my ears. My face and neck are impossibly hot. I can't put my feelings into words. There's sadness, and anger, and questions, and anger.

"I don't want to think about this anymore." My wobbly legs struggle to get out of the desk. "I need to catch the bus."

"If you explore your reactions, perhaps you can answer the question." Ms. Fine softens her voice. "How has life changed for you and your family?"

My lips lock shut. All I can manage to do is shrug. The words stick in my throat. Life slides from okay to worse. Every time I think I'm moving forward, I fall back.

"Jot down your feelings on paper. Tackle these questions a little bit at a time."

"Everything sucks," I say and run out of the classroom.

The meeting with Ms. Fine was a disaster. I ended up with a bunch of emotions that left me annoyed, then gloomy, and confused. How do I put all these thoughts into an essay?

The questions she asked aren't the only things that have me scratching my head. I can't figure out why Lucy gave me a gift or invited me to her party. If she feels sorry for me, the poor scholarship kid of St. Bernie, that's messed up. But so far, she's never called me a name. Whatever the reason, I'm exhausted, and my shift at El Lobo hasn't even begun.

The bus rumbles over the train tracks bringing me to Mela Street. I need to call Mom and tell her I want the twenty-five bucks back. It's time she took over worrying about the money for school. I can't do it anymore. I don't want to do it. I want to be a regular teenager, go to parties, have fun. And I'm asking Olga to let me have Saturday off for Lucy's party, too.

I push open the door to El Lobo. The jukebox booms El Chicano's *Brown Eyed Girl*. Jerry moves his shoulders to the beat and catches me staring at him.

"Bitchin', huh?" He begins slapping the counter in tune with the song.

"Yeah, I like that one too. Olga around?"

"In a meeting. Private."

Thump, the red doors swing open. Jerry's dad, El Lobo, strides out of the bar and into the last booth, clasping his burly hands on the table. Henry slides in across from him. Olga trails them and takes their order. She chews on her bottom lip and scurries away.

"Turn that music off," El Lobo shouts.

Jerry hurries to the jukebox, pulls the plug. El Lobo glances at me.

"Tell Olga to bring our food to the office. *M'ijo*, bring us coffee and chips."

After Jerry and Olga leave to serve El Lobo, the café side is empty. With no one around, I head to the phone.

"The City of San Solano, accounting," Mom answers.

"It's me," I whisper. "I need my money back."

"I'm working. We'll talk at home."

"The principal said I need to bring them more money."

"At home." She hangs up on me.

"Dang it." I slam the receiver down.

"What's the matter." Jerry walks back into the café area and plugs the jukebox back in.

Like I'm going to tell him my problems. "Nothing."

Someone knocks on the front window of the café. Lucy.

"Hey," she waves as the door closes behind her.

Jerry and I wear the same expression. Open mouths. She's
ditched her school uniform and wears jean flares with a gauzy
cream blouse. She slides into a booth. "Menu, please."

"Pretend you don't know me." I hiss out the words near her
ear and drop a menu on her table. "Please."

Her forehead creases when she puts her index finger to her
chin. "Miss, I'll take a Tab and a couple of tacos." She smiles
up at me with a huge grin. *Loca.*

I've never seen Jerry move so fast. He shoots over to the
booth with a glass of water and a basket of tortilla chips. He
stares at her, his eyes bugged out like he's gaping at a movie star.
Lucy is pretty with her light-brown waist-length hair. She fills out
her bra like a grown woman and has a small waist accentuating
her hips. I'm a flat board. I'm Olive Oil next to her.

An insane grin spreads over Jerry's chipmunk face. "You're
a cheerleader at St. Bernadette."

"Love this song. Play it again," Lucy says.

I hand Lucy a cold Tab while Jerry drops a quarter into the
jukebox and selects *Brown-Eyed Girl* and a couple of other
songs.

"He's a junior, right?" Lucy asks.

"Yeah, his dad and uncle own this place. They think I'm
older, and my name's Marie."

Olga walks in, plops herself down on a counter stool. Her
cheeks are extra red. I can't tell if she's wearing new blush or
if someone slapped her face. The smudged black liner beneath
her reddened eyes makes her look like a sad clown. She sighs
and fishes a cigarette out of her denim vest pocket.

"Give me my matches."

I hold up an empty matchbook.

"Need a light?" Lucy takes a red cigarette lighter out of her
purse.

Olga eyes Lucy, reaches for the lighter. "You're too young to smoke."

"Nah, I'm eighteen."

A ring of smoke billows out of Olga's mouth as she watches Jerry rest utensils and a small bowl of salsa on Lucy's table.

"We need another waitress. Wanna job?" Olga says.

"Sure, I can work." Lucy glances at me. "But not on Saturday nights."

What the heck is Lucy doing? She doesn't need to work.

"Bitchin'," Jerry says. "Bring her an application, Olga."

"Wait here." She rushes down the hallway and returns with the sheet of paper.

"You have a ride?" Jerry says. "I mean, I'm sure you'll get the job."

That lovestruck *pendejo*. I don't know what kind of game Lucy's playing, but she better not ruin this for me.

"Yeah, I do. Excuse me, but is my order ready yet?"

Jerry sprints to the kitchen.

"Listen." I slide into Lucy's booth. "Are you crazy? Why'd you ask for an application?"

"Aw, I'm just playing." She giggles and fills out the paper. "Let me hang out here for a while, okay? I'll be cool."

The office door slams. I spring out of the booth and back to the counter. Lucy fills out her application and returns it to Olga, who disappears into the office. Jerry hangs out with us, wiping the counter down over and over.

"Jerry," Lucy says, "I'm having this huge party. You wanna come?"

His black marble eyeballs jump, his thick lips spreading so wide, his eyes close. This game of Lucy's is going too far. The dumb cluck is going to fall in love with her, and then what? Jerry's geeky, but he's an okay guy, too.

"Yeah, sure. When?"

"I'll bring you an invite in a few days," Lucy says.

"Almost five and dinner rush," I tell Jerry. "Grab us more napkins from the back."

"Going for a smoke," Lucy says as she slides out of the booth. "Come on."

We stand on the sidewalk for a few seconds. She checks out the street. "You live here?"

"In the neighborhood. How'd you find out where I work?"

"Asked Petey. He said you worked at the Mini-Mart, but I asked a friend to drop me off at the corner, and I saw you through the window." She wraps her arms around her chest. "I'm freezing. Where do I catch the bus back to school?"

"There," I point across the street. "What about the job you just applied for?"

She wrinkles her nose like she caught a whiff of dog poop. "I'm not working here. I was messing around." She tosses her hair back and laughs.

"Damn it, Lucy. Working here isn't funny to me. And what about Jerry? You invited him to your party." I could slap the silly grin off her face.

"Catch you on the rebound." She jogs across the street.

When I return inside, Olga's walking back and forth from the hallway to the café side.

"Where's that girl? Henry's going to interview her."

"She wanted to know where to catch the bus." I pick up a dishrag and begin cleaning.

"If we don't get help by tomorrow, you guys are working until eleven on weekends," Olga says.

"Not me, I have homework and stuff," Jerry says.

"You can use the extra hours, right?" Olga asks me. "Good tips, *mucho dinero*." Olga rubs her fingers together, winking her racoon-looking eye.

The station wagon rumbles toward me. Good, Mom's alone in the car. I drop into the front seat, throw my stuff on the floorboard.

"Mom, I really, really need the money back."

She turns her face to the driver's side window. In the reflection, the edges of her mouth turn down. "I already gave the housing office the money. We won't have this problem next month. I promise."

My shoulders slump deeper into the worn upholstery. From the look on her face, this isn't easy for her, either. She used to sing and smile all the time, but now her forehead folds into two lines, and the spark in her eyes has faded. I wonder if she used to have dreams, too, before four kids came along and Dad died. I want to tell her I feel bad for her, but I can't make the words come out because, without those twenty-five dollars, I feel bad for me too.

Afraid to let loose with what I feel about this whole damn mess, I keep my mouth shut. Saying anything now will hurt her even more. I hate that Dad's gone. I pull a pen out of my purse and scribble my thoughts in my notebook like Ms. Fine suggested.

"Please try to understand." Mom exhales and turns the key into the ignition. "I'm thinking of you and the kids."

I end my paragraph of thoughts and put away my pen. Right now, I have other things to worry about. I either quit St. Bernadette or take the extra hours at El Lobo's.

CHAPTER 17

The car engine moans like Mom's poking a sleeping giant.
She turns the key again and guns the gas pedal. A squealing
whine falls into an exhausted whimper.

"Stupid car," Caroline says from the back seat.

"I think it's flooded," I say. "Let it be for a minute and try
again."

Mom hits the steering wheel with the heel of her hand.
"Caroline, walk the kids to school. Jacqueline, catch the bus."
She flings open her door. "I'll find a ride from a co-worker and
ask your *tío* to fix the car later."

We all stay in our seats, mouths open. I hate the morning
bus. So crowded with kids.

"*Ándale*," Mom shouts. "Out."

The boys run down the sidewalk with Caroline dragging
her feet.

"Don't forget to call Sister Mary about the letter," I beg
Mom.

She flicks her wrist and hurries back inside the house. I
book it in the other direction to the bus stop. Mom's so scattered she'll probably forget.

Just like I thought, the bus is packed. I edge around out-stretched legs clad in stiff khakis and cuffed jeans. A girl wearing a red crop top eyes me up and down before elbowing her friend.

"Them clunky shoes are sooo cool."

Loud giggles follow me while I work my black and white Oxford-covered feet to the middle of the bus. This time next year, I'll be in college, wearing black PF Flyer tennies with jeans and cool peasant blouses.

"Jacqui," a voice calls out.

I glance up and see Mrs. Washington and a cute little boy sitting beside her, a stuffed lion in his hands. A white pail filled with pink and yellow flowers is at her feet. Every week for the past few months, she's taken flowers to her son's grave, where she decorates his headstone. She does this for all the other soldiers in the cemetery, too, leaving one flower on each grave. Everyone in the neighborhood cuts roses from their gardens for her to take. When she has leftovers, she takes them to the hospital for patients.

"On your way to the cemetery or the hospital?"

She lifts the toddler to her lap and gives me the seat next to her. "Both today. This is my grandson, Jerome Junior. Say hello to Miss Jacqui."

"Rawr, rawr." He thrusts his lion at me and waves his pudgy little hand before he burrows deep into Mrs. Washington's navy sweater. His huge chocolate-drop eyes follow me.

"Going to see my daddy. Rawr." He releases a string of giggles like tiny bubbles of joy.

My eyes mist. I glance away so he doesn't see me cry. His dad's dead, but he's happy to go visit his headstone. His grandma keeps her son's memory alive. I can't even visit my dad at the cemetery when I want. Grandpa insisted we bury him in El Paso, where he lived before he came to California. I know it upset Mom, too, but she didn't say anything. Maybe in her grief, she couldn't. I couldn't either.

Mrs. Washington pats my hand, which makes me sniffle because she understands how it feels to have someone you love die far away and not be able to be with them or see them. I pull out my notebook and scribble those words and more for my application. We stay quiet until we change buses to our destinations.

At school, I spot Lucy at her locker. "Olga at El Lobo's wanted to hire you. That's messed up. You filled the form out!"

"I wonder who answered the phone when she called and asked for Miss Gladys Knight." She throws her head back, laughing until she snorts.

"Dang, you're cold shit. You got Jerry all riled up with your flirting and the party invite."

"Okay, okay. I owe you, then."

Lucy's pretty good at acting, and I wonder if she can pull off tricking Sister Mary Graceless. "Pretend you're my mother and call the office at lunchtime."

She rehearses the line I give her about receiving the tuition letter. "No problem."

"You're a lifesaver. Thanks."

"Why do you work at El Lobo's, anyway?" Lucy says, slamming her locker door shut.

"Have to, I need the money."

"Bummer." She rummages inside her purse, brings out a pot of lip gloss. The strawberry fragrance rises to my nose as she covers her lips in a berry shimmer. "Want some?"

That's all she can say? She doesn't even ask me why we need money or anything. She and most of the seniors know my dad died. What do they think happens after that? That everything's the same. Well, it's not. I want to scream at her and tell her how messed up things are now.

"I said, do you want any lip gloss?"

"No, I don't want any of your smelly gloss."

"Pssh," she says when the first-period bell rings. "You ask me for a favor, and then you act like you don't like me."

Her comment stays with me all through first period. Lucy's okay, and she's been cool with me, but I don't know why I get pissed off around her sometimes. I write down a few more sentences on my notepad and sigh. A heavy feeling comes over me like I want to drag myself into bed and sleep everything away.

The lunch bell rings, signaling it's time to head to the library. I need to be alone. I duck Lucy, which is easy since she sits with Margot Sanders before she proceeds to the pep squad girls on the right side of the quad. Jerry's easy to avoid. The Chess Club sits in the far corner, practically in the breezeway. Petey and the jocks commandeer tables in the center of the yard.

Having lunch in the library and a free fifth period gives me uninterrupted time to add more stuff to my application. Not much time, considering my future rides on this scholarship.

A stream of sunlight comes through the library window-panes putting Sister Agnes in a warm spotlight. She's taking a snooze. Sister doesn't allow eating in the library, so I pull half my tuna sandwich out and take a quick bite.

"Psst." Petey moves through the doorway.

My foot and heart tap faster the closer he comes. He pulls out the chair across from me and sits. Oh my god, I'll have fish breath if I speak.

"Coming to the game today?"

Covering my mouth with my hand to curtail any fishy smell, I answer. "Um, I'm working."

He flicks the drooping curl on his forehead back. "I never see you when I stop by the Mini-Mart."

My face flushes hot. I drop my gaze to my paper. "I must be in the storage room or dumping trash."

Sister Agnes clears her throat, "Shhh."

Petey leans forward within inches of my face. His warm breath slides over my cheeks. "You're off at eight or nine tonight? What if I come by the store then?"

Every butterfly in my belly releases. My skin feels like someone turned up the blow dryer on high against my neck. I swallow and straighten up in my seat, but I can't stop my leg from jiggling. I nod my head. "Nine."

"Students. Silence in the library," Sister Agnes says now fully awake.

Petey stands. "Ms. Fine asked to see Jacqui, Sister. Here's the pass."

My chair scrapes against the floor when I rise, dropping my sandwich on the floor. I scoop it and my lunch bag up, find the apple inside and bite into the sweet flesh to rid my mouth of the tuna taste.

Petey pauses at the door and motions me to follow. I catch up to him in the hallway.

"Did Ms. Fine really ask for me?"

"Yeah, I wouldn't lie to you." He turns to me. "So, I'll see you tonight?"

Is this really happening? I'm dazed by this whole thing. Tonight? Nine? "No, wait. Today, I'm working 'til eleven. We're short a worker."

His broad shoulders droop. "Bummer. I gotta be home by ten. My mom and dad work an evening shift cleaning offices with Petra. Maybe tomorrow?"

"Oh, okay." I choke out the words.

A slow smile spreads across his face and ends in one deep dimple. We walk together another few steps until he veers off to the gym, and I continue to Ms. Fine's classroom.

This is psyching me out to the max. I don't know if he's messing with me or not. He's not like that. . . is he? Could he really want to go out with me, a brainiac who's also a liar? Maybe he does like me, like Caroline says. She knows more about romance than I do. Must be from all those *True Confession* magazines she reads from Mousy's sister.

"Come on in," Ms. Fine says, waving me over to her desk and an empty chair beside her own.

A few kids glance up from their books. Must be the silent reading time she allows during the last twenty minutes of class.

"Let's go over your essay."

"I'm not finished with all the questions, but I'm jotting down my thoughts in another notebook, as you suggested. I'm having problems with this one because I don't have much to say. I point to "'Share a project you participate in to enhance your community.'"

Ms. Fine hands me a magazine from the top of her desk. "New preview issue. Take a look while I read what you've written."

The cover has the giant letters *Ms* with a blue eight-armed woman holding a telephone, an iron, a steering wheel and a bunch of other stuff. The drawing reminds me of Mom. I scan the headlines. "Gloria Steinem on Sisterhood," "Sylvia Plath's Last Major Work," "Women Tell the Truth about their Abortions." A gasp catches in my throat. Abortions?

"A-hum," a snort comes from across the room.

"Good afternoon, Sister Mary Grace," the class says as she waddles to Ms. Fine's desk.

"Yes, Sister?" Ms. Fine brushes a strand of hair behind her ear, exposing a small earring in the shape of a circle with a plus sign. I've seen that symbol on the TV news. I think it's the one that feminist's wear.

All eyes, including my own, observe Ms. Fine, dart to Sister and back. The magazine is like a hot potato in my hand. I throw it back on the desk, put my hands on my lap.

Sister moves to the desk and thumps a thick finger on the magazine cover. "What's this?"

"There's an article about a poet I'll discuss with the class," Ms. Fine says.

Sister snatches up the issue, peers at the cover. "What in God's holy name? Mrs. Fine, this is unacceptable. Come to my office."

The magazine disappears under Sister's arm as she marches out of the classroom. An article about abortion is way worse than Ms. Fine wearing feminist earrings and flare jeans.

"I, uh, I'm sorry, Ms. Fine. I shouldn't have thrown the magazine back on your desk."

"Class, you're dismissed. Take your books to the library until next period." She chews on her lower lip. "You did nothing wrong, Jacqui. Neither did I. I'll talk with you about the rest of the essay later."

CHAPTER 18

Sister Mary Grace acted like Ms. Fine committed a mortal sin the way she ordered her to her office. I'm worried about her. There's already been gossip about Sister talking to Ms. Fine about her "inappropriate" clothes.

The bus stops on Mela Street, and I cross over to El Lobo's. Jerry throws me an apron as soon as I walk inside. He points his chin to the last booth, where Henry sits with his back to me. Olga sits in front of him biting the corner of a fingernail.

"I called lots of times. There's no Gladis lady there." Olga holds up a sheet of paper and points to the name at the top. "María, you know this girl, Gladis Night?"

"No." I shake my head and see that the names are misspelled.

Henry laughs. "She's a singer, *pendeja*. Gladys Knight and the Pips? Olga, you don't know shit."

"Jerry!" Olga calls, scrambling out of the booth, click-clacking her way to the front counter. She shoves Lucy's application up to his face.

Jerry peers at it, then at Olga. "Gladis Night?" A ruby glow of anger or embarrassment spreads across his full cheeks.

Poor guy. He's bummed out for sure. Probably started shopping for new polyester flares and matching vest to wear to Lucy's party.

Henry plods by us, pushing open the front door to the café. "Gladys Knight my ass." His laughter roars into El Lobo's while he stands on the sidewalk and puffs his cigar.

"Going to the bar. Nobody bother me," Olga says just before hitting the red doors so hard they swing open and shut twice.

"Man, why would Lucy do that?" Jerry asks me.

What can I tell him? I'm not supposed to know her, so I shrug and serve the two men who come in and take a booth. They're not dressed like construction or field workers. All they order is coffee.

Officer Palermo strides in the front door and takes an empty stool at the counter. "Hey Marie, Jerry. Coffee and enchiladas, please."

The two men glance at him, gulp their coffee and move into the bar.

"You're early." I place a water glass and chips in front of Palermo.

"Haven't seen Barbie in a while. Doesn't she work here anymore?"

"Took off sick too much." Jerry brushes past me and sets a cup of coffee in front of Palermo. "Fired."

Palermo's forehead wrinkles. The slow stir of his spoon into his cup tells me he's thinking about what Jerry said.

"Jacqui, going to the office for a minute," Jerry says and ducks into the hallway.

"She's sick, huh? Too bad," Palermo says.

"Here's your enchiladas." I set the plate in front of him and grab extra napkins. "I met Barbie once. She came in to give Henry a letter. Last week. You related to her?"

"No. It's just I'm sorry to hear she's been sick. She told me she was expecting."

"Expecting what?"

Palermo stares at me with his pretty eyes. "A child."

"Oh. Uh, okay." Dang, she didn't look pregnant. Hard to tell in the coat she wore.

"If you see her again, tell her Palermo asked how she's doing."

He eats quickly and pulls out a five-dollar bill from his leather wallet when his walkie-talkie crackles. "Keep the change, Marie."

"He had two dollars coming to him. Palermo said to keep it." I hold up the change for Jerry to see when he returns with an armload of supplies. "Oh, he asked about Barbie, too."

"Wonder why?" Jerry scratches his chin, ignoring me with the bills in my hand.

"What do you know about her?"

"Real pretty. Super cool, too. Worked here for about a year. I guess she was Palermo's waitress," he says.

"She wasn't your girlfriend, was she?"

His thick eyebrows shoot up. "Not mine." He glances behind his shoulder. "Don't tell anyone? Barbie and my uncle Henry had a thing going on."

I keep my mouth shut. Now's not a good time to tell him Barbie's pregnant.

"Was Palermo here?" Olga yells as she shuffles out of the bar.

"Left five minutes ago," Jerry says.

Her false eyelashes flutter, her eyes dart from Jerry to me. "Did he ask for me?"

"Nope, but he asked for Barbie."

Olga's head shrinks back with her fuchsia-colored lips open. She bolts back into the bar, doors swinging.

CHAPTER 19

"Prima, I'm in town again," Bebe shouts into the phone. Her tone surprises me so early on a Saturday morning. I cover the phone receiver and wave off Mom, who's drying the breakfast dishes and stops to listen. "Cool. What's up," I say.

"CBA meeting this afternoon. Rudy asked me to make sure you're there."

"Me? Why?"

"I told him how you're applying for the alumni scholarship to UCLA and how smart you are. He's impressed. Maybe you can ask him for a letter of recommendation for your application. Javier and I can pick you up at one. Okay?"

"No, I'll meet you there. I start work at three today. Later."

"Wait. What are you up to?" Mom asks.

"Gosh, Mom."

She hates it when I cross-examine her and calls me a *metiche*. Now it's my turn. Plus, she's gonna be pissed if I tell her the truth about where I'm going, but I need to be at the meeting. The community participation section of my application is blank.

"The meeting's about building a bridge over the train tracks."

"You mean the Chicano group they talked about on the radio?" Mom holds the dish towel in the air and shakes her head. "*Ay*, no."

"Why not? We need to have ambulances or fire engines over here. You need to be at work on time. A bridge will help."

She narrows her eyes at me. "What if someone sees you there and thinks you're a troublemaker?"

"This meeting is for a good reason, not to make problems for anyone. I'm going so I can write something in the community projects for my alumni application. You can tell that to anyone who asks."

"Join the youth group at the church."

I make praying hands and bow my head, which is cheesy, but I need to go to the CBC meeting. "Come on, Mom. I only have a couple of more weeks to turn in my essays. Please?"

Her lips slide into a smirk while she crosses her arms. "Don't make trouble. *¿Entiendes?*"

⚜ ⚜ ⚜

A few kids carrying brown missalettes run across the blacktop to the entrance of St. Patrick Elementary. They're late for Saturday Catechism instruction in one of the classrooms. I make my way to the quiet end of the building, to the location of the meeting. The door is propped open.

"Glad to see you, *hermanita*." Rudy stretches his hand out, grasps my fingers in his own, then clasps my hand again. "Here, let me teach you the Chicano handshake."

Awkward, but I feel like I'm in a special club when I watch everyone else doing the same thing. The room fills up quickly. A girl walks in late, stands near the door and glances around at the crowd. A Mexican flag is stitched onto her denim purse.

"Glad to see a representative from the high school MEChA club. Her name is Angie," Rudy says to me.

A guy close to her gives her the Chicano handshake, which she does like an expert before she makes her way to the front of the room.

Rudy goes up to the podium and starts summarizing the last meeting with the school principals and how they agree the train often makes students late. He glances at his notes and continues, "They maintain that they give the students detention slips so the tardies don't mess up their school funding. We'll continue our discussions on alternatives to after-school detention. Okay, now about the bridge idea. . . Chicanos for a Better Colonia needs everyone in the barrio to buy into our idea and help spread the word about our mission. We need help from all of you to talk to people: the store owners, people with medical problems, anyone who can help this cause."

I glance around to see what other people are doing and find them nodding. Talk with a bunch of store owners? I sure don't want to get that involved.

Rudy takes a piece of chalk and writes on the board. *We cannot seek achievement for ourselves and forget about progress and prosperity for our community.* —César Chávez

"Not for our own success, but for the improvement of our community," Rudy says.

Murmurs rise up from the group. Javier pumps his fist in the air and shouts, "*¡Viva la Causa!*" Others respond, "*¡Qué viva!*" Then the group claps fast and loud to his proclamation.

Angie raises her hand. "I'll talk to a couple of teachers and ask MEChA chapter members to talk to people they know."

Three more hands rise. My chest tightens while my stomach sinks. It's like I'm excited and scared at the same time. Mom told me not to get into trouble, but this is a good thing. How much trouble can I get in for doing something to help our neighborhood? I chew on my bottom lip and stare at Angie, who's scribbling something in her notebook. If she's willing, I should be too.

I raise my hand. "My neighbor's husband had a stroke, and the ambulance couldn't enter our barrio because of the train. Now he needs a cane to walk and has trouble speaking. I'll talk to her."

"*Eso.* Those are the types of examples we need," Rudy says. "Ask your people to speak about their experiences in person or write a letter that we can give to the city council. We'll meet again next Saturday. *Adelante.*"

All the way to El Lobo's, I think of who else I can talk to about the council meeting besides Petra. Right before I reach the Mini-Mart, a line of cars stretches up the street to the train tracks.

Saturday afternoons people go uptown to the markets or to the matinees at the movie theaters. I'm sure a few people are standing there waiting to go to the bank on the other side of town. I make a note to bring this up at the next meeting.

A police car and a motorcycle sit at the curb outside of El Lobo's. A bunch of kids hang out on the sidewalk, trying to peek in the window. Two old ladies stand on the corner, craning their necks to see what's going on.

A boy about my brother's age stretches his arm across the front door and blocks me from entering. "Don't go in. The *jura*'s inside."

I hesitate. The police? Maybe Henry and El Lobo got into a fist fight or there was a robbery.

"Did you know that girl?" the boy says. "The one who's missing?"

Olga's missing? But she's not a girl. "I work here, move aside."

I push open the door and find Palermo in a booth with a lady police officer and Olga. So she's not missing. But something bad must've happened.

"Marie, a cup of coffee, please," Palermo says.

He lifts his hand, shakes his head. "Marie, take a couple of cups down to the office, too." Turning back to Olga, he says, "I have a few more questions for you."

He and the lady cop take turns asking Olga questions. I need to focus on pouring the coffee but can't help listening in on their conversation.

"I don't know Barbie outside, just here. Maybe she have boyfriend problems. Yeah, I remember she said the boyfriend didn't want the baby."

"When did you last see her?"

"Last week, two weeks? The boss fired her 'cause she don't come or call him."

I set Palermo's coffee cup and saucer on the table. "Marie, you mentioned you met Barbie last week?"

Olga swivels her head up at me. Her black-rimmed eyes taper to inky lines against her bright blue eyeshadow.

"The lady asked for Henry. You were in the bar, Olga," I say. "She left after a couple of minutes." I hurry off with the coffee tray to the hallway and the office.

A man dressed in brown corduroys and a T-shirt leans on Henry's messy desk. His thick blonde hair makes him look like a surfer guy from television. An older Black man in a police uniform stands close by taking notes on a small spiral notepad. Henry's forehead is creased into three lines as he leans back in his chair, his arms crossed, his legs stretched out like he's at home concentrating on the football game on TV.

I peek into the open door, clear my throat. "Officer Palermo asked if you want coffee?"

The blonde guy waves me inside. "I'm Detective Roberts. That's Officer Jones." He moves behind me and shuts the door. "What's your name, and how old are you?"

Pushy guy. I tell him my fake name, Marie Monsivais, and that I'm eighteen. Officer Jones jots down my information.

"Um, I only work the restaurant side, not the bar," I add.

"You know this girl, Barbara Ríos?" Roberts thrusts a school photo in front of my face. "The picture's a couple of years old, but does she look familiar?"

Barbie doesn't have on a bit of make-up. She looks my age. "I don't know her, but she came in and asked for Henry." The cup slips from my sweaty hands and hits the table hard. Coffee spills over the rim. "Sorry. But Henry wasn't here. I think she left a letter for him."

Henry shrugs and wipes up the spill with a tissue. "What letter? Didn't see one."

"Your boss says he fired Barbara two weeks ago," Roberts says, scrunching his nose like he's trying to decide who's lying.

I try to keep my shaking hand out of the detective's sight. I paste on a smile. "Need any more sugar for your coffee?"

"You can leave," he says. "For now."

You don't have to tell me twice. I jam out of there and back to the café. Olga sits on a counter stool and watches me as I put the empty tray on the counter.

"What's happening in there?" she whispers.

"They're asking Henry questions."

Olga bites on her bottom lip, swiveling her stool, when we hear a door close. Henry, Roberts and Jones come out of the hallway. Palermo flips his memo pad closed.

"I can go?" Olga hops off the stool.

Jerry comes through the front door, followed by his bull-dog of a dad, who's wearing a tan trench coat and a pissed-off look on his face. He moves like a mafia gangster past Olga and Henry, right up to Roberts, then turns and sits in a booth.

Palermo stops Jerry before he sits across from his dad. "You see this young woman around?" He holds up Barbie's picture.

Jerry's Adams apple bobs. His fingers grip the edge of the table. "Got fired, I heard."

"Is that all, Officer?" Jerry's dad says. "My employees need to return to work."

"We'll be in touch later." Roberts flips out a business card and holds it up to Jerry's dad. "If you remember anything, call me."

The lady cop tapes a flyer to the front window. "Barbie Rios, age 17. Missing 2-9-72."

"The girl's gone for a week, and they send out the Mod Squad?" Henry says. "Everybody back to work."

He and Jerry's dad take off to the office as Olga scurries to the bar section. Jerry waves me over behind the counter.

"Barbie said she was twenty-one," Jerry says. "She worked the bar on weekends. Wonder why the cops are so involved, even if she is missing?"

"Her family must be worried because she's only seventeen. And she's pregnant," I whisper.

Jerry steps back. "Who'd you hear that from?"

"Palermo told me the other day."

Jerry's shoulders slump forward. Poor guy, he must've had a crush on Barbie, and now he realizes his own uncle probably got her pregnant.

"So that's why Olga's pissed all the time." He nods like he's figured it all out. "Olga would mad dog her, they'd argue, until Henry stepped in. He always sided with Barbie."

"Yeah," I nod. "And now she's pregnant and missing."

CHAPTER 20

Walking the final block to school, my mind becomes consumed with thoughts of Barbie. The sight of her outside El Lobo's, looking jittery and unsettled, replays in my mind. The way she flicked her cigarette and glanced around as if deciding whether to enter. And now, she's gone, missing without a trace.

I take the stairs up from the school's lower lot, dragging my feet, thinking about being seventeen and pregnant by a married guy. I thought I had it bad.

Mrs. Jasper raises her curly-haired head when I enter the school office. A couple of students sit on the bench near the principal's door, bouncing their feet against the linoleum. Waiting, I'm sure, to be yelled at or otherwise embarrassed.

"Brought my tuition payment, Mrs. Jasper."

"Good, let's see here." She counts the bills, blows out her breath. "You're short by seventy dollars. Thank goodness, Sister Mary Grace finally heard from your mother. She promised to pay the entire bill by March."

Next week! Dang it. March is next week. I did not tell Lucy to say all that but only to pretend she was my mom and reassure Sister that she received the letter.

"Remember, Miss Bravo. Full tuition by March first preferably, but the fifth is the absolute latest."

She could not be any louder, unless she used the PA system. I wince, pull my neck into my blazer. "Yes, Mrs. Jasper." The dates are emblazoned in my head. She doesn't need to remind me. By my calculations, I'll have sixty more dollars tomorrow and maybe thirty in tips this week. A total of ninety dollars by the fifth.

"I'll be back Friday with more." I rush out of the office and into the closest bathroom.

"Hey, where you been?" Lucy says from her perch on the windowsill.

"On my way to the library. Gotta work on my alumni application." I head into a stall.

"Newspaper this morning had something about a missing pregnant girl. Her family says she got a death threat and worked at El Lobo's. Know her?"

"Death threat?"

"I overheard my dad tell my mom that the girl was pregnant from the manager. Some guy named Henry."

"Dang, they sure know the gossip."

"My parents know somebody who knows somebody. I heard the guy was going with the other waitress, too, and she went ballistic when she found out about the girl being pregnant. I don't think you should work at that shady place anymore."

"What's shady about selling tacos?" I exit the stall, go to the sink.

Lucy jumps down from the windowsill, rustles through her purse, and hands me a large envelope. "Here."

The heavy card stock is soft, the color of cream, with a black fancy script on the front.

"Open it, dodo."

"Mr. and Mrs. Jácquez cordially invite you to a Debutante Ball for their daughter, Lucila A. Jácquez at the Royal Order of the Elks Club April 8, 1972 at 6 pm."

Inside is a smaller RSVP card in equally fancy writing. "A debutante ball introduces a young woman into society. . . ." Lucy's voice comes out heavy, like someone who thinks they're better than others because they have money. "I understand what a debutante ball is. I read. And what society? St. Bernadette's?"

Lucy's cheeks flush bright pink. "You know how my mother, Mrs. Holly Jakes, is." She takes out two *Vogue* magazines from her folder.

"Why pronounce your name as Jakes when other people say it's supposed to be in Spanish, Ha-quez?"

"Mom says Jakes is easier to say." Lucy throws the magazine aside, crosses her arms and glares at me. "If you don't want to come, just say so."

Problem is I do want to go to her party. I want to hear a live band, dance with Petey. I don't know if I can trust Lucy, but she did a favor for me, so I'll go for it. "I feel guilty for wanting to have fun when my family barely makes it. You know, because my dad died. I can't spend money on a new outfit."

She glances out the window. "I get it. It sucks."

"But I do want to go to your party."

"Good," Lucy jumps down from the windowsill. "Because if you didn't, I'd have to let Petey Castro know, and he might not come."

"You don't have to play matchmaker. He doesn't like me like that." I slide the invitation carefully into my folder. "At least, I don't think so."

"He would, if you acted interested." She clasps her hands together. "Hey, I'm thinking of these two dresses," Lucy says, pointing to photos in the magazine. "Or this one. I can't decide."

The hoop skirt with a taffeta bodice is something out of *Gone with the Wind*. The lacy one resembles a wedding dress.

The last gown is white satin with a baby blue silk sash. Tiny seed pearls run along the scoop neckline, with more scattered near the bottom like ice crystals floating. It's the most beautiful dress I've ever seen. It would make anyone look like a queen.

"The satin one is sharp. Reminds me of Olivia Hussey from the movie *Romeo and Juliet*."

"I like the lacy one and the one with a hoop skirt. Oh, I got it. One for my party and one for the prom. You're going to prom, aren't you? It's in late April."

Prom? I don't even have a dress for her party or know whether I'll still be here at St. Bernie. "Don't think so. If you're not choosing that satin one, can I keep the picture?"

She shrugs, tears out the page. I fold the picture in fours, slide it into my Pee Chee. "Gotta book it to the library."

"Wait, I'm coming, too."

Sister Agnes eyes us as we take a seat. When a teacher comes in with several students, she heads to the back. Good.

Lucy pulls out a *Teen Beat* magazine from the back of her World History book. A chair scrapes the floor. Jerry stands over us and pulls out a chair. A scowl covers his face.

"I knew I recognized you from somewhere." He crosses his arms in front of his pocket protector. "You're a senior here, and your name's not Marie."

Damn it. The muscle at the back of my neck tingles. Don't freeze up, I tell myself and scrape my hand through my hair. I glance at Lucy.

"So what?" Lucy says.

"She lied," he says. "So, did you. Not cool."

"Evidently, you guys don't check the applications. That girl Barbie worked in your bar and she was seventeen," Lucy says.

Jerry ignores her and glares at me. If I'm fired, I'll never be able to pay my school bill. I can't let him mess up my plans.

I straighten my shoulders, lift my chin up at him. "You better not tell anyone, Jerry. Not your dad, or Olga, or your *tío. ¿Entiendes?*" I kick at his chair leg.

"Geez. Relax," he says and sits down next to Lucy and faces her. "You had the waitress Olga going crazy with your fake application."

"Sorry, I was just messing around." She leans toward Jerry. "Hey, guess what? I got my invites. Wanna see?" She pulls one out, hands it to him with a glistening pink smile. "I have one for you."

Jerry spazzes out. His arms drop to his side like limp spaghetti and his face lights up like a little kid who's just gotten three scoops of ice cream.

"You gotta bring my friend Jacqui here with you, okay?" She bats her sooty black lashes at him.

"Sure, I'll give her a ride." His eyes dart from Lucy to me. "Right, Jacqui?"

"And you're not gonna hassle her, are you?" She says with a purr. "Or I won't have any place to go after school if she leaves."

He shakes his head. How easily she cast a love spell on the poor guy. He won't tell my secret now.

CHAPTER 21

Time is short. I set my stuff on my bed and jot down notes about the CBC's plan and how I'm helping by talking to community people and writing letters. My bed shakes. The pen in my hand jumps off the paper. Earthquake? I glance up and see Caroline bounce on the end of my mattress.

"Mousy's coming over."

"You're still grounded, and I'm not watching the twins. I need to work on this essay before my shift."

"We'll stay inside, I promise. Just gonna practice hairstyles in the bathroom and check out what's on TV." She clasps her hands in front of her. "Come on."

"Tell her to get lost before Mom comes home. Now scram, so I can finish." I settle back on my headboard and keep writing.

Mousy and Caroline giggle in the bathroom every few seconds. I creep to my door to eavesdrop.

"Hey, check this out." Mousy says. "Lena said *putas* work at El Lobo's and they sell *mota* and *chiva*. That missing girl, Barbie? She did too. That's why the cops are looking for her."

Caroline better not let Mousy know I work at El Lobo's, too.

"Damn. Weed and heroin? No way," Caroline says.

"If Lena said it, it's true. Barbie's on the run because she doesn't want those guys who own El Lobo's to mess with her."

"Nah," Caroline says. "Heard the girl was PG. She probably went to one of them pregnant girl homes in LA."

"But why would the cops snoop around El Lobo's? You think she snitched on them?"

Good question. Lucy said Jerry's dad had a crooked business. And now Mousy's info? Prostitutes are one thing, but drugs? I remember the time Cha Cha looked doped up until that guy from the bar came and gave her something.

"The cops went to El Lobo's because the girl worked there," Caroline says. "If she's pregnant, maybe she ran away with her boyfriend."

"Hunh, hadn't thought of that," Mousy says. "I'd do that, too."

Mousy would say that. I need to convince Caroline to stop hanging around that girl, and I need to pay more attention to what's going on at El Lobo's. As soon as I pay off the remaining seventy dollars this Friday, I'm out of that place.

⁂

There's a mound of red-rimmed cigarette butts in the tin ashtray next to Olga. She blows out a stream of smoke and sighs while I fill the napkin dispensers. Finding out Barbie's pregnant with Henry's baby must've bummed her out big time.

From the front window, I spot Palermo parking his motorcycle at the curb. Olga sees him too, and beats it to the bar.

"Marie, how're you doing?" Palermo greets, as he scans the café, glancing down the hallway before he sits in the front booth. "Sit a minute. I have a question for you."

What does he want now? *Play it cool.* "Coffee?" I pour him out a cup and rest my butt on the edge of the booth in case Olga comes in, and I need to look busy.

Palermo sips from his cup but keeps his eyes on my face. I swallow, press my lips together and try not to panic.

"You're not in trouble, but you're not eighteen, are you?" he says.

"Uh. Why do . . ."

"I know your real name and your mother's name. You wait for her at the Mini-Mart after work." He takes a breath. "Your brothers and sister attend St. Patrick Elementary. Am I correct, Jacqueline?"

Dang. Did he do an investigation on me? And why? I jump up, shake out my hands.

"Sit, please. I'm not here to bust you."

"I needed the money, so I lied on my application. But I don't serve any liquor, so I'm okay. Right?"

"Why do you need the money?"

He should be able to figure that one out himself. But since he asked. . . "For my tuition at St. Bernadette. And we owe St. Patrick, too. My principal will kick me out if I don't pay the bill, and I'll lose out on an alumni scholarship to UCLA. That's where I want to go." I exhale, out of breath.

Palermo takes another drink. I can see my scholarship circling the drain as he keeps staring at me. He doesn't nod or sigh or anything. I gulp. I guess he wants more of a reason.

"You probably know my dad died, and my mom struggles to pay the bills. I need to help out. If my sister ends up in public school, she'll get mixed up with the wrong crowd, drop out because no one cares to push her to do better. Plus, she's boy crazy. For years, I've wanted to go to a university, and St. Bernadette has this alumni scholarship I'm up for. My mom even went to St. Bernie, so it's like I have to graduate from there. You see?"

There, I said the whole truth out loud. I steady myself to hear him say how I should go to vocational school, be a secretary or a wife and help out my family.

"Those are excellent schools. So, you want to go to college? Good for you."

"Do I have to quit working here now?" A thick knot wavers in my throat while I wait for his answer.

The walkie-talkie on his belt crackles, repeating his name. "Gotta go. Don't quit, Marie."

My shoulders lower into an exhale as he scoots out of the booth to the front door. Since he didn't tell me to quit, this place must be legit, and the gossip Mousy heard is all rumors. I'm relieved Palermo's gone, but a cop knowing my personal business leaves me confused.

Customers trickle in and out of the restaurant, with most men going to the bar. At eight thirty, Coco prances in wearing tight jeans.

"Hola," she flicks her wrist at me.

"Hi. Where's Cha Cha?"

"Flu or something."

She disappears into the bar as Olga pokes her head out. "María, not a lot of customers tonight. Go home at nine. Take the trash out to the alley before you leave."

Without Jerry, I'll have to haul the trash cans out myself, and they weigh a ton. Stupid Lucy, if she didn't put in a fake application, there might be someone else hired here already.

A few minutes before nine, I drag the garbage down the hallway to the back door, prop it open with one trash can and pull the other one to the huge metal bins that line the half wall. After I dump three cans, I lean against the wall for a breather. An overhead light flicks on. The back door to the bar opens and slams shut.

Olga's voice soars over the wall. "Psst, not my fault she's sick."

"You gotta have something, ¿qué no? A stash somewheres?" Coco says. "Cha Cha needs it bad."

"The town is dry. Henry needs to find another mule, someone young," a high-pitched voice says.

"Talk to him, then, not me," Olga says.

"The cops are all over this place, watching my house, too," the squealy voice says. "You guys better do something, ¿sabes?"

The door bangs shut. Henry needs a mule? Is that slang for girlfriend? I wait a few seconds, go back inside and toss my apron in the bin of dirty dish towels. At nine o'clock, I book it around the corner to the Mini-Mart.

Mr. Young Singh must've put in a new light at the corner of the store because I can see the whole sidewalk in front of me. Two guys in khakis half squat on the ground at the edge of the parking lot. One of them looks like the guy Caroline likes, but I don't know the other one. I rush to the door of the Mini-Mart and duck inside, where I make my way to the nickel candy aisle.

"Hey, Mr. Young Singh, do you have any more Big Hunks or Mr. Goodbars?"

"No, my friend. The delivery man couldn't come here this afternoon. Train. So, no candy. Maybe tomorrow." He rings up a customer while I pick up a couple of Hershey bars, make my way to the counter.

"That train's a pain," the customer says. "Couldn't get to the bank on time. Had to go to Casa de Cambio. Rip off."

"There's a committee trying to convince the city to build a bridge into the neighborhood," I tell them. "You want to come to a meeting next Saturday? They'll tell you about it."

The man shakes his head, pockets his change. "Sorry, can't take off work."

"What about you, Mr. Singh?"

"Saturdays are my busiest days."

"What if you write a letter about how your business is affected by the train?" I say. "You can sign it, and I'll take it to the meeting. I'll come by in a couple of days for it, okay?"

That wasn't so hard. Now, I'll have two letters from the community. I push open the door and wait outside for Mom to show up.

"Hey, you," a voice calls out.

I glance up and see Sleepy and another guy walking toward me.

"Where's Cooky?" Sleepy mumbles as he sways a little to the left and then begins laughing. The brown paper bag in his hand slips down. He's drinking MD 20-20, which Uncle Mario calls Mad Dog. Nasty tasting stuff, he says. "You're her *carnala*, right?"

"Forget the sister. This one is *fine*," the other guys says.

I heard that squeaky voice in the alley ten minutes ago. He's the one who said cops were staked out at his house. I've seen him with Cha Cha and Coco.

Our car horn screeches like a squeaky toy as it enters the parking lot. The guys bust out laughing, holding their hands to their stomachs. I book it to our car and jump in the empty front seat. Caroline rolls down the passenger window behind me, waves at them. They don't say a word and keep on laughing.

"Roll that window up," Mom says. "Don't ever let me see you wave to those bums again."

Up in our bedroom, Caroline complains, "He didn't even wave back." Clutching P Bear to her stomach, she adds, "I saw him this afternoon, too."

"He called you Cooky. What's the other guy's name?" I ask, putting on my pajamas.

"They call him Weasel. Mousy said he's a friend of her oldest sister."

"Looks like one, too. Sleepy looked loaded. Does he know you're not even fourteen?"

Caroline shakes her head. "Mousy told me he smokes *yesca* and takes bennies, but I didn't believe her until I saw him tonight. But he's so sweet."

"So caring that he didn't even wave back, just stood there swaying in the wind and laughing. Should've called him Dopey."

Caroline throws her pillow at me. I duck and hit her a good one across the head. We giggle until my pillow erupts in feathers.

"Dang it, Mom's going to have a cow."

"Give it here." Caroline takes a spool of thread and a needle out of our nightstand. "I'll sew it back up."

Sometimes Caroline can be really cool when she's not giving me grief. I feel bad for her, since her first crush is on a guy who uses dope.

"Hey, look at this." I wave the invitation from Lucy in front of her face.

She reaches for the envelope and turns it over in her hand. "So heavy and soft." Her finger traces over the lettering. "Is Mom letting you go? What're you gonna wear?"

"A new dress and shoes would be great, but I don't want to spend the money. I'll borrow something from Bebe."

"I'll make you a dress."

My sister is almost as good at dress-making as my mom. But a homemade dress? Then I remember the magazine picture in my folder. I whip it out and show it to Caroline. "Don't you think this looks like a dress Juliet wore in the movie?"

"Sharp. I love it," she says. "We need to find a pattern, buy satiny material and blue ribbon."

"After paying St. Bernie, I might have twenty bucks left. Enough for a couple of yards."

"Right on. You'll put Olivia Hussey to shame wearing the dress I'll make," Caroline says. "Hey, see anything weird at work?"

She must be talking about the gossip Mousy gave her about the drugs.

"Nope. We serve booze, but I don't go into the bar area."

"Probably *chisme*, then," Caroline says. "You're right, that family does love to gossip."

CHAPTER 22

The week flew by. On Friday, I paid the seventy dollars I owed using my whole paycheck and every dime and quarter of my tips. Mrs. Jasper took my name off the ding list but reminded me that I still had twenty dollars to pay by next Friday and March's tuition by the first.

"Dang, not even ten dollars left over?" Caroline says as we walk home from doing laundry. "What about material for your dress to Lucy's party?"

"I'll figure out something." I sigh and kick at a rock on the sidewalk.

"Messed up. . . you gotta borrow a dress or find a two-dollar one from the second-hand." She tugs our beat-up red wagon over the sidewalk and up to the corner store, where she stops and checks out the clock inside. "Hey, it's almost eleven. Hurry up."

The full laundry baskets rock and roll as I jog behind the wagon, ready to pounce on overturned towels if they hit the street. All I need is to bring home dirty clothes and hear Mom yell at us. There's no time for that because I need to shower and change before I book it to Bebe's for the CBC meeting this afternoon.

"Slow down, Caroline."

"No, I don't wanna be late," she says, her long hair flying behind her like a brown kite.

She veers around the corner of our block, keeps running. I wave to Petra's husband sitting on his bench, viewing the world whiz by. He gives us his lopsided smile and raises his bent fingers in a wave.

I'm a sweaty mess when we get to our front porch, where Caroline abandons the wagon. She makes a beeline to the television, turns it on. Inside, we flop on the couch, out of breath and kick our shoes off.

"The Soooul Trrrainn!" Don Cornelius, the announcer says into the microphone. "The hippest trip in America."

"Man, look at his cool Afro. And check out those pink hotpants that girl's wearing," Caroline says. "Mom would kill me if I walked out of the house in those things. But, super sharp."

We stare, mesmerized by the guys in flare pants and platform shoes flipping girls in the air, gliding down the soul train row and doing splits. They're better than any cheerleaders I've ever seen.

"I wish we could spend all our Saturday mornings watching *Soul Train* and *American Bandstand* instead of going to the laundromat."

"For reals," Caroline says. "Or buy make-up at Woolworths or a new outfit at Sanders."

"Just once, could we go out and eat hamburgers at Wimpy's or catch a double matinee at the movies?"

"We're teenagers. This is supposed to be our fun time, huh, Jacqui?"

"And now the number one R & B hit, James Brown's *Talking Loud and Sayin' Nothing*," Don Cornelius says.

"Cool, my favorite," Caroline jumps up, snaps her fingers to the song.

Our fun time. Caroline's dream sounds good, but those things never happen in real life, meaning in my world. I glance over to my little sister, who's rocking side to side to the music, her eyes closed, screeching the lyrics. "You can't tell me. . . how to run my life. . ."

Fat chance that our Saturdays could ever be like our dreams. At least not this year. I don't want Caroline and the boys to end up feeling like me. They should enjoy being kids. I want to dream big, as Ms. Fine says, and I want them to be able to dream, too. If I need to keep working at El Lobo's plus go to school, then I need to suck it up, as Dad used to say. I can't quit so soon. One more month, and our family will be safe from money worries.

"Hey, I gotta go shower and split to the library before work."

"Why?" Caroline stops dancing. "Does Mom know?"

"If she asks, tell her I'm working on my essay."

"You're lying, huh?"

"Nah," I shake my head.

Not fibbing, but I'm not telling her the complete truth either. I have a letter signed by Petra and one from Mr. Singh for the CBC meeting.

This afternoon is the last meeting I'm attending. All I wanted was a little community work to put on my application. That's all.

⚜ ⚜ ⚜

The CBC meeting takes place at St. Patrick, my sister's school. But half the amount of people from the last CBC committee meeting shows up. Javier and Bebe aren't here either. I take a seat at one of the school desks in the middle of the room next to Angie, the girl from Solano High. A large projection screen sits in the front of the eighth-grade classroom.

"Hi. Glad you're here," she says, grasping my hand, shaking and releasing it. I fumble the last part of the Chicano handshake, but she overlooks my ignorance.

The door opens, and in walks Rudy, followed by Sister George, the principal. They're talking like old friends before she takes a seat where the teacher usually sits. That's all I need. What if she tells my mom I'm here? I sink down in my chair. Maybe I can sneak out without anyone noticing.

"I want to thank Sister George and Father Armando for allowing us to meet here," Rudy starts, nodding to Sister. "As promised, I brought the film on the Chicano Moratorium for you all to watch."

Everyone straightens up in their seats while Sister and a guy fiddle around with the film projector. The classroom lights go out.

The reel starts with the words "August 29, 1970." A narrator says President Nixon intensified the Vietnam War, and thousands of Chicanos were dying on the front lines. The Chicano Moratorium was the largest anti-war action where over twenty thousand people assembled in Los Angeles to protest and call attention to civil rights abuses.

Brown Beret members, looking sharp, march together, in step with girls in suede knee-high boots and khaki uniforms. They call out "Chicano" and others answer "Power." My pulse quickens, hearing them shout, seeing them proud and smiling. Other people carry banners that say "Indians of All Tribes," "Brown Is Beautiful," "*Raza Sí, Guerra No.*"

People hold placards showing where they're from: Utah, Colorado and Texas. They're held high by men, women and teenagers. I see a few priests, a group of nuns with their arms linked together and chanting. Kids of all ages walk and ride bikes. The march stretches for long blocks through East LA and into Laguna Park.

The camera person sweeps the crowd. There must be a thousand or more people walking into the park, where several families sit on the grass, everyone listening to the guitar players on the stage. A group of little girls in traditional Mexican dress dance to *folklórico* music.

Police sirens blare. The camera shows a long shot of the park. Silver helmets glare in the sun. The police start advancing, batons out. People move back. Some run, but the cops keep moving forward after them. Everyone's scattering. Police clubs strike heads and backs. Over and over.

My breath halts. I'm gasping. Around me, people mutter in disbelief. I glance at Angie, her face in a grimace. What we're seeing is unbelievable. Something I have never seen before.

In this film, I can clearly count how many times a cop hits a man on the ground. My heart squeezes in my chest as another one hits a woman in the back of her head. She drops like a broken statue. A cloud of tear gas erupts. Cops with gas masks advance on crowds of people running, screaming and choking from the fumes.

Buildings are on fire. At the Silver Dollar bar, a Sheriff holds a thick shotgun aimed at the door. The narrator describes how the cop shot a wall-piercing tear gas projectile into the bar that hit and killed Rubén Salazar, a *Los Angeles Times* reporter and community activist. The film stops.

Sniffles and angry words break the quiet in the classroom. Angie wipes a tear from her eye. I can barely catch my breath.

Rudy takes a deep breath and says, "After the coroner's inquest, not one officer or sheriff was held accountable. No one was charged with the crime of killing Rubén Salazar. But hundreds of marchers were arrested and put in jail. We lost three people, one a fifteen-year-old young man, Lynn Ward Enciso."

I glance around at a classroom full of bowed heads and scowling faces. A fifteen-year-old? A teenager like me? Damn. "My parents and I attended the protest. I know it's hard to believe, but it happened and will keep happening unless we advocate and take action for change," Rudy says.

"Martin Luther King Jr. was beaten with hundreds of others in Selma," Sister George says. "César Chávez marched two hundred and fifty miles in 1965, and in 1968 thousands of high school students in East Los Angeles walked out of classes."

"That's right, Sister George. They were models of action," Rudy says. "The Chicano Moratorium is an example of what freedom fighters have done for centuries. When all the smoke cleared away, we had to make a decision. Do we give up, or do we continue the fight?"

Angie holds her head high, her shoulders squared. "Emiliano Zapata said it's better to die upon your feet than live on your knees."

Die on your feet than live on your knees? That's commitment. I'm in awe of Angie, of everyone who Sister said stood up for freedom. There were students who walked out of their high schools in protest four years ago. Kids my age.

"The question I ask you, *carnales* and *carnalas*," Rudy says with a low, steady voice. "If the city council doesn't pay attention to our petition, will you march? Will you risk criticism, arrest or a punch?"

"*La unión hace la fuerza*," a guy shouts.

Unity makes strength. The only way we're going to make change happen is to be united. My heartbeat speeds up. I don't know if I'm worried or motivated by what everyone is saying. I think both.

"I know it's a lot to take in. Especially for the youngsters or people who haven't seen the film before." Rudy exhales and takes a seat on the desk. "But now we have work to do. Who brought letters from the community?"

Angie raises her hand, waves three sheets of paper above her head. "From teachers."

"Great job," he says, then points to my half-raised hand. "Jacqui, right?"

Oh God, Sister spots me sitting there, letters in hand. She cranes her head. "Yes, Jacqui Bravo. She was the eighth-grade class president when she attended St. Patrick."

Everyone's attention turns to me. I work up the courage to raise the letters into the air. When I lower my arm, I slide way down into the seat. What if Sister tells Mom she saw me here, and Mom brands me a radical or communist? She'll never let me come to another meeting or go off to college.

"Yes, our future leaders," Rudy says. "*Mil gracias*. Let's hear it for our *hermanitas*."

The committee members clap in unanimous approval. Angie and I glance at each other. She fiddles with her long bangs; her cheeks flush mauve to match her lips. My heel taps faster on the linoleum floor.

Rudy draws several circles on the chalkboard. One says "Mini-Mart, Hermanos Market, Loli's Pan" and the other says "St. Patrick." He makes five hash marks next to a circle labeled "Community Members." I'm guessing for the teachers, Mr. Singh and Petra.

"These people are all connected to the community. Think of them as our partners. We need a few more allies from outside the community. The hospital is an idea as well as more businesses."

That's really smart of Rudy. I wave my hand in the air. "Last week the train held up a bunch of people on their way uptown. Happens every weekend. I bet the markets, movies and department stores lose business. A man told me he couldn't make it to the bank on time."

A broad smile breaks out on Sister George's face. "Excellent examples, Jacqui."

"She's right. I'll try Sander's store," one of the women says.

"If they don't ignore you," a woman my mom's age says. "They act like we're invisible when we shop in stores across town."

"Or they follow you, thinking you're going to lift something," Angie says. "But I know a friend of my mom's, a saleslady who works there."

Someone else raises his hand and says he's a relative of a bank teller. Another man says the local labor union could use more work if construction is done in the neighborhood. Guys start bumping shoulders, shouting "*Eso*" and "That's right."

Angie grins, her eyes sparkling. "Check it out. Everyone's coming together."

"Okay, *carnales y carnalas*, let's bring the letters in by Tuesday, the date of the next meeting. Let's show the City Council that the barrio cares about what they do or don't do. People here pay taxes just like everyone else in town."

Everything Rudy says is so right on. My chest tingles, thinking of all the letters we can gather. He makes me believe change is possible and that I have something important to contribute. Me, a seventeen-year-old high school girl.

"Last thing. I need volunteers to read the letters."

Wait. What? Everyone's quiet. No one raises a hand. I glance at the bulletin boards surrounding the classroom to avoid Sister's gaze.

"How about our future leaders, Angie and Jacqui?" Sister George says.

I'm no leader, and talking in front of people makes me break out in a sweat.

"Uh, umm. I'm not a speaker. I mean, not good," I confess.

"You can read the letters you brought," Rudy says. "What do you say?"

Rudy's throwing me right into the action, but Mom said not to become involved with Chicanos. The last time I spoke in front of a group was at my eighth-grade graduation. That was a two-minute reading from the Gospel of St. Peter. Even then, I fumbled through the scripture. I planned to turn in my two letters and quit the CBC. But the film about the Chicano Moratorium, the high school students who walked out, the leaders who risked everything for their cause flash through my mind. Rudy and Sister's encouraging smiles and the way they nod make me believe they need me and that I'm important to the cause. But still, I hesitate.

Angie doesn't miss a beat. She says yes to Rudy. He watches me with an eager smile, and I want to say yes. I want to make a difference, but truthfully, I'm afraid of how Mom will react if she finds out I'm speaking to the city council with the CBC. But this is important.

"Okay. I'll do it," I say in a low voice while my stomach sinks.

CHAPTER 23

What was I thinking when I agreed to speak at city council? Part of me believes in the cause, but the other part remembers what Mom said about protesting: nothing will change. Worse, I'll be labeled a troublemaker.

But what if things do change? And so what if I'm called a troublemaker? The CBC is doing a good thing for the community. Still, I weigh the pros and cons of continuing with the group because Mom's already stressed. Do I tell her now or later?

I continue walking to the projects and hurry to my uncle's place. The front door's open. The aroma of refried beans in bacon grease drifts over me as I peek inside. It's the best way to refry beans if you ask me.

Uncle Mario's upper body is halfway into the hall closet, showing his baggy olive army pants and red bandana hanging from his pocket.

"Hey, *tío*. Is Bebe upstairs?"

"In the shower." he pulls out a bucket, hose and chamois cloth. A Dodgers hat sits backward on his head. "Come outside."

Uncle Mario still works out with weights in his backyard with his friends and neighbor kids, so for an older guy, he has bulging biceps, which make his eagle tattoo stand out when he carries a full bucket of water over to his old Ford truck.

"Heard you work at the Mini-Mart?" he says. "Been there a few times. Never seen you."

"I was probably in the supplies room or taking out trash." I glance at my feet because Uncle Mario has this way of staring you down if he thinks you're lying. "I like my job."

"Don't forget to keep up with homework. A job's no good if your schoolwork suffers."

"I will. I promise."

"You make sure to tell me if someone gives you a hard time." He dips his bandana in the water. "Okay?"

"Hey, Jacqui." Bebe steps out on the porch with a fluffy towel wrapped around her head.

"Yeah, sure. Later, Tío." I step onto the porch.

"Here," he throws me the wet bandana that smacks me in the neck. "Wipe that make-up off your face."

"Geez, I was practicing, Tío."

He waits while I smear my perfectly good shadow and liner off my eyes. Bebe giggles as I pass by her and trot up the staircase.

"Do I look stupid or what?"

"Not at all. I'm laughing 'cause my dad busted you, and it reminded me of when he'd get all parental with me."

"He's doing a lot of that lately."

"'Cause your dad's gone. He feels responsible as your mom's older brother."

"Mom and I can handle stuff."

Bebe shuts her bedroom door. "You're seventeen, you're not supposed to handle adult stuff."

"Tell that to my mom." I hop on her twin bed. "Why weren't you at the CBC meeting?"

"Stopped by the cops on the way. Why else? So frustrating."

"Because Javier has a lowrider, huh? Another fix-it ticket?"

"After ten minutes of show-me-your-registration bullshit and checking out the car to see what else he could write Javi up for, he let us go."

"Why didn't you tell him you guys are in college?"

"Jacqui, the cop didn't want to hear anything about us. He wanted to give us a ticket. Plain and simple. To him, a lowrider is a criminal."

"Messed up. Like you're not a real person."

"Exactly. See what we're up against?" Bebe sighs and braids her hair. "So, what happened at the meeting?"

I tell her that she missed the film.

"Javi and I went to UCLA to see it. How did you feel watching what happened?"

"Sad, mad. Everything inside me twisted up. Why did the cops react that way, as if the protesters had guns and were hurting people when it was just a bunch of ordinary people marching?"

"Yeah, a non-violent march. We didn't kill anyone, but the cops did. Who really are the violent ones?"

I think of Officer Palermo. "They're not all like that, though."

"Maybe not. But we shouldn't have to be afraid to use our voices, especially when we're following the law."

She's right. Why should I be afraid to give my opinion or do something if I'm not hurting anyone? "Yeah, I think I've been scared to use my voice in a lot of ways with a lot of people."

"Your mom?" Bebe says.

"Yeah, and with my grandparents, school, classmates."

"You have every right to speak your mind as long as you're not violent about it." Bebe winks her eye. "Rudy's going to show the film at all the community colleges. People need to know the truth. What else happened at the meeting?"

I explain the circles and partnership stuff Rudy showed us and tell her the date of the next city council meeting.

"*Prima*, I need a favor." I pull out the thick invitation to Lucy's party from my folder. "Check this out. I'm invited to a debutante ball."

"Fancy. What're you wearing?"

"I'd like a new dress, but I won't have enough money to buy a new one. Could I borrow a dress or shoes?"

"Bummer, I got rid of my old prom dress already." Bebe opens the door to her small closet. The space is packed with shoe boxes. "Those aren't all shoes. They're old letters and photos. No room at my new pad. Next time I'm down, I'll bring you a couple of dresses, okay? Oh, check out these cute Candies or these black platforms. They're sharp."

She holds up one of each shoe in front of my face. The velveteen cloth on the four-inch shoes is super cute, but what if I can't walk in them? But they're too cool to pass up.

"These," I say, pointing to the velveteen ones. "I'll need them in April."

"You got 'em, cuz."

"My shift starts soon. Have any eyeliner and blush I can borrow?"

Bebe glances around her room. "Damn, I left my make-up bag in Javi's car."

Without my face painted up, I can't transform myself into eighteen-year-old me. Too late to go back home.

"Did you finish your alumni application?"

"Almost. Oh yeah, forgot to ask. Is 'mule' slang for girl-friend or something?"

Bebe cocks her head. "Why?"

"I overheard someone use that word."

"Mule can mean a stubborn person," she pauses. "Or it can mean a person dealers use to carry drugs like heroin. Where'd you hear that word?"

Weasel must've been talking about drugs, and Henry needed to find someone to be a mule. And Cha Cha must be a heroin addict. Palermo must not know, or why else would he let me work at El Lobo's? I'm not saying anything to Bebe until I know for sure. I can't lose this job yet.

"Heard some older girls at the laundromat talking. Thanks for the shoes, Bebe. And remember to bring your dresses the next time you're in town. Got to run to work."

Uncle Mario's gone by the time I go outside. I jog up the street and pass Petey's place. His younger sister sweeps their front porch while the other one waters the pots of bushy cilantro and yellow chile peppers. Both of them wave.

Through the open door of Louie's Laundromat, the harsh odor of bleach drifts out onto the sidewalk while the overworked machines churn and grind. On the next corner, the sharp vinegary smell of pig's feet gusts out the door of the butcher shop. Grandmas in their floral aprons go in and out of the shop to buy tripe, that gross furry looking meat for Sunday-morning *menudo*. Uncle Mario makes the stuff, but I'd rather eat oatmeal or *arroz con leche* any day. Even Spam, if it came down to choosing between that and *menudo*.

One minute to four o'clock, and I make it to El Lobo's. Olga ogles me as I enter the café.

"I'm not late," I say, my eye on the beer clock.

She circles her long red fingernail around my face. "You look like a kid."

What can I say, except shrug? "Jerry coming in today?"

"His *papá* says no more work. Uff, if I had it so good. You gotta be the busboy and waitress today. *Ándale.*"

"Aren't you going to hire someone to replace Barbie?"

One dark eyebrow arches above her turquoise eye shadow. "What? What chu mean?"

"A waitress. Hire another waitress for the bar section."

"Oh, up to the boss to say okay or no." She turns away and hurries to the bar.

I wonder why her face is pastier than it usually is with all her pancake make-up. Just the mention of Barbie's name makes her stutter.

The men in clean Wrangler jeans and Western shirts come in around eight o'clock. The ladies arrive at eight-thirty, and Cha Cha is skinnier than ever in her platforms and black hot pants. A few new customers, younger guys in silky shirts open at the chest, wearing flared polyester pants, come into the bar at nine.

Weasel strolls in with his creased khakis and a stiff blue Pendleton shirt. Two other guys follow behind. They're dressed the same but in different colored flannels. He takes a seat at the counter, where I'm wiping it down. His piercing black eyes follow me.

"You're Cooky's *carnala*, Jacqui." He rubs his thumb and index finger against his short goatee and leans forward.

"Yeah, I'm Caroline's sister."

He's so close I see his pock-marked skin. He's older than Caroline guessed. I move away from the counter to the water pitcher and fill glasses. The way he stares at me gives me the creeps.

"Give me and my homies Miller High Lifes."

"I can't serve beer. You have to buy them in there." I point to the red door.

"Let's go, then," his friends say, sliding off their stools.

"You *vatos* go. I'm staying." He flashes me a toothy smile of incisors pointed like the fangs of a vampire. "Lemme have a Seven-Up, chips and salsa."

A shiver runs through my chest. I grab a dish bin and hurry to the last booth to bus the table. His beady eyes follow me to the cooler, where I grab a soda, pull a basket of chips from under the counter and slide them in front of his seat. He eats them one by one, dangling them from his fingers, chewing the tips first. I swear he looks like a tall skinny rat nibbling on cheese. Yuck, disgusting.

I push open the kitchen door and call for the cook, "Pepe."

He comes to the doorway, knife in hand, a look of surprise on his face. "*¿Qué pasó?*"

"Oh, it's just we need more salsa," I tell him.

Pepe glances at me and then at Weasel. "I bring it right out, María."

The door from the bar swings open with a thump. Olga, her face damp and flushed, appears with a full tray of glasses. She glances at Weasel, gulps, lays the tray on the closest table and hustles back to the bar.

This is my chance to get away from this creep. I pick up the tray. "Gotta give these to Pepe."

"Want me to go with you?" Weasel's lips curl into a leer and his eyes narrow.

"No."

I glance over my shoulder to make sure he's not walking behind me, but even inside the kitchen, I can hear him snickering.

CHAPTER 24

The city council meeting came so quickly. Before tonight, I'd never been inside City Hall, except to one of the outside windows to pay our utility bills. I'm not ready to read my letters in front of a bunch of strangers, but I gave Rudy my word.

Several members of the Chicanos for a Better Community are here for the meeting, even though it's six o'clock on a Monday night. Even Bebe and Javier have come down from college to be at tonight's session.

The inside of the room is nothing exceptional, just rows and rows of gray seats covered in nubby material that's rough to the touch. Large brass framed pictures of the past mayors line one wall, and the other is blank. Must be for the future mayors.

"Check out those photos," Angie nudges me. "All white men. What does San Solano have against women or brown and black people?"

I nod, but I hadn't thought to ask myself why our city has whole neighborhoods of Mexican Americans and black people but no mayor who looked like them.

Seven city councilmen sit in a semi-circle in front of us. Their blonde and grey-haired heads and navy suits are all I see as they flip through papers on their table and talk with each other. A woman at a small desk to the right of them loads paper into her electric typewriter.

Rudy, Bebe, Angie and I sit in the middle row, waiting. Bebe elbows me, points to the councilmen. "This is why our people need to be college-educated and come back to serve their communities."

To that remark, I don't say a thing. She can come back and be a teacher here, marry Javier or whatever, but once I'm out of the neighborhood, I'm not coming back unless it's to visit the family, who I hope will have moved to a better house.

"Listen up, everybody." Rudy leans forward. "After I speak to the reasons for another entrance in and out of the neighborhood, we'll present your letters. Speak clearly." He points to the desk. "That lady's the recorder. Everything we bring up has to go into the minutes."

I reread the letters Mr. Singh and Petra wrote. The edges of the paper crinkle from holding them so tight. I place the letters on my lap. My fingers bounce off the edge of my seat. Angie doesn't seem nervous at all. She's bent over an index card on her lap.

"What're you doing?"

"Bullet points for my presentation." She slides the cards onto my lap. "So I remember the most important arguments."

That's real smart of Angie. "Who taught you that trick?"

"Public speaking tip. I take an evening class at the community college."

"You attend college while you're still in high school?"

"One of my teachers told me I could, so I signed up. I earned all my credits already, and I'm eighteen, so why not?"

Last semester, I finished all my credits, too. That's why I have a free period. But no one told me I could take college classes. I guess Solano High isn't as backward as I thought.

"This meeting is called to order." An echo from the microphone sounds into the room. The balding man in the center has a sign in front of him: Mayor Harris. "Let's begin."

They start talking about the agenda with each other, and after a couple of minutes, the mayor announces that the order is switched around. The CBC issue moves from number four to number seven. Last on the list.

"Don't be discouraged," Rudy says. "Moving us is a trick to frustrate people. Focus."

The meeting drones on with the city council members calling items to order, talking about electricity and the budget, and a bunch of other stuff I don't care about. I shift around in my seat and tap my feet to wake up my numb butt.

Two hours later, Mr. Harris glances at his wristwatch. "We're almost out of time. I move to adjourn and table the last agenda item for next week."

Rudy leaps to his feet. "Point of information."

We stare at him until he clears his throat and runs down some rule about council meetings, Robert's Rules of Order, and how we're here and ready to speak. The mayor glances to his left and right, nods to Rudy.

The audience sits up as Rudy takes out his folder and taps the microphone at the podium. Most of the councilmen don't even glance at him when he speaks; they fumble with papers instead.

"We have signed letters from the community, which our high school students will read." Rudy motions to me. "After that, I'll present my motion."

"We're running out of time. Your presence is noted," Mayor Harris says.

"Two minutes each for the letters. I'm sure you'd agree that your constituents' needs should be heard."

Murmurs rise in the audience: "Yes, what about us?" "We want to be heard."

A couple of the councilmen fidget with their papers. The mayor drags his hand over his thinning hair and adjusts his tie. "Proceed."

My nerves prickle up and down my spine as I rush to the front. My hands shake so much I grip the sides of the podium. "My name is Jacqueline Bravo. I'm a senior at St. Bernadette High School. My letter is from Petra Gonzales, my neighbor, which I'll read:

"My husband used to work construction—a good job. Now he walks with a cane, and his hand doesn't work anymore. He can't speak good either. It's been two years since his stroke. The train stopped the ambulance from crossing into our neighborhood. They had to take the long way around. Took twenty more minutes. He lost oxygen to his brain. Now he can't work. I must work two jobs. You must do something to help before more families suffer."

My breathing speeds up as I examine the blank faces of the city councilmen. Only one man pays attention to me. I go on with Mr. Singh's letter:

Dear Sirs,

I own a small store three blocks from the train tracks. My customers depend on me for basic food items. Often times, a delivery truck can't come to my store because the train is stuck on the tracks for 30 minutes or more. The delivery man doesn't know the other route. He returns my supplies. This causes financial loss to me, and customers can't buy food. This damages my reputation as a business owner. I'm sure you can understand my predicament. I humbly ask you to build a bridge to alleviate these problems for the community.

Angie strides to the podium and tells them she has three letters from teachers who are concerned for their students who often arrive late because of the train.

"Students who are late because of the train are disciplined. If they're not in class, the government doesn't pay the school district."

That information perks the men up, as well as me, because I didn't have a clue. Mayor Harris thanks her as soon as she stops.

"Dang, Angie, that was great. I didn't know about the money."

"Found that out from Rudy. I looked it up at the library. It's true."

Rudy steps up to the podium and asks the city council to find another way in and out of our neighborhood for emergency access, telling them they could receive state or federal funds to create a bridge over the railroad tracks.

Every council member begins talking. One says the project will be too expensive, that maybe next year they can consider it. There needs to be a study first, and then they can consider it. Mayor Harris motions to adjourn, the man next to him seconds him and bam, the meeting's over.

"They can just do that? Ignore us?" I ask.

Bebe and Angie shake their heads and sigh. My heart sinks. What am I going to tell Petra and Mr. Singh? That the city councilmen don't care enough to take the time to listen to our communities' concerns? People nearly die, students are blamed for things beyond their control and the school district receives less funds because the elected men don't want to listen past eight o'clock?

My stomach churns with these questions. I don't dare tell Bebe and Angie what I think. They're already shuffling down the aisle. They feel as bad as I do. And then I think of Petra and her husband, and the life they live because of a train delay. A few of the CBC members bombard Rudy with questions. He holds up his hands, his shoulders erect. *"Calma.* This isn't over until we say so," he says in a clear, strong voice. "We'll meet again on Saturday and strategize."

This isn't over until we say so. A light flicks on in my head. It's like everything's clear about my participation in the CBC. My mind's made up. I'm in this organization until we're heard, and the changes we need are made.

CHAPTER 25

A group of sixth-period students crowd the entrance to Ms. Fine's room, stuck outside like a bunch of lost souls. Margot and Lucy have their noses pressed against the tiny window on the door like they're spying on some secret society. Larry towers over them, trying to peek into the classroom as if he's looking for buried treasure. They're crammed together like sardines. Whispers bounce around like they're in some sort of conspiracy movie, waiting for the big reveal.

"What's happening?" I ask over Larry's shoulder.

"Sister Mary and Ms. Fine," he whispers and points to the classroom.

Margot presses her finger against her lips as Lucy cracks the door open wide enough for Sister's strident voice to soar into the hallway.

"I've warned you, Mrs. Fine. You must stick to the curriculum and the dress code."

"I'm preparing the students for college, Sister."

"Abortion is preparation? It is a sin, Mrs. Fine."

Petey nudges my shoulder. "Hey, what's going on? Why's everyone out here?"

"Shh. Sister and Ms. Fine are going at it."

Petey presses closer to the door, shoulder to shoulder with me. I glance at his side profile and gulp.

"We discussed this the other day. . . ." Ms. Fine's voice grows louder. "I wasn't teaching on the topic. Although I must say abortion is an issue students need to understand and discuss. Or else how can they make decisions?"

"Tell her, Ms. Fine," I whisper.

That's another reason I like her. She treats us like young adults, not little kids.

"*Ms.* magazine is propaganda and not part of the reading curriculum, *Mrs. Fine*," Sister's voice booms.

"Let me repeat, Sister, I planned to teach about the poet Sylvia Plath, not on abortion. An article on the poet was in the magazine you took from my desk. Personal property, I may add."

A few kids start giggling. I wish I could see the expression on Sister's face. The way Ms. Fine defends herself, cool and collected, is how Rudy from the CBC behaves. She's not backing down from Sister Mary Graceless.

"Your feminist reading material has no place in St. Bernadette."

"I need to prepare the students in the best way I know. If that means a slight deviation in reading material, I think that should be permissible."

"Most certainly not. From now on, you must clear every lesson plan with me in advance." Sister's clunky shoes sound on the floor, growing closer. "My office. Each Monday morning at seven-thirty."

The group backs up in sync before the door flings open. A grimace fills Sister's round red face. We scurry back into the hallway and press against the lockers.

"I can't teach under those conditions," Ms. Fine argues, following behind Sister.

The nun stops in her tracks and whips around, her black habit swooshing through the air, and shouts, "You will follow our rules unless you want to be suspended."

A gasp escapes my mouth as if someone's socked me in the stomach. Ms. Fine can't leave St. Bernie. She's the bridge from here to UCLA, my guidance counselor, a person who cares, a person I want to be like.

"Ms. Fine," I shout.

Petey grabs my arm. "Shhh, you're gonna get in trouble."

She can't leave. She can't walk out of these hallways and out of my life. Not now.

Ms. Fine pauses for a second. Her eyes scan the crowd of students watching her. "Half of you go to the library, the other half go to Study Hall. I'll be there shortly."

"Follow me." Petey takes my hand.

I stand there, gawking at his hand in mine. He lets it drop and scratches the back of his neck, a flush growing across his cheeks. God, I really ruined the moment.

"Yeah, let's go." I work up a smile to let him know holding my hand is okay. I just freaked out for a minute.

More students than tables fill the inside of the library. Sister Agnes scurries around like a headless chicken, trying to corral all the kids.

"Back here." Petey tugs my hand.

We slip past the tables and rows of shelves to the back of the room, where we settle against the wall between bookcases. He motions me to sit next to him on the floor. We're shoulder to shoulder, hip to hip. Petey folds his legs up to his chest while I sit cross-legged on the scratchy carpet.

"Jacqui, don't get mad, but I need to ask you something."

A date? To be his girlfriend? At last. I take a deep breath. My "yes" fills my mouth.

"Why'd you lie and say you worked at the Mini-Mart?"

"Wha-what?"

"Been there a few times, you're never around. I asked the man at the register, and he says you don't work for him."

Honest Mr. Singh. Dang it.

"If you don't work there, where do you go every night?"

"I am working. Just not at the Mini-Mart."

A lump grows in my throat while the back of my neck kinks into knots. How could I think Petey would ask me to be his girl-friend? I'm trying my hardest to keep it together, and right now, everything's falling apart. School, the application and the job. Something or someone is always in my way. I didn't expect it to be Petey, though. Who does he think he is asking all these questions? He's not my brother or my boyfriend.

"Where do you work at, then?" he asks.

"At a restaurant near there, okay?"

"El Lobo's? That place is a dive. A girl who's missing used to work there, too."

"Shhh. It's the only place I could find a job. They think I'm eighteen, pay me in cash, and I make tips. Please don't tell my mom."

His lips twist to the side before he relaxes them and sighs. "I guess you've had it tough with your dad gone."

The comment hits me right in the chest. He understands. I nod.

"I get it." Petey slides his warm hand over mine. "Don't worry. I won't say anything."

His brows draw together. All of a sudden, I want to tell him everything that's weighing on my shoulders. "If I don't pay our late tuition bill, Sister will transfer me out of here next month."

"You'll lose out on the alumni scholarship. Bad enough she put your name up on the ding list."

Oh, my god, he's seen my name on the bulletin board. It's like I'm wearing immense sticky labels all over my uniform blazer. *Poor girl. Dead Dad. Scholarship kid. Ding list.* I bite my lip to stop the tears from brimming.

"Gotta go." I struggle to stand in the tight spot. My books fall onto the carpet, but I leave them there, run to the bathroom, climb onto a toilet and lock the door. I'm so tired of walking around with knots in my shoulders like a ball of tangled twine.

My dad's instructions bombard me. He reminded me every time in his letters home: "Help your mom." "Take care of the kids." "Keep your grades up." "I'll be home before you know it."

I did what he asked, but he didn't come home.

I'm trying my best to help out, to stay at St. Bernie so I can win that scholarship, move out of this town and into a new life. And now, Sister Mary Graceless threatens to suspend Ms. Fine when I need her the most.

Lucy plans for her silly party, Petey only has to play sports and everyone else has a fine and dandy time going to school events, except for me. I'm the girl who doesn't belong at Saint Bernadette, and now, without Ms. Fine, UCLA is farther away.

I'm exhausted from sucking it up, toughing it out. There's no relief. Tears spill into the wad of toilet paper against my eyes. Maybe I shouldn't feel sorry for myself, but I do. I'm sitting in the toilet stall because I don't even have my own room to cry in at home.

Get up, I tell myself. *Get it together.* But these are just empty words. I splash water on my face, stare into the mirror. I'm too tired to keep fighting. My mind is numb.

I push open the lavatory door and find Petey waiting by the entrance. He holds my books in his hand.

He stayed. For me.

His eyes meet mine when he hands me my books. A warm, prickly feeling sweeps over my fingers and up my arms. The blush on my cheeks must match my bloodshot eyes.

"Thanks. For my books and for understanding."

A crooked smile lights up his face. He glances at the ground and rubs the back of his neck. "Listen, uh, about Lucy's party. Do you want to go together?"

CHAPTER 26

Finally, Petey has asked me to go out. Not to study or see a game but to Lucy's big party. I sit on the bus, taking steady breaths, reliving every second of meeting Petey outside the girls' lavatory. My first date with the one I've liked since forever. Me. Jacqui Brainiac Bravo.

I'm thrilled but also dreading the whole thing. Will Mom let me go? What am I going to wear? How do I act on a date? How do I afford a dress, shoes and a gift for Lucy's party? What if the night turns out badly, and I never have another date with Petey?

At the same time, there are a lot of important issues I need to deal with that make thinking about Petey trivial. So many questions fill my head that I miss my stop. I yank the cord and jump to my feet. The bus lurches to a stop a block past El Lobo's.

A '68 Chevy Impala rolls past me in slow motion. A Midniters' song booms from a cassette player. The car backs up in reverse, but I keep walking. The motor rumbles like a stalking lion as it cruises next to me. The rear window has "The Town I Live In" written on it in fancy script.

"Psst, Jacqui or Marie, whatever your name is. Wanna ride?" Weasel's shrill voice rings out. His arm hangs outside the front passenger window, his body reclining into the seat. A stocky guy grips the chain-link steering wheel. Weasel bobs his head to me.

"No, I'm going to work." I point to El Lobo's right across the street and keep walking.

"Take a ride with me." He swings open the car door.

I jump away from the edge of the sidewalk. "You crazy? I'm seventeen." I didn't mean to tell him my real age, it slipped out.

The driver whoops a laugh. "She's just a kid, *ese*." He guns the motor.

"*Órale*, Jacqui," Weasel says, slamming the car door. "Catch you on the rebound, then."

"You're not catching me anywhere, fool," I shout.

I haven't shown him the least bit of interest. I push open the door to El Lobo's and, for once, I'm super glad to be at work.

"María, come meet the new guy, Carlos. Show him what to do," Olga says and walks away.

Jobs must be tough for this older man to work as a busboy. Even though he wears a baseball cap and T-shirt, I'd guess he's around my mom's age. I smile at him, since I don't know whether to speak to him in English or Spanish.

"Nice to meet you, María. If I do anything wrong or you need me to do something for you, just say so."

"It's Marie. I don't work the bar side just take orders and serve the food. Olga's the waitress for the bar, and you bus the bar tables. In here, help me fill up the napkin dispensers, bring in clean silverware and fill the water pitcher. The last guy, Jerry, used to help me, but he quit."

"Don't worry. I can handle it. I'm quick." Deep dimples appear at the corners of his mouth when he smiles.

"Wait here, I'll grab you an apron from the supply closet."

"Marie, just the person I want to see," Henry says from his office across from the hall closet. He waves me inside. "We're expanding the restaurant. Gonna sell *pan dulce* up front. I'll give you more hours."

This is the first time Henry's said more than one sentence to me. "Really?"

"You know how Officer Palermo's always asking for pie or donuts? That gave me the idea for *pan dulce*. Maybe we'll sell Mexican candy too."

Henry continues to talk about remodeling the café and the chance to work more hours. "Tomorrow, early, Olga's going to Tijuana to buy supplies. You want to go with her?"

"To Tijuana? Too far."

I don't go to the corner store with Olga, why would I go with her to TJ two-and-a-half hours away?

"She needs the help. . . lots of supplies. Olga drives there early, you stop for lunch, and you're back by two, three in the afternoon. If I wasn't so busy, I'd go myself. . . . But with the remodeling, I need to stay here. Fifty dollars for easy work."

Fifty dollars? It takes me three days to earn that much. I can pay the rest of my tuition with that, plus my regular check. And, I'll have a few bucks left over to buy a dress for Lucy's party. I'll have to ditch school, but it's for a good cause. I'm doing this for the greater good. Okay, maybe my greater good. I need that money to stay at St. Bernadette and graduate.

"Sure, I'll go."

"Meet Olga here at the restaurant at six-thirty tomorrow," he says.

That's earlier than I leave for school. I'll have to think up some excuse to tell Mom.

I refill chip baskets while Carlos hustles back and forth to the bar. A lull in customers doesn't come soon enough.

"Time for a break, Marie. I asked Pepe to make our tacos. I'll go grab the plates."

He returns with two dishes while I grab two bottles of Coke out of the cooler and sit down. I spoon red salsa over the lettuce and shredded cheese before I bite into a crisp corn tortilla. Carlos tries to hand me a grilled jalapeño.

I wave it away. "No way. I'll choke."

The front door swings open. In walks Coco and Cha Cha with Weasel. They're earlier than their usual eight o'clock entrance. The three of them act like they're friends, although I've never seen them all buddy-buddy before. Weasel glances at me like I'm supposed to be jealous.

"Hola, *chica*. Coffee and tacos for us," Coco says.

"Sure thing, ladies," Carlos says, springing out of the booth and into the kitchen.

"Where's that guy from?" Weasel asks. "What happened to Jerry?"

"Pfft, how do I know," I say. "Ask him."

Carlos is handsome in an older man kind of way. Weasel blows his breath out, rolls his beady black eyes at me when I set water glasses and utensils on their table.

"Hey, Jacqui Marie, this fork's dirty. Get me a clean one."

I check the fork out and see that it's not dirty. "It's only water stains."

"Give me a clean one." Weasel's voice rises like he's a boss, and I'm a peon.

Carlos picks up a fork from the clean dishes bin and places it in front of Weasel. "Here you go."

Weasel's hooded eyes give Carlos the slow once over. "Where you from, *vato*?" He lifts his chin at him like he's out on some street corner.

"*Tejas*," Carlos says.

"Oh, *Tejas. . . me encanta*. El Paso?" Coco asks.

"El Paso? That's an ugly-ass town." Weasel says, glaring at Carlos.

Everyone knows you don't disrespect Texas unless you want to fight. But Carlos picks up the dish bin like no problem. "Amarillo." He strolls to the kitchen. "Pepe, three orders of tacos."

"Where the hell is Amarillo?" Weasel asks Cha Cha, whose shoulders rise in an I-don't-know shrug.

"Wherever it is, they grow good-looking rugged men," Coco says with a shiver.

Cha Cha giggles, nodding her head like a bobble-headed Chihuahua.

"Tell that *vato* to bring our food to the bar," Weasel says.

"You go. I'm gonna take my time here," Coco says, fingering the silky ties on her blouse.

Weasel scoots out of his seat, yanking Cha Cha's hand. I want to tell her, thank you, because now he won't bother me anymore. She pulls him back down to the seat and whispers in his ear. He reaches inside his Pendleton, brings something out. Cha Cha takes whatever it is, gulps coffee and smacks her dark lips. They saunter to the bar together.

"He has a new girlfriend, huh?" I ask.

"Just business, no boyfriends." Coco shakes her head. "Carlos, sit down, rest. Talk a while."

He takes a seat, which surprises me. I overhear them talking about Texas and the Mexican food they compare to California's. They talk until Olga comes out of the bar and holds the swinging doors open. The sounds of guitars and trumpets blast out of the jukebox in the bar.

"Coco," Olga says like my mom when she's pissed off, "we're waiting."

"Yeah, yeah." She scoots out of the booth and blows Carlos a kiss. "When you get off?"

He laughs. "I'm married."

Her full shoulders slump forward at the same time as her red lips mouth, "Too bad."

Olga rolls her eyes. "Back to work, Carlos. And you, María. . . . Remember, six-thirty, *mañana*. Be on time." She disappears into the bar.

"You work early tomorrow?" Carlos says.

"No, I'm helping her out with something."

He tilts his head. "That's pretty early."

"Some errands she needs help with. Tell you later."

Things are looking up. I'm going to make fifty dollars to put toward my tuition, and tonight I don't have to worry about Weasel.

CHAPTER 27

I roll out of bed before six o'clock, put on jeans and a sweatshirt. I lied to Mom last night, telling her I have a meeting with Ms. Fine before first period to talk about my scholarship application. In the kitchen, I make myself a peanut butter and grape jelly sandwich for the road. I rush outside before Mom's alarm goes off at six-thirty.

The sun hasn't risen over the chilly morning yet. I can't see the sky, only the grey darkness around me. I wrap my arms against my chest, walk fast. The cool air is clean and fresh, and no laundromat or pickled pig's feet stink drifts out the shop doors yet.

A rickety van rumbles past and jolts over the potholes in the street until it stops on the corner. A group of farmworkers, straw hats and lunch sacks in hand, climb into the vehicle. Thank goodness I'm not going off to the fields. Once, on a weekend, Mom took me with her to pick strawberries. I came home sweaty, dusty and with a backache.

At the corner of Mela Street, I spot a station wagon at the curb in front of El Lobo's. The car's not as old as our beat-up wagon but it's not shining new either. The pinpoint of a glowing cigarette illuminates the driver's seat. The window rolls down a few inches. Smoke billows outside. It's Olga.

She wears a blue scarf over her hair like those ladies in the old movies, the ones riding in convertibles. I tap on the window. She reaches over to the passenger side, unlocks the door.

Without her bright lipstick and pancake make-up, she doesn't look like Jayne Mansfield anymore. Her lips and brows are so thin they fade into her pale face. She wears a sweater that comes up to her neck. Unusual for Olga.

She catches me staring. "What?"

"Nothing. You look younger without make-up."

"*¿De veras?* How young?"

"I dunno, like twenty-eight?" I take off a few years, so she'll get off my case.

"*Ay.*" A smile grows in her eyes before she starts up the car. "Let's go, *ya.*"

Olga speeds onto the freeway, driving fast and talking faster. "I like going to Tijuana. I came to the United States by myself, around your age. My parents died and my older brothers they came here and sent me and my little sister money."

"That's cool."

"My brothers said everybody could have a car, a house, in the US, because there was so much work, so I came. But a girl can't work in construction like the men, so my jobs were not that good."

By the time we cross the border into Tijuana, I hear everything about her boyfriends and heartbreak, her favorite Mexican and English songs, and how much she likes the food in Tijuana.

I visited TJ once before the boys were born when my dad brought us for a vacation at Rosarito Beach. TJ's the same, down to the zebra-striped donkey and the psychedelic cart splattered with the words Tijuana, Mexico.

We drive in circles after we leave Avenida Revolución and pass the same bank, stores and church three times.

"*Ay, ay*," Olga says under her breath, "why don't Henry give good directions to the *botánica*?"

On the fourth attempt, we find the tiny place sandwiched between two larger stores. A small sign above the arched doorway says, "Botánica Lynda."

"Come on." Olga unties her scarf, wraps it around her neck and fluffs up her dyed blonde hair. "Let's go."

The store is the size of our living room, jam-packed with herbs, jars of oils and five hundred statues of saints scattered on tables, shelves and on the red-tiled floor. A heavy pine scent hangs in the air.

There are candles to get rich or for love, jars of crumbled herbs for stomach pain, headaches and bad feet. The colorful jars crowd together on folding tables. This doesn't look like a place to order bakery items or Mexican candy.

Olga picks up a candle labeled "Fall En Love." She studies the back label and carries it to the counter, where a girl around my age sits on a stool, snapping her chewing gum. An older man in a *guayabera* shirt walks out of the black-curtained hallway. He tips his brown hat at Olga, and they talk while the girl rolls up the candle in butcher paper. The man returns to the back room.

"*Deme dos botellas de Fanta también.*" Olga hands the two bottles of soda to me and tucks her wrapped candle under her arm.

The old man returns with items in a bundled paper bag, hands them to Olga.

"*Vamos*," she says. "*Ándale.*"

"But where's the restaurant stuff?"

"They deliver next week. Now we go to buy baking supplies." She shuts the car door and hands me an orange soda.

We find the *panadería* right away. Sheets of *pan dulce* sit in the front window, assembled in a rainbow of colors. A bell chimes when we open the door. Red plastic trays sit in a tower on one side, with metal tongs in a canister on the other. I breathe in the warm air of the sugar-coated domes of bread until my stomach rumbles.

"Pick twelve pieces of *pan* and wait for me here." Olga hands me a tray.

The woman behind the counter yells out, "Catarino."

A man in a white apron and sweaty T-shirt pokes his head out. "*¿Y la Barbie?*"

Olga shakes her head and walks into the kitchen of the bakery. I wonder why the baker would be expecting Barbie?

There aren't any chairs in the place, so I lean against the wall after the lady packs the sweet bread into a pink bakery box. Five minutes later, Olga walks out.

"Okay, let's go. *Adiós*," she waves.

She's moving so fast to the car I jog to keep up with her, balancing the box in my hands.

"You like *tacos de carnitas*?" Olga asks as I climb into the station wagon. "I know the best place in town."

Olga weaves in and out of traffic for a couple of miles until we pull onto a side dirt road. Corrugated tin roofs over wooden lean-tos cling to rocky slopes. Mom used to tell us we were lucky we lived in a decent apartment, even if it was government housing. If we were in Tijuana, we might be in a rickety shack up on a hill with a view of a trash heap.

A palm-covered fruit stand comes into view. Next to it is a shed with a huge copper kettle in the front yard. A pile of glowing firewood blazes under the pot. Three men sit on a slanted wooden table eating tacos.

"*Carnitas* Coka Cola," a sign on the shed announces in red paint. Does that mean pork meat and Coca-Cola soda, or what?

Olga catches me staring at the sign. "They make their *carnitas* with Coca-Cola soda. Sit down, I be back." She disappears into the covered area.

A citrus-scented tang fills the air along with the lime aroma of ground *masa* and charcoal. A thin man in a dirty apron stirs the kettle, occasionally dumping in liquid from a plastic bucket. A syrupy fragrance floats toward me like the melted caramels we had once on Halloween.

Olga comes out of the shabby hut with two plates in her hands and two more bottles of soda under her armpits, shuffling so she won't drop them. I run over and take the plates. We lean against a shady wall and eat our tacos. She's right. They are the best.

"Eat quick. We got one more stop. Then we go. Wait here, I bring some for the road."

She wolfs the tacos down, licks a finger. When she returns, she carries out a large woven yellow and green tote bag, the kind the Mexican grandmas use for shopping.

"*Ándale*, let's go," she says.

The dirt road runs into the paved one heading back to town. We pull into a circle of green canopied shops ringing an enormous three-tiered fountain. Fancy. Several well-dressed women browse the windows showing mannequins in outfits, complete with hats and purses.

"Last stop, *la farmacia*."

Olga slams the car door and ducks into a shop. In five minutes, she's out with a white paper sack. She opens the tailgate, puts the bag into the woven tote, then lifts out a foil-wrapped plate of tacos. The car rocks side to side when she stuffs the tote into the back.

"What are you doing?" A knot forms in my stomach. Olga's up to something, but I don't know what it is. Who puts stuff in the spare tire area except for a crowbar?

She hops back into the driver's seat, glances at her wristwatch. "I need room in the back for the pots. Uh, for the restaurant. Plant flowers, make the place look pretty."

Long lines snake across the lanes at the border crossing. Olga rolls down her window, lights a cigarette. Man, I thought I was poor, but the kids walking through the lanes wear ragged clothes and dirty shoes without laces. Several of them are my brother's age.

"If you see pots, like for plants, call the man over," Olga says.

Within minutes, she bargains for two huge blue and yellow ceramic pots. Then she buys a scary looking clown piñata that an old woman pushes through my window. I shove it onto the back seat.

"When we get to the border agent, talk English. Tell him you're an American citizen." She adjusts her headscarf, dabs at her sweaty face with tissue paper. "Hand me a *pan dulce*, the *cochinito*."

"I am a citizen," I say and reach for the other brown piggy pastry.

The car creeps up to the border patrol window as we munch on our *pan dulce*. A couple officers in green uniforms walk around the cars in the adjacent lanes. Olga fingers the driver's license in her lap.

"What was the nature of your visit in Mexico, ma'am?"

"Shopping."

The young officer glances at me, walks around the station wagon, and taps on my window. I roll it down.

"Where were you born?"

"Near Los Angeles. San Solano."

He nods. "How old are you?" I don't know whether I should say seventeen or my pretend eighteen and sit silently for a second. Olga glances at me. Her eyes pinched together.

"Seventeen," I blurt out.

"We buy her piñata here for her party," Olga says.

The officer focuses on my eyes. I'm trying so hard not to bust out laughing. How could he believe that a seventeen-year-old would want that ugly clown piñata at her party? He steps back to her side of the window and waves us through.

"Thank you, officer." Olga waves, and peeks in the rearview mirror while we drive away. "Put this back in my purse."

Before I put her license away, I glimpse Olga's photo on the card. The picture resembles her, but the name on the card is Barbara Ríos.

CHAPTER 28

The city bus jiggles over the train tracks and heads to St. Bernie. I ignore any stares from the other kids and take a seat near the front. The girl who previously remarked on my Oxford shoes doesn't say a word. Her eyes are closed as she leans against the window.

Questions roll around in my head, trying to make sense of the trip I took with Olga yesterday. We stopped at a pharmacy, a bakery and an herb shop, and all she ended up with was a candle, *pan dulce* and paper bags she stuffed in her tote bag.

Weirder is how and why she'd have Barbie's ID card if she's missing? I mean, I'm super happy about the money I earned, but something isn't right. The rumors about El Lobo's being a front for drug dealing look like they could be true. Should I quit? Or ask Bebe first and see what she thinks?

If Bebe says El Lobo's is shady and a front for drug dealing, I'll have to quit. But if I do, I won't have any money to pay the rest of that tuition. By next week, Mom will be paid again, and I'll have enough from work to pay all of March's tuition. I need to hang on for one more week. Like Dad said, sometimes you gotta do what you gotta do.

Cars and groups of students make their way through St. Bernadette's parking lot before first period. I run up the stairs to the school office before the bell rings. The forged signature on my sick note has to pass Mrs. Jasper's examination.

"Hey," Petey says from the top of the stairs and comes down to walk beside me. "You sick yesterday?"

I'm out of breath and pause. Was Petey waiting for me? "Yeah, I didn't feel good."

"Check it out. We heard Ms. Fine has a meeting next week with Sister Mary Graceless about her threat to suspend her."

"Sister sure messed things up. Ms. Fine's the best teacher here."

"A few of the students feel like that, too. Come to the quad at lunchtime, okay?"

The bell rings, and Petey veers off to his class, leaving me with a stomach full of excitement and disappointment. Excited, he invited me to lunch, but sad that Ms. Fine is in trouble. She's the only teacher I'm able to talk with like a person.

In every period, the class gossip is Sister Mary's threat to suspend Ms. Fine. Larry exaggerates when he retells the story, saying she went up to Sister Mary Grace's face and yelled at her, while others say they heard Ms. Fine crying when Sister stormed out of the classroom.

After fourth period, I find Petey waiting in the hallway for me. "Let's go to the quad."

My pulse speeds up as fast as my vibrating heart. I swallow to wet my throat and croak, "Sure."

He finds an empty picnic bench in the center as if it's reserved for him. Soon, Larry, Lucy and Margot join us. I half expect Larry to call me a name, but he lifts his chin at me and sits on the top of the table next to Petey. Lucy nudges me with her arm and smiles when she sits next to me on the bench. Margot doesn't even look at me.

It's weird hanging out with them, eating lunch together. Strange but cool. I peer into my lunch bag and examine the bologna sandwich inside. I can tell without taking my sandwich out that Caroline slathered on too much mustard. Gobs of yellow dot the waxed paper. I pull out a bag of Fritos instead.

"You guys," Margot says, "I've been thinking about Ms. Fine's situation and how wrong Sister was to threaten to suspend her over a magazine article. So not fair."

I'm surprised by Margot. She could afford to go to any college, even if she doesn't win the alumni scholarship. Why would she care?

"You know what's not fair?" I say. "When we go into your department store, and the sales ladies ignore us. This lady I know complained about that."

Margot's mouth drops open. Petey and Larry twist their necks in my direction.

Lucy presses her finger on her chin. "Yeah, every time I go in there with my mom, she has to chase down a sales lady."

"Oh, that's not true." Margot flicks her hand at Lucy.

The smirk on Lucy's face and the glare in her eyes tells me it is true.

"If this lady, who I don't know, said so and Lucy too, then it's happening. I think you should check out your salesladies. See if you catch them being prejudiced."

"We're not racist," Margot shouts and tosses her long hair aside. "Don't say that, Jacqui."

Larry jumps off the picnic bench and rubs the top of his buzz cut. "Geez, calm down. Weren't we talking about Ms. Fine?"

I glance around to the other benches and see a bunch of kids watching us. Everyone definitely heard us. Margot hangs her head, picking at the table with her fingernail.

"I'm not accusing you, just your sales ladies," Lucy says before biting off a hunk of her Twinkie. "I've been wanting to tell you for a while."

The guys chew on their sandwiches while I nibble a corn chip. This is the first time I've had lunch with these kids, and it might be my last, if I don't say something quick. "Margot, you were telling us about Ms. Fine's situation?"

"Uh, yeah. We need to make sure she stays here." She pulls out a sheet of paper from her three-ring binder. "I wrote up a petition."

"That's a brilliant idea." A rush of adrenaline tingles in my stomach.

Margot's face lights up. She tosses her lunch bag aside, pulls out her binder and several sheets of paper. "We need a bunch of signatures so we can give it to Sister Mary Grace in time for the meeting with Ms. Fine next week."

"What's a petition gonna do? Sister's the principal. What she says goes," Larry says.

Lucy jumps up, lobs her lunch sack in the trash can. "Yeah, Sister never listens to any of our ideas in French Club. She couldn't care less about us."

Meeting with the CBC this past couple of weeks has made me realize that working to change things isn't easy; it takes effort. Rudy also said we can try to change things, even if there's no guarantee what we do will work.

"Don't we count?" I throw my Fritos bag down. "Ms. Fine's a great teacher, and it's not fair she's threatened with suspension for treating us like young adults. All she had was a magazine on her desk."

"Yeah, and we're going to college soon," Margot says. "Why shouldn't we discuss important topics."

"Don't get me wrong," Larry says. "I like Ms. Fine, but I don't think petitions will help. We'll be kicked out of school."

Petey rubs his chin like he's deep in thought. "We should try, though."

"He's right. We need to make what's wrong right," I say. "I'm in, Margot."

"Hell yes, count me in, too," Lucy says. "Down with Sister Mary, up with Ms. Fine."

"Shhh," Margot says. A rosy blush spreads over her freckles. "Thank you, guys. I didn't realize I was the only one who felt like this."

"Hold up. What happens if Sister puts us on probation? I can't get pulled off the baseball team. My dad will have a cow," Larry says.

My stomach takes a dip. What if Sister threatens to suspend all of us? I'm hanging by a thread already.

"St. Bernie has a winning baseball team. Sister's not going to piss off the coaches by suspending you two," Lucy says.

"She's right." I grab a piece of paper out of my Pee Chee folder. "Check this out."

Rudy's idea of community allies reminds me that we can tackle Ms. Fine's problem the same way we're doing with the city council. I draw circles on the paper as Rudy did at the meeting. In the middle ring, I write Ms. Fine's name, and around it, I draw another and write in the words, "students," "teachers" and "parents."

"See this? They're part of St. Bernadette's community. Think of them as partners in the petition. This school isn't for Sister Mary Graceless but for all of us."

Everyone crowds around me. Margot flips over a petition paper and makes the same circles.

"There's strength in numbers," I say.

"Add alumni to a circle," Margot says. "My sister graduated from here, and Ms. Fine was one of her teachers."

"So did my brother," Lucy and Larry say.

"Those people who don't attend our school can be our allies."

"Hey, I like that, Jacqui." Margot fills in the circle. "Partners and allies in a common cause."

"Exactly. Let's get started today," I grab the petition sheets from Margot. "If each of us takes a sheet and asks kids to sign, we should have at least one hundred signatures by next week."

CHAPTER 29

What was I thinking? Getting one hundred signatures from classmates I rarely talk to isn't going to be easy, and I already have so much to do. First on my list is to ask Olga about Barbie's ID. I take a breath and push open the door to El Lobo's. The pink bakery box from yesterday sits on the counter. I find a couple of pieces of Mexican bread inside and slide the box under the counter for break time.

"Hey," Olga bangs through the bar doors and holds out a broom. "Take this and bring me some napkins. I'm in the bar today."

Dang it, I won't have a chance to ask her about that ID. She'd tell me none of my business, anyway.

Officer Palermo walks in and slides onto a stool in front of me. "Hi, Marie. Coffee, please."

"Sure. Guess what we got in today?" I remove a sugar-topped *pan dulce* from the box and place it on a plate. "We got them in Tijuana yesterday. They're still kinda soft."

"Tia-Juana, Mexico?" He bites into the sweet bread, scattering white crumbs over the plate. "These are good, but we have Mexican bakeries here in town. Why go to Tijuana?" He leans back and waits for an answer.

"Henry's gonna put in a bakery, sell *pan* and candy. You can have dessert now with your coffee."

"Hmm." He finishes the sweet bread in three more bites and another gulp of coffee. "See you later."

Palermo didn't seem concerned about the errands, so maybe my imagination is running away with me. And Olga probably stole Barbie's ID so she'd have a card to show she has papers to be in the US and legally drive.

Several workers come in for a bowl of soup or enchiladas, and Carlos and I are busy working the front by ourselves. By the time seven o'clock rolls by, we slow down long enough for a break.

"I'll grab us a few tacos," he says and hustles into the kitchen.

I sit at the counter sipping a Coke, watching people as they walk by the front window. Petey rides up on his three-speed bike, hops off and wraps a long length of chain-link around the front tire and the streetlamp outside. Oh crap, I'm a sweaty mess in a greasy apron. He catches me watching him and waves before he walks into El Lobo's. Too late.

He leaps onto a stool. "Thought I'd stop by and visit you on my way home. Plus, I'm hungry. You said the cook makes good tacos here."

I look gross while he's looking fine with his glossy hair, even if he parts it on the side like a little boy. I press my lips together to stop smiling so wide.

"Had a baseball game earlier," he says.

"You guys win?"

"Slaughtered them. What time are you off?"

"In about an hour and a half. Nine."

"Call your mom, tell her I'm taking you home."

"What?"

The way he says, "I'm taking you home," is like an order. That doesn't sit well. Too many people give me orders, and I don't want Petey to think that's okay with me. I cross my arms and glare at him.

"I mean, my mom said your mom has a side job on weekends, and she needs to rest. So, how about I take you home?"

"Oh, okay."

I telephone Mom and tell her Petey's walking me home. She sighs, mumbling, "He's so nice," in a sleepy voice. She's pooped, her feet probably throbbing from walking door to door and up hills delivering heavy telephone books this past weekend.

"Ready?" Carlos says, his hands holding two plates.

"Hey, Carlos, this is Petey Castro. He came by for tacos."

They shake hands, and Petey tells him we live near each other in the projects and have known each other since the sixth grade. He tells him I'm so smart, I make the dean's list every semester.

The way he goes on about me is embarrassing, but it makes me happy, too. Who knew that the boy I have a crush on would brag about me?

"I'm impressed. Here you go, two taco plates. I'll grab another order."

"Wait a sec," I tell Petey and follow Carlos into the kitchen.

"Please don't tell Olga or Henry that I'm seventeen and in high school. Henry said he doesn't like to deal with work permits," I say in a low voice. "I really need this job."

"Don't worry, your secret's safe with me and Pepe." He lifts his chin to the cook.

Pepe nods.

"We understand," Carlos says. "Heard you went to TJ yesterday."

"Yeah, to help Olga because Henry's going to remodel the front of the restaurant for a bakery." I tell him about the errands but don't mention the fake ID.

"Nice. Go on back out there. Petey's missing you already." He winks at me.

When I step back into the café, Weasel sits on a counter stool. He's one space away from Petey and giving him a mad-dog look.

"Hey, Marie Jacqui," he snickers his idiotic laugh. "Thought maybe you went home already."

"Nope. Your girlfriend Cha Cha's in the bar."

"Psst. She's not my *jaina*, too old. Lemme give you a ride home."

"I'm taking her home," Petey says.

"Who are you? Her boyfriend?" Weasel leans close to Petey, who doesn't back away.

"He's my *primo*," I say.

I don't want Weasel knowing any of my business and I don't want Petey saying we go to St. Bernadette. The less Weasel knows, the better.

"Taking care of your cousin, huh?" He bobs his head. "I remember you. Saw you on your old bike once."

"Here you go." Carlos walks in with another plate and a bowl of salsa. He sets them in an empty booth. "Go on, take your break. I'll be in the kitchen with Pepe."

Weasel glances at us. I scramble to the booth where Petey joins me.

"Later, Marie Jacqui, Jacqui Marie." Weasel drags out my name and gives Petey a last glare while he saunters to the bar doors.

"Don't pay attention to him. He's a jerk," I say, digging into my food.

Carlos drops some quarters into the jukebox. "You kids enjoy."

"It's A Shame" by the Spinners starts playing. Petey bobs his head, moving his shoulders to the guitar strums.

"It's a shame, the way you mess around. . . " he sings.

Makes me giggle, but I join in too. "Sitting all alone. . ."

We're singing while sitting in the booth with half-eaten tacos and beans. The song ends way too soon and we bust up laughing. Another song clicks to play. The Five Stairsteps.

"Ooh child," we both say.

"Things are going to get easier. . ." We sing. "Ooh child, things will be brighter. . . Someday. . ."

We keep going on for the next song that Carlos chooses for us. This is the best time I've had in two years. Petey and I, together with the music playing, is like having a date. A really good one.

"María," Henry's voice burst into the dining room from the bar doors. He lumbers to the booth, hands me a long envelope. "For your time."

He glances at Petey. I slide out of the booth and take our empty soda bottles to the counter.

When he leaves, I slide five ten-dollar bills out. Fifty bucks just for taking a ride with Olga and having lunch.

Petey eyes the envelop. "What's that for?"

"Side job with Olga. Help me clean up, okay?"

We hightail it out of the café at nine o'clock. Petey unravels the bike chain and makes room for me on the cross-bar.

The hard bar between the bicycle seat and the handlebars chills my butt. If Petey had a Stingray bike, I could sit behind him on a comfy banana seat with my arms around his waist or put my hands on his broad shoulders. Instead, I'm wedged between his arms with the scent of his Brylcreem swirling around my head, making me woozy.

White puffs of breath from Petey's mouth float by while he pedals and talks. His letterman jacket brushes against my arms each time he makes a turn onto another street. I'm in a warm nest between his arms, smiling like a fool, my teeth icy from the rushing air. He glides his bike around cars and curbs. The porch light grows as we ride closer to my place.

"Let me get off first. I'll hold up the bike for you." Petey scoots backward off the seat near the rear tire while holding onto one handlebar.

My legs are tight as I try to straighten them out. They don't unfold fast enough and the bike tips toward him, with me still sitting.

"Jump," he says.

I bend my legs to leap onto the sidewalk, but my nose hits the top button of his jacket. I stumble back, my hands grasping for his. Within a second, he wraps his arms around me to hold me up.

Dang it, I'm so dorky, but he doesn't laugh. He holds onto me tighter. My arms, tucked by my side, freeze in place. His heartbeats thump against the side of my face. I must look like a hot dog inside a handsome brown bun. Petey's warm breath ruffles the top of my head. He doesn't say anything, just keeps holding me.

"Sorry." I bend my head back to look up at his face.

He doesn't roll his eyes or push me away. Instead, he lowers his head. His warm lips press against my forehead, then move to my right cheek. I shut my eyes because I don't know if he's going to kiss me on the lips or not, and all I think of is that I've been eating tortilla chips with chile all night. I hold my breath until his lips slide over mine.

The sensation tingles every nerve in my body. Forget the chile, my mouth seems to say. My lips part like they understand what to do. His warm tongue slides against mine and flicks across the top of my mouth, sending a shiver down my legs.

This isn't gross at all. Not like I imagined. I pull my head back because I'll faint from being so close to his body. His head lifts just enough for an inch of cold air to drift between us. The tiny space breaks the moment.

I don't remember saying goodbye, walking to the porch or knocking on our front door. But I do remember this is my first kiss from the boy I've loved since sixth grade.

I wake up Caroline, telling her I need to go to work early today. She murmurs and swats me away. She's dead asleep since we don't have to do laundry today, and Mom left for her telephone book delivery job an hour ago.

Downstairs, I make myself a PB&J sandwich and see a note on the kitchen table. "Go to Confession today—Mom." Nope, I have other plans. With my extra money, I'm going shopping. I telephone Lucy to ask her to call Jerry so we can go to the mall before my shift at noon.

"It's only eight." Lucy yawns. "Let's go at ten or eleven."

"By then, we won't have much time to shop. This is the only time I can look for a dress. I need your help."

Lucy liked that I said I needed her help. I could hear her leap out of bed. She must have a telephone in her room. Lucky her.

We agree on nine-thirty. I wind my way through the streets, cross the park, pass the laundromat, which is already busy, and wait for Jerry on the corner of El Lobo's.

All night I thought of Petey's kiss. Does this mean we're boyfriend and girlfriend? If I trusted Lucy, I'd ask her, but what if she blabs to someone? She and Margot are cheerleaders. I'm sure they had their first kisses two years ago. I can't ask Caroline. She's another big mouth. She'll tell Mousy, who'll tell her oldest sister Lena, who has a crush on Petey, and then she'll try to fight me. I need to keep this to myself.

Riding in Jerry's car is sure faster than taking the bus to the north side of town. Lucy sits in the front while I sit in the back. We all yak until we park at Sanders Department store right when they open.

"Here?" I ask Lucy. "The clothes are way expensive."

She glances at Jerry, then back to me. "Let's just see what they have, and then we can go to the mall."

"I guess." I don't want to sound ungrateful, but my budget is ten dollars for a dress because I need to buy Lucy a gift too.

Jerry splits to the men's section to look at slacks and shirts. Lucy stops at all the racks and examines the dresses. She's all excited like she's looking for her dress, not mine.

We begin at the back of the store and make our way up to the mannequins wearing the latest stuff. I pretend I don't like any of the expensive dresses she pulls off the racks for me. After the tenth dress, my eyes are crossed, and my feet hurt. I'm tired of looking at dresses I can't possibly have and hearing Lucy say, "But this outfit is only twenty-six dollars."

Jerry rushes toward us with two pairs of slacks over his shoulder. "Check out that lady behind you."

An older woman in a blue blazer and matching pants peers at us over her cat eyeglasses on a chain. She doesn't say a word, but every time we move, she moves. But she never comes close to us or asks us if we need help. I glance up at her from time to time and see her flashing a pink-lipped smile at other people.

"Let me know if I can be of assistance," I hear her say to another woman.

Lucy holds up a super cute dress and shakes it at me. "Should we take this one?"

I look for the tag on the dress but can't find one.

"We don't do layaways," the woman says from a distance.

A few ladies glance up at us from the clothes racks. They're standing right in front of the sign that says, "We Do Layaways."

"The dress cost more than at the mall. And if I had the money, I wouldn't buy it from a snotty place like Sanders," I tell Lucy.

"That's right," Lucy says in a loud voice. "Sanders is snobbish."

"Well, you people can't afford our clothing anyway," the saleslady says.

Jerry puts his slacks down at the counter and pockets his wallet. "Let's go."

You people. All the way to El Lobo's, the words repeat like the cassette tape in Jerry's car. I don't even feel like shopping anymore or going to Lucy's party.

⚜   ⚜   ⚜

My feet drag into El Lobo's. The words the saleslady said, "you people," keep repeating in my head. It's like I'm in a separate category because I'm not white. Because I'm not rich. Because I'm young. Because every dollar and dime I make has to go to food, rent or school.

Olga and Henry don't seem annoyed when I arrive late. Olga flashes her three gold bracelets at me. Her jewelry could buy me a year's worth of dresses.

"They match my necklace, see?"

I nod, tie on an apron and start filling the salsa bowls. Carlos is so busy with all the people coming in and out of the bar that he hardly speaks to me but smiles when he comes through to pick up clean glasses.

"*Oye*, Carlos," Henry says, "take care of this side while me and María go to my office."

I jerk my head up and follow him down the hall. "Sorry I was late. Won't happen again."

He waves at me to sit.

He leans on the corner of his desk and says, "Olga says you were a big help on her errands. You're a good worker, María. I want to do the remodeling quicker, so Olga needs to run another errand. Can you come in on Monday to go with her?"

I can't miss another day of school. Plus, I planned to meet with Margot and the others to present the petitions on that day. I can't take off to Tijuana.

"TJ is too far."

"No, not there. The next town over. Thirty minutes there and back, maybe two, three hours of work. I'll pay you the same: fifty bucks. Leave around noon, back at three."

Fifty dollars? That'll really help me get ahead on my tuition. Errands around town don't sound as sketchy as taking off to Tijuana. If I leave school at lunchtime, I can make it here by noon. "Okay."

I return to the cash register to find Carlos sweeping. "Petey picking you up?"

"No, he has a game."

At nine o'clock, Carlos grabs his beanie. "I'll walk you to the Mini-Mart."

We pass the alleyway, where the parking lights of cars near El Lobo's trash bins are on. Carlos stuffs his hands in his heavy army jacket.

"Customers in the alley, too." He shakes his head. "So, tell me about your trip to TJ."

"Not much to tell, just errands for Henry. Olga knew where to go."

Carlos tells me he used to go to Tijuana a lot when he was younger. He asks if I went to the huge restaurant warehouses for baking supplies. When I say no, he asks questions about the other places.

"You know where Carnitas Coka Cola is? We went there for lunch."

"Nope," Carlos says. "It takes so long to cross the border. You guys have any problems?"

Do I tell him Olga lied to the officer?

"Did something happen? You wrinkled up your forehead."

"No problems, but Olga had Barbie's ID card, but with her own picture in it. I thought that was weird. I guess she needs it because she doesn't have papers. Barbie used to work at El Lobo's, so maybe she left it somewhere in the café."

Carlos nods.

"I'm going to help Olga do more errands on Monday."

His head swivels toward me and stops walking. "You're going back to Tijuana?"

"No, the next city over this time. Henry paid me fifty bucks for TJ and he'll pay another fifty more on Wednesday. I'll be able to get ahead on my tuition. Takes a load off my mind."

Our dumb car horn moans at us when we enter the parking lot of the Mini-Mart. Mom cranes her neck at Carlos and waves me over to the car.

"Come meet my mom," I say. "Mom, this is Carlos, we work together."

She scrunches her forehead so much her eyebrows meet. Mom can give dirty looks better than anyone I know.

"I didn't want her waiting by herself," Carlos says. He smiles so wide his dimples burrow into his handsome face, but that doesn't erase the look on Mom's face. "Nice to meet you," he says.

She mumbles, "Thank you," and starts the engine. "Why didn't you wait inside. I'm a few minutes late. No reason for you to be outside with some man. . . ."

Geez, she starts with the third degree and doesn't let up until she parks in front of our place. I let her talk because I've had a great week, and it's about to get better.

CHAPTER 30

At the top of the staircase, Lucy waves to me. I make my
way through the parking lot, dodging cars and kids grouped in
small circles, and jog up the steps.

"What do you mean you can't stay, Jacqui?" Lucy says.

"I'm sorry, but I have a dentist appointment and gotta go
home at lunchtime."

"You can't have your mom reschedule?"

"Nope." I shrug and notice Margot approaching. "Did you
tell Margot about her sales lady?"

The way Lucy presses her glossy lips together tells me she
hasn't brought up the incident. It's been heavy on my mind, so
as soon as Margot comes closer, I bring it up.

"We went to your store on Saturday, and one of your sales
ladies followed us around. Never asked us if we needed help.
And she said, 'You people can't afford Sanders anyway.'" I try
to mimic the lady's voice.

Margot's bright eyes dull. "Hmmh."

"That's it?"

She shifts her feet and glances at Lucy, who nods. "Yeah,
she was snotty."

"I'll look into it," Margot says. "I promise."

"Good." I smile because I don't want to be pissed off anymore. "Here are my signatures. About twenty."

Took a lot for me to ask for those, too. I talked to more kids in three days than I did in the preceding three years at St. Bernadette.

"Made all the flag team and cheerleaders sign, plus the basketball team," Lucy says. "And Margot bugged the Student Body Council and the French Club. Fifty-five signatures."

"Dang, you're really good," I say.

"We tag-teamed them. They couldn't get away from us, huh?" She nudges Margot.

"What about Larry and Petey? Where are they?"

"They talked with the baseball teams and got about twenty signatures. All the junior varsity signed, but only a few varsity players. They're afraid Coach will hassle them, so I said the girls will handle it," Margot says.

"Right on." Lucy throws her fist in the air. "We got this."

The way they're so confident makes me embarrassed that I'm not. "That's only ninety-five signatures, and there's five hundred kids in the school."

"We counted on our parents' signatures, but they wouldn't sign. They said it's a school matter. No use arguing with them," Margot says. "But my sister was home over the weekend, and she signed. And then they all started arguing, telling my sister to mind her own business."

"Damn. You should've seen my mom. She was so P-O'ed she threatened to cancel my party," Lucy says.

Geez, I didn't even ask my mom.

Margot shuffles the papers, begins counting. "Ninety-eight signatures." Her words bubble out.

"Cool. Hey, let's take them to the school office now," Lucy says. "That way, Jacqui can come with us. We don't have to wait for Sister's meeting with Ms. Fine later."

"Good idea." Margot slides the sheets into her binder. "Come on, Jacqui."

Thoughts on how loud Mom will yell after Sister scolds me run through my head and sour my stomach. "Uh, I don't... bell's gonna ring soon."

Lucy grabs my arm. "What happened to partners and allies? You're the one who said we need to make right a wrong."

Margot's gaze focuses on me. She frowns. "I thought Ms. Fine was important to you like she is to me."

Everything they say is true. I urged them on, helped them and now I'm bailing. "Ms. Fine's my favorite teacher, but, uh. . ."

Lucy jolts to a stop and puts her hands on her hips. "Damn it, Jacqui. I liked you because you didn't take shit from anyone, you don't care what people say, and now suddenly, you can't be in this with us?"

They both study me as I shuffle my feet and hide my twitching hands. They're right. I know they are, but they don't realize I'm barely hanging on at St. Bernadette. Still, I said I'd help.

"Okay, let's go."

Lucy and Margot link their arms in mine as they stride into the courtyard. *Please help me, St. Bernadette*, I silently plead when we pass her statue in the courtyard. Lucy flings open the door to the school office. I follow and wait beside Margot while Lucy taps on the desk bell three times.

"Ladies, one ring is enough." Mrs. Jasper lifts her eyeglasses from the chain around her neck. "A payment, Miss Bravo?"

I'm not giving her my last twenty bucks. "Uh, no. On Monday, the first, I'll have March's tuition."

"Then your name remains on the ding list," she says.

Margot and Lucy glance at me. The class bell shrills that it's first period.

I clear my throat and ignore her remark. "Um, we're here to talk with Sister Mary Grace."

Margot steps up to the counter and slaps the papers down. "Yes, we have a petition with student signatures that we'd like Sister to see before her meeting with Ms. Fine this afternoon."

"Over one hundred signatures." Lucy crosses her arms.

"What business do you students have with Mrs. Fine, if I may ask?"

"We want her to stay here as our teacher," I say. "She shouldn't be suspended."

"Girls, that is school business, not yours." Mrs. Jasper sits back down with a thud and begins typing.

Lucy nudges me. "She's ignoring us."

"Excuse me," Margot says. "Please call Sister Mary Grace."

"Mrs. Jasper, you're right. This is school business, and we're part of the school," I say.

Her eyes dart back and forth between us, finally landing on the telephone on her desk. She dials. Good, she's taking us seriously now.

"Dean, please come to the office." She bangs the phone onto the receiver. "If the three of you don't want a week's detention, you'd better run along to class before the Dean of Students arrives."

My neck swivels at Margot and Lucy, both glaring at Mrs. Jasper. Margot gulps, a pink blush rising on her face.

I take a step back, my hands curling. "This is wrong. You can't punish us for giving our opinion."

"We have a say so. She's our teacher and a great one, too," Margot says.

I swear Lucy's brown eyes are blazing copper. "Call Sister Mary Grace. Now."

The principal's door opens. Sister waddles out into the lobby. "What is going on out here?"

"These girls, they, they're demanding to see you."

"We asked politely several times, but you called the Dean instead," Margot says.

"What is the problem, Miss Sanders?"

Margot hands the petitions to Sister. "We collected one hundred signatures asking you to keep Ms. Fine here at St. Bernadette."

"Hmm." Sister glances down at each sheet. "This is a personnel matter."

"We should be part of personnel," Lucy says. "We want Ms. Fine to know we want her to stay."

The dean sticks his head through the office door, looking like a giant turtle with his dark green dickey and sweater vest. He gestures to Mrs. Jasper. "Problem?"

"No, no," Sister Mary Graceless waves him off. "The girls are leaving now."

"But Sister," Margot says.

"I have your petitions in hand, girls. Now don't be late for class."

CHAPTER 31

Margot had a good point when she said Sister Mary Grace stayed too calm when she took our petitions. Neither of us trusts her to show Ms. Fine the signatures, so she and Lucy are checking with Ms. Fine at lunchtime.

As soon as the lunch bell rings, I run to the bus stop. By twelve-thirty, I make it to Mela Street to wait for Olga. My heart's pounding. With this last errand, I'll be able to stay at St. Bernie and quit El Lobo's. This is the final time I help her with anything. I'd rather be at school hanging out with my new friends and Petey.

Olga pulls up, tooting on the car horn and waving her arm out the window. She looks like Rosie the Riveter in the posters with a red bandana on her head.

"What?" Olga snaps her minty chewing gum when I get into the car.

Dressed in faded jeans and a checkered apron over her blouse, you'd think we're on our way to clean offices.

"Were you cleaning your house or something?"

She smacks her lips and starts the car. "At the first place I need to go in, but in the second place, you go. The guy already has what we need. You pick it up and come back."

"What am I picking up, and why do I have to go in by myself?"

"Because I'm tired. You're supposed to be helping. The man doesn't speak English, and your Spanish is not so good. In the second place, the guy only speaks English. Give him our order, *y ya*."

In another fifteen minutes, we're in the next city, driving in and out of alleys.

"There aren't any stores here."

"The man does business out of his house. He don't have an office."

Olga parks in front of a white stucco house with a black wrought iron gate that wraps around the front yard.

She opens the hatchback of the station wagon and pulls out her tote bag. A dishtowel covers the huge bulging purse. A fierce looking Doberman Pinscher runs from the side of the house, barking until he stops and bares his teeth. I roll up my window. Olga puts two fingers in her mouth and whistles.

A burly man comes out to the porch and yells at the dog, "*Ya pues*."

The dog retreats to the porch and lies down. Olga walks through and goes inside the house. In a few minutes, she returns with her tote bag half-full of paper bags. There's no type of restaurant equipment with her, unless those bags have metal tongs for the *pan dulce*. Who sells utensils out of their house?

We pass several stores until we arrive at the other side of town. It's a nicer area with better-looking apartments. Olga stops across the street and writes down an address on a napkin.

"Go across the street, down near the end. Another contractor. A *gabacho*, red hair," she says before she takes a shoebox out of the trunk. There's duct tape across the top and sides.

"What's this?"

The box is heavy, like a few books are inside. I shake it.

"Hey, don't do that." Olga reaches inside the car window, puts her hand on mine. "He forgot some things at my house. Give him the box and ask him for my purse. I leave it over there the other day."

The fake toothy smile she gives leaves me wondering what's inside the taped-up box. The knot in my stomach tightens the longer she gives me that smile. I think it's better I don't know for sure.

"Why's your purse there? I thought he didn't speak Spanish."

"*Ay*, he's just a boyfriend, kinda. Just bring my *bolsa*."

She walks around to the driver's side, slides behind the steering wheel and slams the door. "Go on. We don't got all day."

Little palm trees and flowering red bushes surround the two-story building. The shady sidewalk winds in and out further back to identical apartments. I find number eight and knock a couple of times on the cream-colored door. No answer. I set the box down and knock again.

A short freckle-faced man way older than my mom answers. His red hair is in a ponytail. This must be the guy.

"From Olga?" His blue eyes shift left to right when he speaks.

My mouth goes dry. I nod a few times.

"Wait here." He shuts the door in my face.

He comes back and hands me a brown suede purse that I grab. She must have left her make-up bag and a brick in it because the bag weighs a ton.

Once I'm out on the sidewalk, I look down the street for the station wagon, but Olga's not there. I look in the other direction, and she's not there either. Should I go back to the man's apartment? Maybe I can use the telephone and call Henry.

A car horn toots behind me. The station wagon cruises to a stop.

"Dang it, Olga, where were you?" I swing the purse off my shoulder and into the car.

Olga lifts it by the straps, opens it and smiles before she drops it onto the back seat. "Had to go to the bathroom at the gas station."

She could have gone inside the man's apartment if she dated him. And her purse was there. I sit back in my seat and cross my arms.

"One more stop," Olga says.

"What? I need to get back. You said an errand, not three stops."

She ignores me and turns on the radio. "Find me the Mexican station."

My ribs tighten while nerves prickle my arms and fingers. They tremble as I turn the dial. The station wagon turns into an old junkyard with bald tires stacked up on each other like a huge black sculpture on both sides of a long trailer. A tall chain-link fence covers the entrance to a pothole-filled drive-way. Two German Shepards run and jump at the gate when we stop the car.

I do not want to go into this place.

Olga beeps the horn. A guy with a bushy beard pokes his head out of the trailer and comes to pull open the gate. He walks to Olga's window and stares at me. I gulp and stay still.

"Wait here."

Another man, much cleaner looking, comes out of the trailer with a packet in his hand. It looks like a piece of meat bundled in brown butcher paper. "Who's the girl?"

"Friend's daughter, giving her a ride home," Olga says.

I can't tell if the man knows Olga is lying or not, but he stares at me before he glances in the back seat.

"I'm in a hurry," Olga says.

He goes around to the back of the car, where she joins him. The car moves from side to side. I glance over my shoulder and see that the man has yanked open the inside part of the car's upholstery. A bag rustles and he shuts the door. Besides the sinking feeling in my stomach, my body tightens up.

Olga sits back in the car, peers at her watch. "Almost three. We stop at Wimpy Burger's before we go back to El Lobo."

She grabs her fringe purse and reaches inside. The sound of a rubber band snaps. Olga waves three twenty-dollar bills in front of my face. "You did good, María. Keep the change."

⚜ ⚜ ⚜

During my entire shift at El Lobo's, the next day I re-run the errands with Olga in my mind. The whole time in the car, I was scared. Were we mules? Is Mousy's rumor about El Lobo's selling heroin and marijuana not a rumor but the truth? And Cha Cha always looks doped up.

I feel like I'm living in two different worlds. In both, I'm trying to hang on to get what I want, but one is legal, and the other looks like it's illegal. In one, I have college and a future. With the other, I can get caught and end up in juvie. I need to quit.

"Looks like you lost your best friend." Carlos pours me a soda and leans on the counter across from my stool, his chin resting on the palm of his hand. "You're frowning like you have a lot on your mind."

The door between the bar and the restaurant swings open. Olga struts out wearing a silky red blouse and a black mini-skirt. A diamond ring sparkles on her ring finger. She stretches out her hand on the counter and wriggles her hand.

"Are you engaged?" Carlos asks.

"No, but someone loves me more than anyone." She smiles like she has an important secret.

Carlos lets out a long whistle. "Beautiful. *Mucho dinero.*" He puts away a dishpan. "Wish I had that kind of money to spend on my lady."

This might be a good time to ask Olga for a favor, since she's in such a good mood.

"I know it's late, Olga, but I need Friday night off."

"No, too short notice. The restaurant side's crowded until seven-thirty."

"Can I work until seven o'clock then? This is really, really important." I clasp my hands in front of me in mock prayer. "I need the favor. Please don't say no. I did you a favor."

Olga stops twirling her ring. "Only if Carlos takes over for you."

Carlos winks at me. "Sure, no problem."

"Thanks," I tell them.

Olga grabs a bowl of chips and walks back to the bar. "I better not hear about any *problemas.*"

"No, señora," Carlos says. "See, Jacqui, you spoke up, and she compromised with you."

I bounce on my toes. "I won't get to Petey's game until the end, but at least he'll see me there."

"Hey, what favors did you do for Olga? TJ again?"

I'm telling Carlos the truth. Maybe he can tell me if I'm making a big deal out of nothing. "I ran errands with her. We went to this scary looking junkyard. She said the guys were in charge of the remodeling, and this other guy, at an apartment building was the contractor."

Carlos rubs his chin. "Contractors have offices. Strange you went to a junkyard and an apartment. Did you make extra money?"

"Sixty bucks."

"Sure is a lot of dough for what you're doing. I wonder why she can't do that herself."

I shrug because he's probably caught on that Henry and Olga run a shady business. And I don't want him asking me any more questions. I'll quit, and that'll be the end of any errands.

CHAPTER 32

The week's finally finished. Petey's game is at seven to-night so I tell Carlos that Jerry and Lucy are coming for me. I run to the bathroom to put on more lip gloss before the game. I've already called Mom and told her I'm working until ten o'clock. If Mom wasn't so strict, I wouldn't have to sneak around so much.

"Have a good time," Carlos says and winks.

I wave goodbye and rush out the front door to meet Jerry. Sure enough, he's bought himself his dream car. A '68 Nova Super Sport. The blue paint sparkles under the streetlight like the car is the grand prize in *Let's Make a Deal*. Lucy stands nearby in her cheerleading uniform, waving to me.

"Wow, I love the color." I climb into the back seat and slide my hand over the smooth upholstery. No rips or tears or stains like in our old station wagon.

"Emerald Turquoise metal flake." Jerry's grin spreads across his round face. "Boss, huh?"

"Hurry up, the game's going to be over soon," Lucy says. "We can't keep Petey waiting."

"Did you guys hear what happened this afternoon?" Jerry says.

Lucy shakes her head at him.

"No, what happened?" I ask.

"Someone broke the glass on the bulletin board and pulled everything off it." He stares at me for a few seconds before he starts the car.

The ding list? "Well, it wasn't me. But I'm not sorry that happened."

"Crazy, huh? You should've seen Mrs. Jasper. She had a fit. So did Sister Mary," Jerry says. "She kept using the word 'hooligans.'"

"Oh, yeah, like gangsters lurk in St. Bernadette," Lucy says.

She and Jerry laugh.

"There were three names on the ding list, and I'm sure we're the suspects. Sister Mary Graceless is going to accuse me of doing it." I sigh. That's all I need, for Sister to have an excuse to kick me out of school.

"What's the big deal? She shouldn't be fronting off the students, anyway," Lucy says. "Oh, cool, you have that new Santana cassette."

She pops the cassette into the player. The soothing sounds of the song relax me as Jerry cruises into the back parking lot of the baseball field.

Lucy grabs my hand, tells me to follow her to the bleachers. We sit right behind the cheerleaders. They're so smiley when she approaches, but they lose the smiles and raise their eyebrows when they see me and Jerry behind her. I'm sure they think it was me who broke into the locked bulletin board, too.

"Petey's up next," Lucy shouts. "He's going to be glad to see you, Jacqui."

That remark gets the attention of the girls around us. Petey glances up at the stands. Lucy pushes my shoulder and almost knocks me over.

"Smile and wave." She bumps my shoulder.

My grin comes out all crooked and goofy, but I lift my hand halfway up and give him a quick hello. Then he smiles. A small, shy looking one.

"When the game's over, Jerry's going to ask him to come with us to go eat at Wimpy's," Lucy whispers in my ear.

"No, too obvious."

She wiggles in her seat, laughing. "It's perfect. Don't blow it."

"Where's Margot?" I glance around the stands.

"Said she had to work tonight at their store."

I nod and pay attention to the baseball game, which ends too soon. When I stand to leave, Lucy tugs my hand. "Wait a sec. Jerry's not back yet."

"Do you like him or are you teasing him?" I ask.

"He's okay. We're just hanging out." Lucy shrugs. "He's definitely not my boyfriend."

"I hope he knows that."

Jerry jogs back to the benches. "Petey's coming after he changes. Let's wait in the car."

Petey strides out of the boy's gym. Jerry honks his car horn and waves him over. He steps into the back seat, where I'm sitting, and says hello. The scent of shampoo wafts between us.

"Thanks for coming to see me, Jacqui."

Why didn't I reapply more lip gloss? I swallow to wet my throat. "Sure. Good game."

"Jerry's treating everybody because we won." Lucy slaps his shoulder.

He nods all goofy and blasts Santana on his tape deck. Lucy gabs all the way to Wimpy's, and that's okay because my heart feels like a conga drum. I'd be embarrassed if anyone heard my excitement. Sitting next to Petey is enough for me.

"Hey, you guys, we should go cruising on the boulevard," Jerry says once we're done eating our burgers in the parking lot of Wimpy's.

"Yeah, let's go," Lucy says.

"Can you take me back first?" Petey says.

My heart sinks. He's hardly said a word to me. Lucy tries to talk him out of it, but he keeps insisting. Maybe he doesn't want to be with me, after all. I know I've been quiet, but every time I try to make conversation, Lucy starts blabbing.

Jerry drives into the school parking lot. Petey steps out and holds the door open.

"Come on," he says.

I jump out of the car so fast I become self-conscious.

"Thanks, Jerry. See you, Lucy." Petey touches my hand. "We have a team party in the gym."

Lucy and Jerry mumble something, but I'm in a daze and don't care what they've said. We go over to the gymnasium, where a few baseball players and cheerleaders are standing around. The night breeze, Petey's words and music swirl around me, taking me into the daydreams I've had about me and Petey for years.

We pass the gym's foyer, where the glass cabinets hold all the trophies and awards. We walk to the far corner of the gym. I'm sure the coaches don't want the basketball court messed up, so a few tables of snacks and punch are on blue mats, and the baseball team and cheerleaders are up on the bleachers chatting and laughing.

The closer we get, the stronger the smell of damp towels and rubber mats. A mass of blue and brown eyes follows us as Petey leads me up to the middle bleacher's where we sit down.

"I'll bring us something to drink." He jogs down the row of bleachers.

Larry swats Petey on the back and glances up at me, waving. I lift my chin up to him, hurriedly run my hand through my hair and bend low to reapply my lip gloss. Petey returns with a plate of salty potato chips and cups of Hawaiian Punch. So, this is what the team and cheerleaders do after games. I could kick myself for not coming to see the teams play in the past three years.

I balance the plate of chips on my lap when Petey's hand covers mine. I become lightheaded and freeze up. Thank goodness only half the gym lights are on because I must have cherry tomatoes for my cheeks.

He clears his throat. "Okay if we hold hands?"

"Um, yeah."

Petey talks about the game and points out all the player's positions as if I care, but I can't say a word, which is weird because I'm usually not at a loss for something to say to him. Thirty minutes later, a chaperone flicks the overhead lights. The spell is broken.

"Brought my bike." Petey points to the bicycles locked up on the rack outside the gym.

I glance at the bike because my rear's already sore from sitting on the bleachers, but hey, better than walking the five or six miles home. If this was a sunny day and we were riding at the beach, we'd look like a couple of teenagers in those beach movies. I sit between Petey's arms for a few miles until the bike hurts my butt too much.

"Let me off. We can walk for a while," I say.

Weasel, Sleepy and another guy crouch in the corner of a parking lot, smoking and drinking. Weasel's watchful eyes follow us as Petey and I walk his bike on the asphalt.

"Isn't that your sister's boyfriend?" Petey says. "Caroline needs to stay away from him."

"She's gonna get a bad reputation hanging around with him, but she doesn't listen to me."

"Find a way to make her listen. And when are you going to stop working at El Lobo's? Too many rumors about that place." He tells me the same things Lucy and Mousy said and reminds me about Barbie Ríos missing. "See anything suspicious?"

"Lately, younger men go into the bar or visit Henry in his office."

"That's all?" Petey takes my hand. "Let's sit for a minute."

We rest on the curb under a streetlamp. I glance up at the cloudy glow of the light and watch the moth circle. Can I trust Petey with my suspicions about the errands? What if he tells his mom or his dad, and they tell my mom? I'll be in deep shit. But if Olga gets busted, I'm sure she'd snitch on me, and that's worse.

I pull my hand away and take a breath. "Henry asked me to go on these errands with Olga because he's going to remodel the café and put in a bakery." My rush of words sounds incoherent.

He shrugs. "Okay? Anything else?"

My heart races, just thinking about the errands. "We never leave with bakery equipment, but we always pick up or leave with packages at sketchy places. Olga hides the stuff in the back of the car, where the spare tire goes. She flashes lots of jewelry and twenty-dollar bills."

"She makes *you* pick up the stuff and then hides it in her car?" Petey rubs at his chin and stares at me for a long time.

"They pay me just for going. I think Henry and Olga are using me as a mule."

"What?" Petey shakes his head. "You gotta tell your mom, Jacqui. And you need to get away from them and El Lobo's, quick."

The hamburger in my stomach flip-flops and threatens to spew out. I drop my head into my chest. How am I going to explain this to Mom?

CHAPTER 33

Olga leans on the counter, her heavily mascaraed eyes trailing me while I fill the sugar containers. For the last hour, a wave of unease has washed over me as I've tried to find the right time to tell Olga I'm quitting after today's shift.

"Because I did you a favor Friday, I need a favor too." Olga moves closer to me. "For next week. . . just an hour or two."

"Again?" My fingers fumble with the canisters. "Sorry, I'm busy."

"You don't have to miss school. Twenty-five dollars. Easy work."

I concentrate on not spilling the sugar because my hands are twitchy. "Gotta go with my mom to the doctor."

"I pick you up, bring you back before the appointment. And I let you off at eight tonight."

"Sorry, I can't."

I pick up the tray of sugar containers and hustle over to the booths.

Carlos glances at me from the table he's wiping down. Olga follows me down the hall, where I pick up napkins from the supply closet.

"Oh, come on María, I really need the help. Fifty dollars then."

"Wish I could, but I can't. Excuse me."

I maneuver around her and back to the counter. Her footsteps and flustered exhale are close behind me.

"*Ay*, María, what's a couple of hours?"

I whirl around, tired of her nagging. "My finals are coming up, and I need to concentrate on my school stuff. I'm giving you notice. I can't work here anymore."

Olga's hands jerk to her hips. "You what?"

"Can I help you out?" Carlos says.

Olga shoots him a look that says, mind your own business. She marches to the bar door, hits it open so hard, it swings to the wall with a bang. My breath catches in my throat.

Carlos shakes his head. "What's that all about?"

"I dunno."

But I do know. Those errands are so important that Olga's throwing a fit because I won't go, and it has to be me, not Carlos.

For the rest of the shift, I stay away from Olga, who scowls at me every time she comes into the restaurant side. When she's busy, I hurry behind the counter, start dialing.

"Petey? Yeah, um, it's me, Jacqui. Uh, hi." My whispered words come out all mangled because I'm scared Olga might bust me using the phone, but also because I've never called a guy before.

"What's wrong? Are you okay?"

"Yeah." I rub my throat, trying to ease out the words. "Olga's insisting I go on another errand with her, but I don't want to. I'm, uh, I'm scared."

"Don't go. Tell your mom or your uncle. Today."

"I can't tell Tío Mario. He'll come over here and go ballistic on Henry. That'll make things worse. What if I'm the next one on a missing poster? And what can my mom do?"

"Try to act like you're not scared. I'll meet you at the Mini-Mart later."

The bar door swings open. Henry strides out. I drop the handset.

"María, come to the office."

My eyes dart left and right, looking for Carlos, but he's not around. I grab a rag, wipe the counter. "Let me finish this first."

"Now, María."

I follow him down the hall and stand by the door as he sits down behind his desk. I'm not going into the office. He can tell me whatever he wants while I stand at the door.

Henry takes a pencil from behind his ear and taps it against the desktop. "Olga says you can't help her out next week and you want to quit."

"Yeah, and I, um, need to go to the doctor." My shoulders squeeze my neck as I speak.

"This remodeling business is a pain in the ass. We need your help one more time." He stops tapping the pencil and holds it in mid-air, waiting for an answer.

I don't want to help him or Olga anymore, especially since she's mad-dogged me all evening. I clutch the doorknob.

"Henry, I don't need the extra money anymore. I'm really busy."

"You can't leave us just like that without any warning. We'll need to hire someone else. Stay for the week and go with Olga one last time, okay?" He leans back in his chair with his arms folded behind his head.

We stare at each other for a minute until he sits back up. I want out of his office before I break down and tell him what I suspect. Thank goodness, I'm wearing jeans, or Henry would see my knees knocking.

"What do you say? Help me out one last time?"

I don't know what to do except stall for time. I won't show up to the errand and tell Mom in the meantime. "Okay. Then I have to quit."

"Good. I'll tell Olga."

The hours drag by. The chime on the front door rings. Weasel. My stomach twists as he swaggers in and glances around.

"Jacqui Mah-ree. All alone?"

"No, Carlos is in the kitchen, Olga's in the bar." I grab a dishtowel, head to a booth so I don't look at him.

"Com'ere." He waves me toward him.

"I'm busy, Weasel."

"No, you're not. Come here." His voice changes from a high-pitched sound to a sneer.

My heart thumps and the hairs on my arms rise. I'm not moving.

He cocks his head. "I gotta message for your sister." He sits down and pats the stool next to him, smiling, showing his fangs.

"From Sleepy?" I move toward the seat. "What about?"

His bony hand swipes through the air and grabs my wrist, pulling me close to his surly face. The smell of wool from his Pendleton shirt swirls between us. I want to look away from his ugly smirk, but I can't show him I'm afraid.

"You want to see your *carnala* again?"

My face screws up. "What the hell?" I pull away.

He grabs my other wrist, yanking me so close, his hot breath scorches my neck while he snarls in my ear.

"You do those runs with Olga, or I'll have someone fuck up that sister of yours. *¿Sabes?*"

My wrists throb while he presses them against the stool and brings my face an inch from his long nose. I want to close my eyes so I won't see his sneering face, but I can't, or he'll see I'm terrified.

"Lemme go." I jerk my head and arms back with as much force as I can muster. "What's your problem? I'm already going on Monday." I pull one hand away.

He releases my other hand, sits up in the chair. "Now you're thinking."

"Leave me alone and get the hell outta here before I scream my head off."

"You better do that job." Weasel straightens out his khakis and runs his hands down the sleeves of his Pendleton before he walks to the front door. "Don't forget, I know where you live."

CHAPTER 34

My trembling hand can't hold my glass still enough to drink the water. Heartbeats race through my chest. That *cabrón* Weasel scared the crap out of me, grabbing me like that. I move to a booth because I just might fall off the stool.

What if he uses Sleepy to lure Caroline into an alley or into his car? Or if Weasel shows up at our place and threatens Mom? I need a plan super quick. I pop the kitchen door open. Carlos is scrubbing the grill. "I'm heading out early."

"I'd walk you out, but the *bruja*. . ." He glances over his shoulder. I know he's talking about Olga. "She'd fire me."

"That's okay. I called Petey."

"Your face looks pale. Are you feeling okay?"

"Yeah," I nod a couple of times. "Must be something going around."

I open the front door to El Lobo's real slow and pray Weasel isn't waiting for me. I peek around the corner wall, hightail it to the parking lot of the Mini-Mart and dart inside the store.

"My friend, we have Mr. Goodbar's today."

"Hey, Mr. Singh." I take a deep breath, unclench my fists and grab a couple of bars.

"Tell me what happened at the meeting you spoke of."

"The city council said they'd discuss the idea at the next meeting, but I got to talk about your letter."

"Very good. You let me know when the next meeting is and maybe I can attend." He slides the candy into a paper sack and throws in a few pieces of Dubble Bubble gum. "For your brothers and sister."

The buzzer on the front door squeals. I flinch.

"Something wrong, Miss Jacqui?" Mr. Singh's dark eyes hover over my face.

What's he gonna think if I tell him Weasel threatened me? He might call the cops. Weasel will deny knowing me, and things will get worse for me, Caroline and Mr. Singh.

"No, nothing. Just tired."

He stares at my shaky hand when I reach for the bag and glances up at me. "Whatever is on your mind, you must tell someone."

"Um, I'm waiting for my friend to pick me up."

"Good, you wait in here."

The door opens, and Petey's head and shoulders stretch inside. "Jacqui? I'm here." He rolls his bike halfway into the store.

"My friend's here, Mr. Singh." I point to the front door, head in that direction. "Later."

Petey hops on his bike and motions for me to get on. "You sounded super nervous on the phone. I got here as fast as I could. Should we go to your uncle's house?"

My fingernails are bitten to nubs, and my bottom lip's puffy from biting it so often. I don't want to have Uncle Mario or Mom involved before I think this out and make a plan.

The words "community" and "allies" from the CBC meetings keep bouncing around my brain.

"My uncle's? Not yet. No doubt about it, drug dealing's going on at El Lobo's. I ignored so many signs, Petey, just so

I could pay my tuition bill. But what Henry and Olga are doing is wrong. . . forcing me when I tried to quit. Weasel came in, telling me I better do the errands or else."

He stops the bike. "Did he threaten you or your family?"

"Yeah, uh, he said he knows where we live, too."

"Tell your mom tonight. What if Palermo comes into the place and finds drugs and busts everyone? You'd go to juvie."

My body jumps at his words. "Worse, I'll be kicked out of school and lose any hope of a scholarship. There has to be a way out of this mess without Weasel hurting me or my family."

Petey takes my hand and squeezes it. "I'll help however I can."

We walk hand in hand through the neighborhood, which is alive with music from car stereos blasting and older kids riding their bikes on a Saturday night. The smell of *tripas* for Sunday *menudo* drifts in the air, mixed with the lemony scents of the nearby orchards.

The neighborhood might be run down and poor, but it's rich in other ways. There are good people here, hardworking people who are trying to take care of their families. Bebe's told me so many times that drug dealing kills the barrios. And I was part of it.

"Man, I really messed up, Petey. I was so desperate, I only thought about making money fast." I exhale like I could blow away the past month. "I feel crappy about what I've done."

"Henry and Olga used you. It's on them." He faces me. "I know you. You're going to figure this out."

His words boost my confidence. The beginnings of a plan swirl in my head. I work it out like I do a math formula. Who can be my ally? Mom? No, she'll ground me and never let me out of the house again. Officer Palermo? Can I trust him? Uncle Mario? No, he'll kick Weasel's ass and make it worse. Bebe. She'll know what to do.

CHAPTER 35

I can do this. My family is my community. They're my allies. All night, I repeated this as I worked out my plan. Once I had it figured out, I called Bebe, and she agreed to drive to her dad's place and meet me after my afternoon shift at El Lobo's.

My family is my community. I repeat this to myself all the way down the block and into the housing projects. I will myself into Uncle Mario's house, scared he and Mom will go ballistic after I tell them about El Lobo's.

"Hello." I hope no one notices the shaking in my voice. "Tío? Bebe?"

"Is it four o'clock already?" Mom pokes her head out of the kitchen. "Bebe's upstairs. Your *tío*'s working on our car out back."

"Yeah, uh, I need to talk to you guys. Can you call him inside for me?" I run upstairs to Bebe's bedroom and knock on the door.

"*Prima*, this is going to be hard, but you have to tell them everything. Quick before Caroline brings the boys over," she says.

"If Mom tries to throw her *chancla* at me, I'm booking it outside."

"She won't." Bebe laughs.

Keeping secrets eats me up inside like never-ending heart-burn. They're not going to like the truth, but it's all I have now. They've always had my back, and I need to trust them.

I sit down on the couch closest to the front door, in case Mom becomes so angry, she throws her shoe at me. Bebe sits next to me and gives me an encouraging nod. Mom dries her hands on her apron and sits next to Bebe.

Uncle Mario sits in his black recliner, leaning forward, hands on his knees. "What's this about?"

In a rush of words, I tell them about waitressing at El Lobo's and not working at the Mini-Mart. "Sorry, I lied."

"Jacqueline Monsivais Bravo." Mom's hand flies up to her chest.

Uncle Mario's palm hits his forehead; his eyes roll up toward the ceiling. "You're working at a bar?"

"No, I said I was eighteen, so I only waitress on the restaurant side." I need to tell him we owed money, so he'll understand how desperate I was. "We owed St. Bernadette and St. Patrick almost two hundred dollars. I had to do something, or they'd kick me out of school. I'd lose my chance at the alumni scholarship. Now, I'm all caught up."

"Two hundred? Why are you so behind?" Uncle Mario swivels his head to Mom and back to me. "Don't you know what kind of a place El Lobo's is?"

Of course, now I do. I crumple into the sofa and hang my head.

"They sell drugs there." Uncle Mario jumps to his feet and paces in front of me. "Pills, marijuana, heroin."

"You are *not* going back there," Mom says.

"I have to." My voice comes out trembling and louder than I want. "Just a couple of more days."

"You quit, NOW. Do what your mother says. And you," he points to Mom, "if you can't afford the tuition, take her out of that Catholic school, put her in public." He slaps his hand on his thigh. "This is what happens when mothers aren't home to take care of their kids. They get into trouble."

Mom shoots him a withering stare. "My kids need to eat, and Jacqueline's not the one selling drugs, Mario."

"I need to stay at St. Bernadette, so I can go to UCLA. And, Tío, you're not my dad."

Uncle Mario moves closer to me. "Your dad would want me to keep you safe. You, your mother and the kids are my responsibility, too. You're my family."

Bebe clears her throat. "Jacqui, tell them about the plan."

I'm taking a huge chance by pissing Uncle Mario off, but what if Weasel really does get someone to beat up Caroline? Everyone will be doubly mad at me. My fingers grip the sofa edge. If I could disappear under the seat cushions, I would.

Uncle Mario peers into my face. "Listen to me. Barbie was Henry's mule. The girl was pregnant from him, and he wouldn't divorce his wife. She got mad, said she'd quit delivering drugs for him, but he wouldn't let her stop. Who knows what happened to the girl?"

My foot's practically tapping out Morse code on the linoleum floor. I can guess what happened to her, and it's not pretty.

"Tell them your plan," Bebe nudges me.

I tell them about Henry's fake story to remodel the bakery, how he duped me into going to Tijuana with Olga and paid me fifty dollars for the trip, all of which went to pay tuition.

The acid in my throat rises. I'm out of breath, but I need to say everything. I wet my lips and then tell them how Weasel grabbed my wrists, threatened he'd get Caroline beaten up.

"Henry wants me to do one more job tomorrow. I'm telling you all this because I need to be safe. Caroline and you guys need to be safe."

"Jacqueline, you are quitting now. Don't go near that place," Mom yells.

"But Weasel knows where we live."

"We have to go to the police," Mom says.

Uncle Mario jumps to his feet and paces around his chair. "*¿Estás loca?* What do you think will happen to Jacqui then? Or you? Think."

"I used to go to high school with Palermo. He's a good man. I can tell him," Mom says.

"They'll bust Jacqui for being a drug mule. Do you want her to go to Juvenile Hall? Ruin her life?"

I'm doubly scared now. Uncle Mario understands how things go with drug dealers. They find out you give the police information and they'll label you a snitch until the day you die or someone kills you, whichever comes first.

Mom and Uncle Mario keep arguing about calling the police, her eyes watering and his face turning mauve.

"Stop!" I jump up from the sofa. "I was tired of being on the late tuition list at school. We never have enough money for the things we need. And then you'd decided to pay the kid's bill first. And we had rent and the overdue water bill."

"You're the one who said St. Patrick was the priority, that Caroline needed a chance at the scholarship. I agreed because if she doesn't go there, she'll be distracted with boys. . ."

"What about me, Mom? The harder we work, the further behind we get. It's like we're being punished for Dad dying. I'm so stressed out about everything I'm not thinking straight anymore. Sometimes, I want to give up and say, yes, life, you kicked my ass."

I fall into the sofa, exhausted. This isn't going the way I planned. Mom moves to sit next to me.

"Your dad chose to re-enlist in the Army so he could learn more about repairing the newer helicopters. He loved that job. He also wanted to earn more. For us." Mom pulls me into a hug. "He didn't know he'd end up going to Vietnam. Or have an accident. No one knew."

"I don't want to go to public school this late in the year. I don't want to be satisfied with what's around me. I can't stop hoping, stop dreaming." I sniffle, trying to hold back my tears.

"I'll ask Palermo to help us," Mom says.

Uncle Mario flings his arm up through the air. "Just because you went out with him in high school doesn't mean he's a good guy."

My neck whips around to my mom. "What? You dated Palermo?"

"Mario," Mom shouts. "We're old school friends. *No más*."

I need to leave. I jump up, reach for the front door. Uncle Mario blocks it. My mom pulls the back of my blouse and yanks me back.

"Oh, no, you don't. You sit your butt down. We have to figure out what we're gonna do and fast."

"Jacqui, tell them your idea," Bebe shouts. "Everyone, sit down. Please."

No one sits except for me and Bebe. Mom and Uncle Mario pace through the living room.

"Now." Bebe nudges me again.

"My plan to run the last errand and keep out of trouble with Henry, Olga and Weasel will only work if I have help from both of you and Bebe's friend Rudy, he's a lawyer. And we have to keep it a secret from everyone. Can you do that for me?"

CHAPTER 36

The dinner in front of me is untouched. I push food around while Mom and the boys eat and talk about a school project. Caroline stands at the stove, flipping more tortillas on the *comal*.

Last month I was dying to leave this city, go to UCLA and make a new life for myself so I could be me, not Jacqui, the oldest kid who's in charge of three others. Me, not Jacqui Bravo, daughter of a dad who died. This month, my plans are screwed up so badly that I might end up in Juvenile Hall for years or die in Solano.

The telephone rings. Caroline runs to the phone ahead of Mom.

"Pfft. For Jacqui." She rolls her eyes. "Bebe."

"*Prima*, I talked to Rudy about your idea. He's in."

I still haven't told Mom about the committee, only that Rudy is Bebe's friend. There's only so much news she can take, and I'm not about to give her more to worry about.

"I called in sick to work tomorrow, so we can meet then," I tell Bebe. "That pissed off Olga, but she was glad to hear I'd still go with her."

"Good. You need to act like everything's normal, okay?"

Normal. After Uncle Mario's and Mom's shouting about El Lobo's, I didn't have to play-act too much when I called in sick for work. The burning sensation in my chest hasn't left since Weasel's threat.

My fingers play with the curly phone cord and my heart starts thumping. I dial Petey's number. What if his mom picks up the phone? Worse, his dad?

From the word, "Hello," I know it's him.

"Hey, this is last minute, but meet me at St. Patrick tomorrow after twelve o'clock Mass? I have stuff to tell you." My words are all rushed, and I'm out of breath.

He doesn't ask why or anything and says okay. That was easier than I thought.

"Was that Bebe?" Mom waves me over to the stove. She points to the ceiling signaling, the kids are upstairs. "Did she talk to her friend about El Lobo's?"

"Rudy's going to help us deal with them. But I need your help too." This is the hard part, because I have so many conflicting feelings about this piece of strategy. "Would you call Officer Palermo and ask if we can meet with him?"

Her forehead lines grow deeper when I fill her in on the plan. "It's been a long time since we talked, but if that helps, I'll do it."

⚜ ⚜ ⚜

"Can I go with you to visit Bebe?" Caroline asks on our way out of Sunday Mass with the family.

"No, you need to go to the laundromat, since we didn't finish yesterday," Mom says. "A couple of loads are in the car. Jacqui can go on to Bebe's."

"Always about Jacqui, isn't it?" Caroline stomps to our car in the parking lot.

She's usually dramatic, but this is extra. Maybe something happened. While Mom's jabbering with ladies from church and the boys are running after their friends, I find Caroline standing at our station wagon.

"Hey, what're you so mad about?"

"All you think about is your own self."

I lean on the car next to her. "Why do you say that?"

She stares off at the sky. "Every day, you get closer to going to college. You're going to get out of here and leave me to be the junior mom. . . to take your place."

"But I need to go to college."

Caroline stomps her foot. "Why so far? Why can't you live here like Tío made Bebe do when she started? I'll be alone, taking care of everything. Mom will make me work and go to school so we can afford the tuition. I'll never go out, have fun, do normal teenager stuff."

Everything Caroline says is true. Every complaint she has is the same one I've had but never had the guts to tell Mom. What if I live here and attend community college? Caroline would be older by the time I'm a junior in college. But what if I can't concentrate on college because I don't have time to study? I swallow hard and try to find the words.

"But, I, uh. . ." A sinking feeling from my heart to my feet comes over me.

She moves in front of me. Her chin trembles while her eyes get glassy. "Oh, go to Bebe's and plan out your life. Forget your sister and brothers."

Her words stab me in the heart. "I gotta go," I say as Mom and our brothers reach the car.

My chest feels like a dozen giant rubber bands are tightening until I can't breathe. How come I feel so guilty for wanting to go away to college? Why does this have to be so hard?

I spot Petey standing in the basketball court of St. Patrick Elementary. We sit on one of the shaded benches, and I tell him everything that happened at Uncle Mario's house.

"Your family wants you safe."

"The other thing I lied about is being part of the Chicanos for a Better Community. The CBC. I started out trying to get information for my scholarship application, and then I got kind of caught up in what they were talking about. Things like justice, speaking up and making a difference. I even attended a city council meeting." I glance at my tennis shoes. "My mom hates the word 'Chicano'. . . thinks they're a bunch of hippie radicals."

"Lots of older people think it's a bad word, but I don't think so. The CBC's trying to help the community. Right?"

I nod. "There's a meeting now. Bebe and her boyfriend are waiting for us in one of the classrooms. Come with me?" Petey's brows pull in, his finger rubbing his chin. I chew on my bottom lip and think of the people at the LA park marching, smiling, then running, grimacing from blows on their bodies.

"I saw the Chicano Moratorium film," I tell him. "There was more to it than the TV showed or told us. Pisses me off. I'm angry, it's unfair the system lets an officer of the law murder someone. People died in the protest, a kid my age, and no one was punished."

Petey nods. "Okay, let's go."

We walk from the CBC meeting to the laundromat. The whole time, Petey and I talk about Rudy's question. He told us he scheduled a special meeting with the city council and asked who could attend on Tuesday night. He warned us that they might not listen again. If that happens, we'll stage a sit-in until they talk with us. I said, yes, but Petey didn't volunteer.

We stop in front of the laundromat, where Caroline sits, reading a magazine. The two full baskets of clean clothes are at her feet. I don't see Mom anywhere.

"I gotta go in and help. My mom should be here in a few minutes."

"Arizona State is where I want to go, but the draft is still going on," Petey says.

The smile on my face wavers. "What do you mean?"

"A sit-in? I can't risk an arrest, and neither can you. How's that going to look to the alumni committee? They decide who wins the scholarship."

"No, I mean, uh, you said the draft," I stammer. "To Vietnam?" My temples thump so hard I'm dizzy. I sit down heavily on the curb.

Petey moves next to me. "It's something I've got to think about. The next lottery is a year away, but it's for the year I was born."

I search his face. He can't go. Not to Vietnam. Not to war. Not to disappear from my life forever. Not to end up like Dad.

"If I'm drafted, I gotta go. My father said it's my duty." His face screws up, and he shakes his head.

"No! Get a deferment. Don't they give those to college guys? Go to Mexico or Canada."

Petey's Adam's apple bobs. He drops his head to his chest. I take a breath and think.

"What do you want to do? In your heart?"

"Play baseball at Arizona State."

Every nerve in my body winds up. I squeeze his hand. "Then you gotta get that athletic scholarship. Ask for a deferment once you get it."

His broad shoulders relax from his sigh. "I guess I shouldn't worry about that right now, but it's on my mind every day."

Why does everything in our life conspire to keep us from going to college? If he doesn't get into college, it really is a life-or-death situation. I can continue living if I miss out on the alumni scholarship. Petey might not.

I grab his hand. "I understand if you don't participate with the CBC. There's a lot at stake for you. But it's not right that Petra's husband can't talk because he didn't make it to the hospital in time. It's not right that people can't stand for something without getting beat down. The CBC has organized for six months already. Rudy's tried to speak with the City Council twice before. They didn't want to hear what we had to say. They don't care about our neighborhood or us."

"But you can agree with the CBC without marching," he says.

"I think of Ms. Fine and how she stood up to Sister Mary Graceless. How Emiliano Zapata said he wasn't going to live on his knees. How César Chávez and Dolores Huerta marched two hundred and fifty miles. How men, women and teenagers protested the war at the Chicano Moratorium. How we got to fight and claw our way above the obstacles in our lives. This issue means a lot to me. I listened to the people who wrote letters. I've seen what happens when medical help arrives too late. I believe in this project."

"You're risking too much, your whole future." Petey rubs his neck. "I'm not trying to put you down. I just want you to think about what you're getting into."

I jump to my feet. "I respect your decision, Petey, but if I never risk anything, I'll never gain anything either. Now, I need to help Caroline." I point to the door of the laundromat, where she's now standing, gawking at me. "Later."

⚜ ⚜ ⚜

Caroline tugs the laundry wagon behind her as we head to the sidewalk. Mom went to the groceries and told Caroline to take the laundry home if she wasn't back by four o'clock.

"You know why I didn't ask you to come with me?"

"Lying again?" Caroline says. "You were with Petey?"

I fill her in about the CBC, what they're trying to do and that I spoke at a city council meeting.

"So, if the CBC decides to do a sit-in, you guys are joining in?" she asks.

"Petey doesn't want to risk it. He's trying to get a scholarship to play college baseball." I leave out the draft part because I don't need to tell her everything. "He says I might get arrested and lose my chance at college, but I said I'm doing it anyway."

"You told him that? Geez, he's gonna drop you."

"What he does isn't as important as what I do. I'm making my own choices about my life."

She nods. "True. I guess if he likes you enough, he'll understand. But Mom's gonna bust a gut if you tell her."

The screeching sound of sirens rattles through the air. We glance up the street. The signal lights blink red while the train jerks back and forth on the tracks. The sirens continue.

"Train's stuck again," Caroline says.

"What's that burning smell?" I turn in the other direction and peer down the street. Plumes of smoke rise in the darkening sky. "Over there, near Mrs. Washington's house."

A loud howling of a fire engine joins the sirens. That damn train is holding up emergency help. We run down the block, the baskets of clothes tumbling onto the side of the wagon.

Orange flames jump from the roof of Mrs. Washington's place. Her dog, Rider, leaps at the chain-link gate, barking his head off. A neighbor swings it open, pulls a water hose over the lawn as far as he can. It only reaches the front part of the house, but he sprays the side with water while Rider bolts across the street.

A car pulls over to the curb. The driver jumps out, sprints into the garden, grabs another hose and sprays the burning side of the house. Crackling and popping sounds cut through the air.

Caroline stops running and stoops over to catch her breath. "Jacqui, stay here."

"What if Mrs. Washington and her grandson are inside? What about her cats?" I keep running until I reach her front yard.

Another girl runs up the porch steps, pounds on the door, shouting, "Mrs. Washington! Mrs. Washington!"

She picks up a clay pot of geraniums on the porch, smashes the windowpane and unlocks the door. Smoke billows out. She steps back, coughing.

"Mrs. Washington, Junior," I yell into the doorway.

Poking my head inside, I spot a figure sprawled out face down on the floor. A small body, covered in a blanket, in front of the larger one. Bare little legs aren't moving.

"The baby. Junior," Mrs. Washington coughs, trying to lift her head.

"In here," I shout, running inside.

"We need help to carry them," the other girl yells to the men outside.

Smoke swirls into the living room, my nose and eyes. I drop to the floor, scoop up Junior, his body limp in my arms. Two other people rush past me, pick up Mrs. Washington.

Sirens pierce through the air as the fire engine and ambulance grow closer.

Finally, the sound stops. Around me, people cough and gasp.

Mrs. Washington moans, "My baby, the baby."

Jerome Junior's head flops to the side when I rest him on the grass. He looks like he's asleep. I don't know what to do except what I see on television. I feel for his pulse. Nothing. Why didn't I learn CPR? Damn it. Smoke and fear fill my throat.

"I'm Gloria, her neighbor." The girl who helped me lays a wet cloth on Junior's forehead.

"Make way, make way," Yellow-helmeted firemen yell as they drag thick hoses over the lawn.

The ambulance man nudges me over from Junior, picks him up and puts his ear to his chest. He places him on a stretcher. "He's alive. Where did you find him?"

"Inside." I cough, blink my burning eyes.

The man slaps an oxygen cup on Junior's tiny face. "Sit down, take a breath," he tells me.

"Jacqui, are you okay?" Caroline tugs at my hand.

I lift my head, but my chest hurts like a giant bruise. The sidewalk is thick with people. A few of our neighbors gather around until a couple of cops arrive and shoo everyone back across the street.

"Come on." Caroline pulls me up.

"No, wait until Mrs. Washington's put in the ambulance."

We sit and stare as the firemen hose down the flames. Poor Mrs. Washington's garden is a mess of trampled flowers and broken pots. Someone leads Rider back up the street. The ambulance doors slam shut, the vehicle lurches forward and speeds up the street.

"Jacqui, Jacqui." John and Bobby run past the crowd to where we're sitting. Mom follows behind, her hair in a scarf.

"*Ay, Dios*," she says. "What happened?"

Caroline tells her the story while I try to keep my knees from knocking together. My chest feels like a rope tightens against my ribs. My hands tremble. I pound my fist on the concrete. "This is so messed up."

"Do you feel sick? We should go home," Mom says.

Bebe runs to me. I stand on wobbly legs. There's no smoke inside my chest, but I feel like a bonfire's lit in me.

"Bebe, this isn't right. That damn train made them wait."

Grandparents, moms, dads and little kids on bikes fill the street. The whole neighborhood is out here. People murmur, "The train stopped the fire engine."

"I called emergency when I first smelled the smoke," Gloria says. "Took forever."

"Happens too many times," a man shouts. "*La señora* could've died, *y su nieto*."

"*Sí, es cierto*," people around us agree.

Adrenaline surges through my body, up my throat. "We tried to convince the city council to listen to us about the train, but they ignored us," I shout. "Tell them, Bebe."

She explains to them in Spanish about the CBC's work. People nod. Mom bites her lip. She doesn't know what Bebe and I have been up to, but I can't keep the secret any longer.

"We tried to get them to pay attention to us," I say. "We wrote letters, we attended meetings, and still, they don't listen."

Bebe tells everyone to gather at St. Patrick Elementary School this coming Saturday. She'll phone Rudy and other CBC members to strategize the next step.

Mom drags me and Caroline to the station wagon. She and the kids listen while I tell them about the meetings at St. Patrick, including that Sister George and Father Armando attend. Mom clicks her tongue like she doesn't believe me.

"The CBC tried. People from the community submitted letters telling them how they're impacted by the lack of emergency access into our barrio."

Mom crosses her arms and watches me. She's tripping on the words I used, like "impact" and "access," but I keep on speaking until I'm out of breath. "Even Petra wrote a letter."

"Tía, Jacqui did really well at the city council meeting," Bebe tells Mom. "You would've been proud. My *tío*, too."

Hearing Bebe say my dad would've been proud of me makes my eyes mist. I sniffle back tears while Bebe wraps her arm around my shoulder.

"But the city said no. What can a committee do?" Mom says to us.

"We can make the city listen." My hands clench and unclench. I turn to the crowd on the sidewalk and street in front of Mrs. Washington's house. "We need to protest. We need to march!"

CHAPTER 37

"Jacqueline, how embarrassing. Why are you telling every-one to march?" Mom says while she's shooing us home. "It's not like the fire department didn't want to get there."

"If firemen aren't complaining to the city council, then they must not care when they get there."

Mom pulls my arm. "How can you say that?"

I yank my arm away. "How can't you not see that? Peti-tions, meetings, didn't work. It's time for action."

"Those militants have gotten to you. *Ay, Dios*," she says, shaking her head.

"We're going to organize next Saturday, and I'm partici-pating."

⚜ ⚜ ⚜

Whenever Mom has a problem, she prays in front of the small altar under our staircase. The niche has a statue of the Virgin, a candle of St. Jude and four votives. One for each of us. Overseeing the whole thing is the picture of the Sacred Heart of Jesus on the wall.

She lifts herself off her knees, gives them a rub and turns to me on the sofa. "Praying that everything works out and you kids are safe. We need to go see Palermo tonight. Call the kids downstairs."

The boys run down the steps like a small herd of cattle. Caroline teeters on the top step, watching me. "I have a surprise," Mom says. "Mr. and Mrs. Gonzales are taking you to the movies tonight. Go get ready."

"Yay. Thanks, Mom," the boy's shout. "A nighttime movie. Whoa."

Caroline eyes me and Mom. She knows something is up, but she doesn't say anything because going to a Sunday night film isn't a trip she wants to pass up.

Someone knocks at the door. After looking out the window, I see Petra. Her husband leans on his cane. Both of them are dressed up like they're going to church.

Mom hands quarters and a dollar bill to Petra. "For popcorn and candy."

"*Me gustan los* Red Vines," Petra says. "*A él le gustan los* Jujubes."

Her husband nods and gives a crooked smile.

Mom douses Bobby's cowlick with Tres Flores and glides a comb through his hair, making it all shiny.

"Smells too girly," he says.

The jasmine scent is subtle. I like it better than Petey's hair cream.

"You're going to be a young man, *m'ijo*," Mom says. "You need to do this yourself."

"But I like the way you do it," he says, smiling up at her.

"Sheesh. Let's go," John says.

"What about Jacqui?" Caroline asks Mom.

"She's helping me with an errand. We'll pick you up in a couple of hours."

We drive downtown to La Mode theater and drop everyone off.

"Pay attention to Petra," Mom tells the kids.

They wave as we roar off down the street.

"So, where are we meeting Palermo? Did you remember to tell Bebe?"

"Of course. We're driving to the next town over. We don't want anyone to see us."

"Sorry, I'm just nervous."

Our station wagon circles the parking lot of a new Denny's restaurant. Mom parks in the far corner. We never go to restaurants except for graduations, and that's to the Chinese food place downtown. She turns the rearview mirror toward her and applies fresh lipstick, her Candy Apple Red color.

Mom moves past the counter filled with men eating dinner without waiting for the waitress. I follow her to the last booth, where a man sits reading a newspaper. She slides into the seat. He drops his paper.

Palermo in regular clothes is just like an average guy having a cup of coffee. I stand there staring. Not because he appears so normal in his brown crew neck sweater and blue jeans but because all I see is him straddling his motorcycle, looking like the cops in the film I watched. I'm not sure I trust him enough to tell him about Weasel's threats.

"Sit down, Jacqueline." Mom pulls my hand.

My body drops into the seat next to her. My eyes focus on Palermo's face.

"Everything okay, Marie? I mean, Jacqueline," he says.

Nothing's okay after the documentary about the Chicano Moratorium. I still see police on rooftops with rifles, rows of them blocking off the street during a peaceful march.

Mom's knee knocks into mine.

"Yeah, I'm fine," I mutter.

He signals the waiter, orders us hamburgers and sodas. He knows my mom drinks Tab and doesn't like onion on her hamburger.

"Hey, you guys." Bebe comes up to the table with Rudy. "Sorry we're a little late."

Rudy slides in next to Palermo, and Bebe pushes me over. She introduces Rudy to Mom and Palermo, mentioning to them that he's a lawyer and that she's filled him in on everything.

"Thank you, Bebe, Rudy," Mom says.

"Jacqui, anything you tell Officer Palermo is confidential," Rudy says. "I'm here as your attorney."

I glance to the side and see that two other booths have people, and they're out of earshot from us.

"Yes, whatever you tell me is confidential." Palermo takes a small spiral notebook from beside him and flips it open. "Tell me about the places you visited with Olga and when."

"I didn't know anything about any drugs or that I was a mule. I just rode in the car with her. I swear." I swipe a napkin over my forehead. "You have to promise not to use my name or take me to the police station."

"Your attorney made that clear when we spoke on the phone," Palermo says. "That's the deal."

By the time I finish talking about the Tijuana trip, my mouth is tired. My throat's raspy. The waiter comes, placing our plates in front of us.

Rudy eyes the waiter. "Let's take a break."

Palermo drops his notebook onto the booth seat. After we finish eating, I tell him about the other errand, and he recognizes the junkyard I'm talking about.

"What's going to happen now?" Mom asks.

Palermo pushes his dish aside and leans forward. "I want you to go with Olga this week."

"No," I say. "You have the information, use it."

"Jacqui, I don't want to take you into court to testify. This way, you go on the errand, and we'll follow Olga. Then we don't need your testimony."

"Anthony, the plan is too dangerous," Mom says.

Anthony?

"I won't let anything happen to her. I give you my word." He leans forward a bit and his eyes go soft.

Bebe clears her throat. I don't like seeing Palermo eyeing Mom. I shove my plate aside. He straightens up and looks at me.

"But what about Caroline? Weasel knows where we live," I say. "What if he figures out I said something? Barbie disappeared from town. I don't want to end up like that either."

Mom chews on her lower lip. The thin line on her forehead grows deeper as her eyebrows slide closer together. "Weasel or his friends might hurt one of my kids. I can't risk that."

"Trust me. We'll take care of him," Palermo says. "He'll be in county jail by tonight."

Rudy shoots a glance at me and then at Palermo. "All legal, right?"

"He has an outstanding warrant," he says. "It'll all be by the book."

"You can put Weasel in jail, but that doesn't mean much. He can call or write someone to make good on his threat," I tell him.

"He won't have a chance. Our plan is to follow Olga as she makes her stops. All you need to do is what you did on the last two trips."

"This places Jacqui in danger," Rudy says. "You have to guarantee her safety."

Palermo nods. "We'll do everything in our power to keep her safe. She won't be out of our sight. I give you my word."

Mom lets out a low sigh. "*M'ija*, this is the best choice we have right now."

So much for my plan. I thought telling Palermo and Rudy about the trips would be enough. I could let the cops do their thing: raid El Lobo's and arrest Olga and Henry. End of story. But this is more complicated than I expected.

We go over the type of cars Olga used on her last two errands. Palermo gives me his phone number and asks me to call him after I find out the exact time for the next errand.

"Undercover cops will follow you to make sure you're safe," he says.

"Don't make it a narc car," I say. "Everyone knows which ones they are."

Rudy nods. "Any sign of trouble and you have to call this off."

"Understood," Palermo agrees. Then, looking at me, he says, "Jacqui, don't look out the windows to see who's following. Act like the other times you went along with Olga. You can do this."

CHAPTER 38

This is the first time that Mom's driven me inside the gates of St. Bernadette's parking lot. I glance around to see if anyone can hear our old station wagon creaking to a stop. Lucky for me, hardly anyone's in the lot this early, foggy Monday morning.

Mom's eyebrows pinch together, causing a wrinkle on her forehead. "Make sure you don't look suspicious when you're doing that errand. Call me at work as soon as you can."

"Don't worry. I'll be okay." I shut the car door, speed walk across the parking lot and up the stairs to the school office.

Palermo said he had my back, and Rudy's looking out for me, so I should be fine. Only, I don't feel so great. From the time I got up this morning until now, I'm nauseous. I thought I'd be happier now that I caught up with my tuition, but my last errand for El Lobo's overshadows everything.

At the top of the steps, I glance over my shoulder just to check that Weasel hasn't followed me. Maybe that's paranoid, but I'll be nervous until I finish the errand.

"Hey, Jacqui."

I startle before I notice Lucy and Margot in the courtyard waving me over.

"Come here," Lucy says.

"Why are you guys here so early? It's only seven-forty."

"Sister cancelled last week's meeting with Ms. Fine, but we heard it's going on today. Before first period," Margot says.

"Let's hang out inside the office. I need to see Mrs. Jasper, anyway," I say.

We walk down the hallway, and I push open the office door and plunk my books on the counter. Lucy and Margot sit down in the chairs along the window.

"Oh, no," Mrs. Jasper says. "You girls better not be here to start trouble again."

Lucy blows out her breath. Margot sighs.

"They're waiting for me, Mrs. Jasper. Here's my March tuition." I hand her three twenty-dollar bills.

While she pulls out the receipt book, the door to the principal's office opens, and Ms. Fine strides out, followed by Sister Mary Graceless.

"Ms. Fine," Margot jumps out of her chair. "Did Sister give you the petition? We want you to come back right away."

"Girls, what are you doing here?" Sister says.

"What petition?" Ms. Fine turns to Sister.

"Lucy, Jacqui and I gathered one hundred signatures from our classmates. We want you to stay at St. Bernadette."

"Your signatures have no bearing on a school personnel matter," Sister says. "Go on to class."

"No," Lucy says. "We want Ms. Fine to see the petition."

Sister and Mrs. Jasper gasp in sync. Ms. Fine's eyelids flutter before she smiles.

"Our opinions should count," I say. "Ms. Fine is one of the best teachers here."

"Ms. Bravo, you're on thin ice with me already," Sister admonishes, wagging her finger at me.

"Because I'm late with payments? Well, I'm all paid up, and I brought in my March tuition."

Margot and Lucy crowd next to me.

Their closeness gives me the courage to speak up. "I have just as much right as anyone to give my opinion. And I'm going to college, not vocational school, like you told me because Ms. Fine says I can dream big. I'm smart. I can make it in a university."

The office becomes so quiet I can hear my rapid breathing.

"Girls, I appreciate what you've done," Ms. Fine says. "Everything you said, Jacqui, is true. All of you are capable of excelling in a university. All of you deserve to follow your own path and achieve your dreams."

"See, Sister, that's why you can't suspend her," Margot says.

"She didn't suspend me, but I can't abide by the numerous stipulations Sister Mary Grace requires. So, I've resigned."

Her statement slaps me in the face. My application isn't finished and the deadline is in a couple of weeks. She can't leave. I watch Ms. Fine stride out the door, a smile on her face when she turns into the courtyard. Although this isn't great news for me, I understand that Ms. Fine is standing up for her principles, and I admire her even more.

⁂

When the sixth-period bell rings, I bolt out of class. Ms. Fine's resignation makes me feel like UCLA is a distant dream, drifting further and further away each day. I'll figure out something.

"Wait up, I'll walk with you," Petey calls to me.

He jogs beside me and nudges my arm. "Messed up about Ms. Fine, but at least we tried."

"Seems like I try and try and end up losing."

"But you didn't lose. You're still here. You're not transferred. That counts for something." Petey stops walking and takes hold of my arm. "The petition didn't make a change, but *you* changed. I remember when you were in eighth grade, even as a freshman. You were a friendly person, happier. But during the last two years, you've been a loner, ignoring anyone who tries to talk to you."

"You have some nerve calling me a loner." I jerk my arm away and jog down the steps to the parking lot. "My dad dying changed everything."

"Is that why you stopped talking to me and everyone around you?"

For a second, I pause. "You wouldn't understand."

"Jacqui, I'm trying to understand, so talk to me. Explain."

"Not now. I need to catch the bus." I break into a trot, hoping he stops asking me questions. Petey persists. "I thought El Lobo's was closed on Mondays?" He jogs behind me.

"It is. I'm going to pick up my paycheck."

"I'm coming with you. We have plenty of time before we get to El Lobo's."

"Don't you have practice or something?"

"Yeah, I'll make it back in time."

The bus trip gives us time to talk. He listens to me as I tell him about Dad, why he went back into the Army, and I talk about the helicopter accident that killed him.

"Everyone knew your dad was a good family man," Petey says. "What happened shocked everyone. I don't know, it's hard talking to someone when they lose one of their parents." He wrings his hands together and lowers his head. "I should have said something to you. I was so sorry to hear about the accident."

Lots of neighbors did come over and talk to Mom, but I don't remember much about those days surrounding his funeral, except that my grandparents were upset that Mom wanted Dad buried in Solano, not Texas. They compromised and had the burial in Texas and a memorial Mass in California. We can't visit Dad at the cemetery, which kind of pisses me off.

"My dad died during my sophomore year. That year, none of my friends, the ones some people called the 'scholarship kids,' came back to St. Bernie. They had to transfer to public schools when their families couldn't afford the second-year tuition. I was able to stay because my mom received insurance money but that only covered a few months of expenses."

I told Petey I was angry and hurt after my dad died, that I couldn't lift my head in class and barely made it to school. "Sometimes, I can't bear to bring up those memories. I just go on and try to be normal. That's tough to do."

"The past couple of years must've been hard on your mom. On all of you guys." Petey covers my hand with his. "Have you talked to your uncle and mom about El Lobo's?"

"Yeah. I'm quitting."

I lower my head because I can't tell him I have one final errand to run with Olga and that the cops will follow us. After today, I'm never going back to El Lobo's.

Petey's fingers entwine with mine. His grip tightens on my hand as the bus rocks side to side over the railroad tracks into our neighborhood. I glance out the bus window as we pass Loli's bakery, Hermanos Market and Mr. Singh's Mini-Mart, places where each, in their own way, helped me or my family.

My hand's trembling faster than my foot tapping on the floorboard of the bus. "We'll follow Olga as she makes her stops," Palermo had said. I take a deep breath, try to steady the quaking in my chest and go over what I'm supposed to do on the errand today.

"Are you okay?" Petey lets go of my hand.

I nod. He must think I'm embarrassed or nervous about holding his hand. What if Olga catches how nervous I am? What if I mess up or the cops aren't there when I need them?

What if they don't follow us close enough? I couldn't give them a description of the car we'd use since Olga wouldn't tell me. The only information she gave me was to meet her in front of El Lobo's after I got out of school.

Mela Street comes into sight. My heart races. I pull on the cord and wait for the bus door to open.

"Call you later," Petey says as I step out the back door of the bus and into my uncertain future.

I wave at him as the bus pulls away. It's weird how I still have all the same problems as when I left the school parking lot a half hour ago, but talking about them with Petey makes me feel better.

A few steps down the street, an old lady waits at the front door of El Lobo's.

"Finally, María," the woman says when I approach.

The old lady has Olga's voice, but she sure doesn't look like the Olga I'm used to at the café. She's wearing a loose black dress with a long dark sweater. If that isn't bad enough, she's wearing scruffy brown old-lady shoes with white socks. She's barely recognizable.

"Let's go." Olga pulls a red crocheted hat on her head and shuffles down the block.

I follow when she crosses the street and turns into an alley. "Where are we going?"

She doesn't answer and instead speeds up her steps, like we're really late. Halfway down the alley, she stops and peers through the rickety wood fence into the backyard of an over-grown lot. I can't see a house, just scrawny trees. Olga pushes away the loose slats in the gate and ducks inside. I scan the alley and see two cars pass on the nearby street. Neither of them looks like undercover cars or cops. Maybe I should wait for a minute, so the officers can see where we're going.

"Hey, María? Where are you?" Olga yells from the other side of the fence.

No one drives up the alleyway. I hope the undercover guys see me, even if I don't see them. I try to stall her. "I'm coming. I got a nail in my shoe, wait a sec."

She pokes her head through the empty space between the boards, looks up and down the alley. "*¡Muévete!*"

I slip between the opening in the fence, follow Olga through a backyard filled with weeds and a small tower of old tires. A tiny wood-framed house sits at the front of the hulking lot. This is Mousy's place.

From where I'm standing, I catch a glimpse of Olga at the back door. I can't see who stands on the other side of the dark mesh screen, but a tattooed arm reaches out and drops car keys into Olga's hand. She waves me over. The door closes by the time I reach her.

"Come on." Olga waves me to a lopsided carport.

Inside is a faded black Pontiac GTO. I glance behind me and can't see any cars driving by. No cars in front of Mousy's house either. Those cops are supposed to be watching me. For a second, I think of making a run for the fence.

"You drive." She tosses me the keys, which drop into the dirt yard.

"I, um, I don't have a license, and this might be a stick shift."

"Who cares? You can drive, can't you?"

"Not really."

Not at all is the truth. Uncle Mario tried to teach me last summer, but I jerked the car so much that he said I gave him a headache.

Olga throws her hands up in the air and says, "Give me those keys back."

"What happened to your station wagon?"

"In the shop, *metiche*."

"God, I just asked a simple question."

We get into the car. Olga grabs the steering wheel, starts the ignition and we pull out. As we drive she doesn't say a word. I try not to look out the window to check if anyone's following us. At the stop sign, I look into the side mirror to see who's behind us. Just a guy in a beat-up old truck. Looks like a gardener with his wide-brimmed hat.

Where's the dang slow train when you need it? We drive over the railroad tracks and turn into the boulevard. Olga hums to herself. We turn into a street, and she slows the car when we hit the middle of the block. I recognize the apartment complex where the red-haired ponytail guy lives.

Olga parks and looks in the rearview mirror for a long time before getting out of the car. She opens the back door and yanks out her colorful woven shopping bag.

"Come help me." She hands me a grocery sack from inside her tote and points with her chin to the apartment.

I look around. No one's nearby, except a couple of kids tossing a softball. Maybe the officers have binoculars and are somewhere across the street in one of the buildings. We walk through to the back apartment building, where Olga knocks on a door and then steps back. She scratches her head, then her arms like she has a rash.

A young guy opens the door. He's around my age and holds a lady's pocketbook in his hand, the old-fashioned black ones with a gold clasp. He gives it to Olga, takes the tote and grocery bag. That's it. We go back and climb into the car.

"Now where?" I ask.

"Find a bathroom. I got to pee." She guns the car down the street to a gas station. "Wait here."

I nod, and she disappears into the restroom with her pocketbook. I'm surprised she'll use those nasty toilets.

Five minutes go by. Maybe the undercover cops can see me better if I step out of the car. I shut the car door and step out.

When the bathroom door swings open, Olga steps out and shouts, "Hey, what're you doing?"

"I gotta go pee, too."

"*Ándale pues.*"

I go in, close the door and gag because the toilet's backed up. After a few seconds, I hurry out. We get back in the car, and Olga pulls out of the service station. The next stop is a *panadería* in midtown. We both go in without anything in our hands but come out with two large pink boxes she got both from the back room. I glance up and down the street and don't see anyone I'd think is a cop. We leave and stop at the laundromat.

"That girl over there is taking care of my stuff" she says, pointing to a girl who looks like Mousy's sister, Lena. "She folded my laundry and put it into that box. Go get it for me, María."

I don't want to go in there. Lena's well known in the neighborhood as a fighter. She sits on an orange plastic chair, popping her bubblegum, reading a *True Confessions* magazine. Her feet are on a cardboard box. Maybe she won't ask me twenty questions.

"Um, are those Olga's clothes?"

Lena moves her magazine to the side and arches her thin black eyebrows. "Who wants to know?"

Oh shit, do I tell her my name? "Olga sent me. She's out there." I point to the GTO. "Uh, um, she told me to pick up her clothes."

Lena stares at me with coal-black eyes that match her long hair. One eyebrow relaxes when she looks out of the wide window. I glance out there, too, and notice an old navy-blue pickup truck parked across the street. The gardener guy again, but no one is inside.

"Yeah?" Lena looks me up and down, then snickers. With her foot, she pushes the box toward me. "Tell Olga to pay me. Now."

I lift the box so I can get the hell out of there. Lena waits until I say, okay, then buries her face in the magazine again. I rush to the car and find Olga, without her hat on, slouched into the seat. She's all smiley with her hair down around her shoulders.

"That girl said to pay her."

Olga blows out a loud sigh. "*Pinche* Lena." She hands me a sealed envelope. "Give it to her."

I hand Lena the envelope, hoping she doesn't notice my trembling hand. She tears it open, looks inside and slides it under her sweatshirt.

With that, Lena strolls out the front door and disappears around the block.

I find Olga slumped over in the front seat. "Hey, wake up."
"Wha?"

She must be high, because something doesn't look right in her eyes. They're glassy.

"Hey, I'm done. Let's go, Olga."

"You drive. It's just right there, right there." She swings her arm forward and leans into the passenger seat.

I slip behind the Pontiac's huge steering wheel, push Olga's butt over and try to remember what Uncle Mario taught me. El Lobo's is only three lights down the street. I go real slow, jerk the car past the green lights and park across from the café.

"What's wrong with you? Wake up." I push her shoulder. "I gotta go pick up my brothers from school."

Olga's eyes flutter open, then close. I shake her by the arm. "Get up."

She acts like she doesn't hear me. Do I leave her in the car or not? There are still two pink boxes from the *panadería* in the back seat, and her purse is on the floorboard.

"Hey," I say again louder. "I need to go."

"Oh. . . kay."

But she doesn't move. The navy-blue pickup truck coasts to a stop on a side street nearby. I can't tell who the driver is because the huge hat casts a shadow over the man's face. Must be the undercover cop. I really don't want to leave Olga, but I don't want to stay here in the car either. I drop the car keys by her purse and head across the street to El Lobo's.

The front door to the restaurant is locked since today is Monday. I knock on the window. "Henry?" I yell out. "Henry, it's me, Marie."

The door opens half an inch.

"Olga must be sick or something, she's still in the car. I need to get home."

He pokes his head out and looks both ways, then across the street to where I'm pointing. "She's in that Pontiac?"

"Yeah, and she's asleep."

"Where are the boxes?"

"Inside the car with Olga. Can I go now?"

"Bring them to me, then come to the office so I can pay you."

Palermo told me Henry or Olga has to pay me before I leave. If I can get them to pay me out in the open, even better.

"I'm late and there's three boxes." I start to back away. "Can you meet me out here?"

He nods, and I run to the car, grab two boxes and go back across the street. Henry returns with the bills.

I thrust the boxes at him. "There's one more in the back seat. The keys are on the floor, near Olga's purse."

With that, Henry crosses the street to the Pontiac.

I jog to the corner of Mela Street, duck into someone's front yard and hide behind a large flower bush. I can hear Henry pounding on the passenger window, yelling at Olga to get out of the car. I peek around the bush. Henry stops hitting the window, turns and heads back toward El Lobo's.

A patrol car drives by me in Henry's direction, and another comes up from the other end of the street. One of the patrol cars blocks the sidewalk in front of the restaurant.

"Hold it. Hands up, hands up!" all three officer's yell.

None of them looks like Palermo. Henry looks around, scratching his head like he's confused. In seconds, he's spread eagle against the patrol car with one cop frisking him, a second one behind him. He yells at the cops and struggles to twist around. The third cop glances at Olga's car, then at Henry.

"Grab her," the cop yells.

The second cop dashes to the Pontiac and hauls Olga out of the car. She's out of it. Henry's face down on the asphalt scuffling with the officer while another cop handcuffs him.

My legs and hands tremble when I duck out of my hiding place and turn the corner. Safe on the next street, I book it down the block toward St. Patrick Elementary. Whew, I did it. Henry and Olga are arrested, and I'm okay. I'm never going back to that place.

I slow to a walk and round the corner toward St. Patrick. Mom said she'd pick me and the kids up at five o'clock, and it's already four-fifteen. She didn't want us at the house alone in case Weasel showed up.

A few kids shoot hoops on the basketball court closest to the parking lot of the church. The closer I get, the more yelling and cussing I hear, and it's not from the ball players. A kid bouncing the ball stops, and they all turn toward the school playground. A crowd rings the center of the blacktop. Someone's yelling. I push my way through.

Lena's screaming at Caroline, calling her a slut. Mousy and another girl stand behind Lena like bodyguards. Bobby's behind Caroline, tugging on her school jacket, his face frozen into immense eyes and open mouth.

"What the hell, Mousy?" Caroline yells back.

Lena steps forward and pushes Caroline hard. Bobby catches her before she falls to the ground.

"What the hell?!" Caroline yells when Lena pushes her again.

This time she falls on her butt. Caroline swings her open hand at Lena but misses. Mousy and the other girl rush her, hitting her in the face and shoulders. Someone screams before Caroline hits the ground.

Bobby and John jump on Mousy's back. I shove kids out of the way and get close enough to drag the other girl off Caroline. Someone grabs my hair, kicking at my back. I yank Caroline up by her jacket.

Caroline's stunned, wobbles a bit before she straightens up. Deep scratches, dotted with blood, track her cheeks. She runs toward Lena, swinging her arms like a wild woman.

The other girl swings at me like a man, but I dodge out of her way. The janitor grabs the girl with a strong jerk. Someone takes hold of my shoulder. I turn and see Sister George. A couple of older boys push Lena to the ground and hold her down.

Mousy turns and runs into the lemon orchard across the street. The bulky girl shoves the janitor away and runs too. Lena's still struggling, cussing at the boys holding her down, but they don't let her go. Caroline sits on the curb across from Lena. John and Bobby stand behind her, dusting off their pants.

A police siren approaches with a loud shrill until everyone clears the playground. An officer steps out, yelling, "Everyone back, everyone back!" to the people hovering in the street. He jogs over to Sister and the janitor, who grasp Lena by each arm. She's struggling with them, cussing up a storm.

The officer handcuffs Lena and pulls her over to his patrol car while another black-and-white rolls up.

"Let's go inside. I'll call your mother," Sister George says.

"Come on, Caroline. Boys. It's over now," I say.

They wait outside of the office on the bench. I'm too pissed off to sit. Muffled sounds like whimpers come from Caroline, who has her head down and elbows on her knees. I'm fuming mad and want to scream because this is my fault.

Mrs. Candelaria comes out to the hallway with a few tissues and gives them to Caroline. "Everything will be okay. I'll be back with some milk."

"They told me Sleepy wanted to see me," Caroline says out loud. She looks straight ahead like she's talking to the air. "Mousy said he was in the lemon orchard, and I was supposed to go there. When I said no, she tried to grab my hand. Lena grabbed my other hand."

"I yelled at them to leave her alone," Bobby says. "But they didn't."

"The chubby one said she wasn't going to have Weasel pissed at her and grabbed Caroline," John says.

Weasel. He must've gotten a message to them once he was locked up. I knew he'd do something. My feet stomp on the ground. This is my fault, for my own greediness. I knew something was wrong after the first trip with Olga. I felt it in my stomach, but I kept on going with her anyway.

"Why did they do that?" Caroline's tears streak her cheeks. "I was scared."

I can't answer her. I can't tell her the truth. She'll hate me for the rest of her life. All of them will know I screwed up. They'll never trust me anymore. Instead of the big sister, the second mom, I'll be the one who put them in danger.

Shame overwhelms me like a hot, muggy day. I press my fists against the sides of my thighs to stop my hands and legs from trembling. If I could, I'd rewind back to the time when I saw my name on the ding list, walk into St. Bernadette's office and quit school. None of this crap would've happened. Caroline wouldn't be scared and scratched up.

"Come sit with us, Jacqui," Bobby says.

John pulls me over to the bench and makes me sit down next to them. Their hands are on my hunched back. Their gentle pats release all my pent-up anxiety, and I begin to sob, my chest heaving. I try to make myself smaller and quieter, so I don't scare them, but one of them hugs me tighter.

"Your mother is on her way." Mrs. Candelaria says, as she hands each of us a carton of milk, graham crackers and more tissues. "Why don't you go clean up in the bathroom before she arrives? Okay?"

The boys thank her, and Caroline takes a tissue. The look of concern on Mrs. Candelaria's face surprises me, but I nod and follow Caroline into the girl's lavatory.

"Damn, we're a mess," she says, laughing. "Look at this rat's nest of hair."

"Yeah, we don't want to give Mom a heart attack."

I wash my face and wipe dirt off my legs. Caroline pulls her brush out from her purse and smooths down her hair and mine.

"Okay, let's go." I take a deep breath and stride out of the bathroom and into the hallway. "Mom, Uncle Mario."

"I'm here. I'm here." Mom rushes toward us with *tío* behind her.

The boys leap off the bench and run to her. She doesn't ask what happened. Instead, she brushes the hair out of my face and inspects Caroline's cheek.

"Let's go inside the office and talk to Sister George," Uncle Mario says.

We make our way into the small office. Mom sits down, and we crowd around her. Sister George tells the story of when she heard all the yelling and describes the girls. Caroline speaks up and tells her what she told me. Then John and Bobby tell her more. Mom shakes her pale face from side to side. Uncle Mario rubs his forehead.

"I can't believe it," he says.

"Jacqui came to help, too," Bobby says.

A huge lump rises in my throat.

"Why did they try to trick me?" Caroline says through her tears.

Mom wraps her arms around Caroline. Uncle Mario touches my shoulder and brings me close to his chest, patting my back.

"Everyone's safe now, Jacqui. You did the right thing," he says in my ear. "You did what you had to do. Caroline's safe, everyone's going to be okay."

CHAPTER 39

Every day, Mom has searched the newspaper for the drug bust at El Lobo's, but five days later, nothing has come out. She said she talked to Palermo, and he said the whole thing is under wraps until they have all their evidence together.

"Maybe next week," Mom says, folding the paper up. "That gives us time."

"In a way, that's better."

Now, the kids won't know about what I did until Mom and I talk to them.

At school, I told Lucy and Margot about Mrs. Washington's house burning and how the fire trucks couldn't get through to our neighborhood. I told them all about the CBC, and they were interested in attending the next meeting. But Bebe called this morning to say the special agenda meeting between Rudy and the city council was called off by the mayor.

"MEChA members spent two days telephoning people in community organizations to notify them about a CBC meeting this afternoon at St. Patrick. Be there," Bebe says.

"There's a committee meeting this afternoon," I hang up the phone and tell Mom.

"You're not going anywhere. You have chores, and it looks like it's going to rain."

"This is important. The more people who show up, the better. The city council isn't listening, so we're marching."

"I'll come," Caroline jumps up from the sofa. "Lemme grab my markers."

"Really? Cool." I grab my folder and a jacket.

"No. You're going to get sick, yelling and marching in this weather," Mom warns us.

"I'll be back later, Mom." I say as I head to the door.

"Let's find some cardboard for signs," John says to Bobby.

We disappear so fast that Mom doesn't know who to run after first. The boys and Caroline catch up with me at the top of the block. I stop in my tracks. They need to understand what they're getting into if they're going to protest.

"If you see cops coming into the crowd, you guys run home. Got it?"

Bobby rubs his cheek and glances at John. "I can run fast."

"We'll stick together," John says. "Don't worry, Jacqui."

Several people stand outside of St. Patrick Elementary. A few guys I recognize from the CBC drag chairs out to the asphalt court for the older people in the crowd. Guys and girls in their brown berets help Javier set up a microphone at the top of the basketball court.

A group of college girls stands with Bebe near the building. The tables next to them have poster boards and paints. Gloria, the girl who helped rescue Mrs. Washington, is with the college girls. On closer look, she's around Caroline's age.

"This is Gloria. She's in our tutoring group," Bebe tells us.

"What tutoring group?" Caroline asks.

"The MEChA club at the community college tutors kids from the two junior highs in the area."

"Wow, I'm going to tell Mom. She's always putting you guys down," Caroline says. "We came to help you make signs."

"Right on." Bebe ruffles John and Bobby's hair. "The Brown Berets and MEChA don't protest for the hell of it. They do this work for their community. Be proud, *primitos*."

A couple of guys in tie-dye shirts and girls in bell-bottom jeans greet us. They all give us the Chicano handshake and welcome us to the protest.

"Make the signs like these." She holds up two placards. "We Deserve Medical Access" and "Emergency Care for Everyone."

A record player blasts James Brown out to the schoolyard from the open windows of the classroom. More and more people amble over to the school.

Angie moves slowly across the schoolyard with three large pink bakery boxes. "Señora Loli sent over all this *pan dulce* for everyone." She sets them on the table and says, "I told as many teachers and students as I could. A few are coming."

"Bebe, I'm gonna run home to use the phone."

"*Prima*, I got the keys to the office." She dangles them in front of me. "Make it quick, though, because Sister George trusts me to keep everyone out of the classrooms. Put on another record while you're at it."

The first person I call is Petey because I don't have anyone else's phone number. His mom answers. It's embarrassing, but I tell her it's Jacqui Bravo from school, and she calls him to the phone.

"You just caught me. I'm going to practice," he says.

"We're having a protest march. Can you call Lucy and Margot and whoever you think will come to St. Patrick?"

"Sure. I'll head over there."

"You will? Uh, I'm really glad to hear that."

"What you said the other day made sense. If I really believe in something, I need to show it," he says.

I hang up the phone, stunned that anything I had to say could change Petey's mind. Even if he only shows up, that'll be one more person to march.

Bebe has a stack of 45s and albums next to the record player. I find Santana's *Abraxas* LP and put it on. Outside, the people making posters bob their heads, tapping their feet to the guitar music.

By the time I return to the sign-making table, there are so many people over on the school grounds. Several seats are ringed in front of the microphone. I spot Sister George and Father Armando seated in the front. I recognize a couple of teachers from St. Patrick, too. Someone placed a couple of picnic benches in front of the seats, which serve as a stage. Rudy stands on one of the benches above the crowd and taps on the microphone.

"I'm proud to see you all here. I know you want life to get better in the neighborhood," Rudy says into the mic. "This is a non-violent action to protest the lack of emergency services in this neighborhood."

He goes on to tell the crowd about the CBC's work of the last few months, the city council meetings and when they voted no to our request.

"As a result, your neighbor, Mrs. Washington and her grandson, were injured in a fire. After that incident, I had a private meeting with the mayor. He didn't change his mind. And he canceled the city council meeting where we planned to present our issues."

"That's not right," "Messed up," the crowd rumbles with these and other comments.

"Last week, one of the youngsters here said we should march right after the fire," Rudy says, "but we thought we'd give the mayor a chance. That's over, we march together today. Up this street, past the railroad tracks. . ."

"If the train isn't blocking us," someone shouts.

"If it does, we wait for it to leave. Remember what activist and poet Corky Gonzales said: 'the odds are great, but my spirit is strong.'"

Dark eyes gleam while Rudy continues to speak about community unity, solidarity and pride. The confidence he shows grows in me. The fluttery feeling in my chest is only outpaced by the pulsating in my heart. I spot Petra and run over to where she's standing, bags in her hands, and fill her in on everything that's happening.

"I march too. For my husband."

My eyes tear up. Here's this lady, old enough to be my grandmother, who just came from cleaning offices this morning, and she says she's going to protest without any hesitation.

A group of people moves to the front of the crowd where Javier and Rudy stand. Everyone shakes hands. Rudy taps on the mic again.

"Listen up," Rudy's voice booms out to the crowd. "These young men and women are relatives and friends of Mrs. Washington and her grandson, who are still in the hospital. They came from out of town."

One of the young men wearing an Afro and a black and green dashiki steps up to the microphone. "Thanks to everybody who helped our aunt. I'm her nephew from the Bay area. We called her church friends from Bethel AME across town, and they're gonna join in on the march. All of us, too. We have to advocate for change, like the Black Panthers, the Students for a Democratic Society and MEChA. This is how change happens." He raises his fist. "Power to the people."

Everyone breaks out into applause, cheers and many pump their fists in the air.

"If anyone knows who it was who helped save my auntie and little cousin, please tell us," he says.

Bebe nudges me. "Tell them what you and the others did."

"Nah, it wasn't a big deal."

"Rudy," Bebe shouts. "Jacqui was there."

I spot Gloria and motion for her to come with me. She drops her marker and walks up to the mic with me.

"Everyone, Jacqui is in high school. She read letters from the community to the city council. Come here," Rudy waves me over.

"Come with me, Gloria." I tug on her arm.

She's not shy at all, which gives me the courage to move up to the mic and tell the story of how Gloria sprang into action to open the locked door while her neighbors fought the fire with water hoses. I hand her the microphone.

"My name is Gloria Robinson. Mrs. Washington is the sweetest lady. She takes flowers to the cemetery, not only for her son who died in Vietnam but for any soldiers buried there, my uncle included," Gloria says. "Jacqui and Bebe told us about meeting with the city council, and how they didn't listen. Now Mrs. Washington and her grandson are in the hospital, and her house is wrecked. That's why I came here today. To protest to make them listen, like Jacqui said."

People clap and shout, "March! March!" while Gloria hands the mic back to Rudy.

"We have the constitutional right of free speech and assembly," he says. "Bystanders will call us names like communists, long-haired radicals, agitators, but they're trying to bait us. Don't worry about what they say. If you see the cops, keep marching. Hold your signs up high."

CHAPTER 40

We move to the sound of our chanting, louder than our feet, marching past St. Patrick's church, past the sweet aroma of Loli's *Panadería*, the Hermanos Market, Mr. Singh's Mini-Mart and over the dusty railroad tracks of the barrio.

People wave their arms at on-lookers standing on the sidewalk. "Join us," we shout and lift our homemade signs above our heads proclaiming, "We Demand Equal Treatment" and "Power to the People." Bikes, scooters and feet propel us over the iron tracks and onto the boulevard leading uptown.

Rudy and Bebe lead in the front. Bebe shouts into a megaphone, "Equal treatment," while the rest of us chant, "We matter."

The growling sound of a motorcycle goes by. Officer Palermo sits upright, his black-gloved hands on the handlebars, the white headlight in the front blinking. I glimpse his leather boots as he glides by us.

Ahead of me, people spill into the road. I glance over my shoulder and find a hundred or more kids, adults, *viejitos* joining us. Caroline's beside me, her arm linked to Bobby's, whose face is pale. I give her a quick hug, then wrap my arms around my little brother.

"Don't be afraid, Bobby. We have a voice, and now we're using it."

His shoulders wriggle, "Okay, okay. Are Mrs. Washington's cats and dog, okay? And can we go see her in the hospital?"

"I'm sure they are, but I'll ask Gloria, her neighbor, when I see her."

"We count!" Caroline shouts. "We matter!"

"Where's John?" I ask.

"Somewhere behind us."

I turn back, and push through the crowd until I find him, arm in arm with Petra and Mom.

"Mom, you showed up!" My words come out raspy.

"If this is what it takes to keep you safe, this is what I'll do."

The prickling sensation behind my eyes makes me blink. Mom doesn't believe in protests or calling herself Chicana or making a fuss, but she believes in keeping her kids out of harm's way. This is what she's always done, even though I didn't recognize it at the time.

Her way of marching was to keep us in Catholic school, where she thought we'd receive the best education. She took on second jobs so we could have water and electricity and she redesigned clothes from the thrift store so we could have something to wear. Even her prayers to saints and attending church were to help us keep faith and hope during the difficulties of our life.

I try to smile my appreciation that she's here marching with us. "Thanks for coming."

"Jacqui," someone shouts. "Hey, wait for us."

Lucy, Margot and Petey move upstream into the crowd to where I'm walking with Mom. Behind them is Ms. Fine with two other adults. She waves to me.

"We got here as fast as we could," Petey says.

Margot and Lucy stand at his side, both of them bouncing on the toes of their tennis shoes. Ms. Fine hugs me and introduces the others as teachers from Solano High.

"I'm so proud of you, all of you."

Lucy and Margot wave signs above their head. "Build a Bridge."

"Easy to say," Lucy says. "Ms. Fine's idea."

"My teacher, Ms. Fine," I tell Mom and Petra. "And these are my friends."

Petra hands her sign to Petey. "You're taller than me."

He takes it, holding it up high as we continue walking to City Hall, the air growing thicker with the heat and sweat of hundreds of people. The odor of crushed grass and oily asphalt rises as we march.

"Cops," John points to the street corner ahead.

Blue and red lights blink on two police cars parked at an angle blocking off half the street. My breath catches in my throat. Scenes of swinging batons, riot helmets and tear gas flood my memory. What if the cops try to stop us and start bashing heads in? The muscles in my legs tighten like they're going to get ready to run, but I don't. I won't.

Officers in black shirts and pants, silver badges glinting, stand outside the police car between the bank and Western Union buildings. Motorcycle cops sit on their bikes.

The crowd slows its pace. I edge over to the outside of the rows of people and stretch my neck out to see the street corner. No shining helmets, no batons out. Palermo straddles his motorcycle. For a second, I want to yell at him, ask him what he's doing here lined up with the others, but I don't. He's a cop, and I guess he's doing what he has to do, and I'm doing what I need to do.

A few police have their arms crossed, their feet in a wide stance, and others have their hands on their hips. All of them watch intently as we pass us under gray skies.

"Keep marching!" I shout.

The crowd surges forward, bends around the cop cars and moves ahead toward the civic center. A man carrying a huge camera trots alongside the crowd, stopping to take pictures. I can't tell if he's from a newspaper, but the thought of my photo in the paper and Sister Mary Graceless seeing it unnerves me.

We're a block from City Hall. More cops line the side of the civic center. And then I see them. Up on the roof. Policemen with rifles aimed at us down below. I clutch the edge of my sign, jolt to a stop, my knees locking. What if they start shooting? My head swings left and right, looking for a place to run if there's gunfire.

Another man with a camera snaps pictures. I hope they take hundreds of photos, because whatever happens here will be caught in color, forever, like the scenes at the Chicano Moratorium.

The crowd slows to a standstill, taking up the area in front of the building. A cop shouts into a bullhorn. "You cannot assemble in the street."

But there's no place to stand except the sidewalk, and the crowd is backed up all the way down and around the block. The air buzzes with sound. Our whole barrio must be marching.

Rudy jogs up the broad steps of city hall and turns to the crowd. "We have the right to peaceful assembly," he says in English and Spanish. The megaphone carries his voice into the crowd. "Move to the right and left."

Bebe and the Brown Berets direct the masses of people. Half the crowd sways to one side, and the other half slants to the left in front of the steps of the building. Most people are off the street now. Everyone strains their necks high to watch as

Bebe and Angie join Rudy at the top of the steps. They wave their signs: "Medical Access for All" and "Equal Treatment." Margot and Lucy run up the stairs, holding their signs up high: "Build a Bridge." I join them with my sign: "We Count." In a few seconds, every step has someone holding a sign.

The men with cameras crouch low and snap photos. Rudy addresses the crowd, telling them he called Mayor Harris an hour ago and told him we were coming.

"Where is he?" people shout.

"We'll wait until he shows up," Rudy says. "No matter how long it takes."

"Build a bridge, build a bridge," people start chanting.

Their voices grow louder, echoing through the crowd. With each chant, my heart beats stronger, my voice louder.

The glass doors to city hall open a few inches. A woman, the recording secretary at the city council meetings, waves Rudy closer. They talk through the crack for a few seconds. Rudy turns back and lifts his megaphone.

"The mayor will talk with a few of the committee members."

Cheers rise, fists thrust up to the sky and people hug each other at the good news. Rudy waves Bebe and Mrs. Washington's nephew into the building. Before Rudy shuts the door, he sticks his head out.

"Javier, Jacqui, keep everyone calm. Sing, talk, whatever it takes, until we get back."

He thrusts the megaphone into my hands. I turn to Javier, his eyes wide. Lucy's eyes glow.

"Play a song," she says.

Javier scoots his guitar in front of him and strums the strings. I hold the megaphone in front of him while he sings the lyrics to "*Yo Soy Chicano*."

The crowd starts cheering, yelling, "*Eso, órale*."

CHAPTER 41

We assemble at the kitchen table as Mom dishes out scrambled eggs and chorizo. The eggs look like the real thing. A plate covered in foil is on the table. A basket of oranges is on the counter.

"Mr. Reyes gave us a dozen eggs this morning," Mom says. "Friends of Mrs. Washington's brought by this coffee cake and banana bread. Petey's mother brought over the oranges."

"Wow, it's like Thanksgiving," John says, reaching for the plate of coffee cake.

"They all said Jacqui did a good thing by organizing a march to city hall."

"But I didn't start the committee, the CBC did."

"The neighborhood thinks you did it," Caroline says. "You did tell everyone to march when we were at Mrs. Washington's house."

Her comment has me smiling on the inside and outside. I messed up by getting involved with Olga, but she tricked me. I hope the march shows Mom I wanted to help the family and the community.

"Look at this." Mom holds up the newspaper.

Black and white photos of the crowd in front of city hall make the front page of Sunday's paper.

"Here you are," Mom points to a long shot photograph of several people.

I recognize Rudy right away, because the megaphone is at his mouth. Bebe, Javier and Angie are on his left. Me, Lucy and Margot are on the right. We're all holding signs over our heads, the messages are clear in the photo. In another picture of the crowd, Petey stands out because he's taller than Petra. His arms are stretched over his head, holding his sign.

"Oh, man, what if your principal checks out the paper and finds those pictures?" Caroline says.

Friday is the deadline for the alumni application. What if Sister Mary Graceless refuses to accept it or throws it in the trash before the scholarship committee can review my application? My mind runs through our code of conduct in the school handbook. I can't remember if I read anything about protesting, but if there is, I don't care. Staying at St. Bernadette doesn't matter as much to me anymore because I'll find another way to college.

"What I do outside of school shouldn't bother her. Plus, the march was important, something I believe in, and I'm not going to stay quiet about it."

Caroline's mouth drops open.

"No one's going to transfer you if I have anything to do with it," Mom says. "And tomorrow is a free day. No school."

We all jerk our heads up and glance at each other. The kids wait for me to speak. "Tomorrow's Monday. We've never had such a thing as a free day. Not that I'm complaining."

"I'm giving the family a day off from school," Mom says.

"Yay," the boy's cheer. "No school, no school."

"Go change for church."

Caroline and I run up to our bedroom. She peers into our bedroom mirror, chewing her bottom lip. "Damn, my face is jacked up. You think it'll be better on Tuesday?"

Thin welts cover one side of her face, a bluish bruise is on her other cheek.

"Sure, you will. I bet Lena and Mousy will still be messed up from the punches you landed on them."

That makes Caroline smile, which makes me feel better. "Hey," I say. "I'm sorry this happened."

"Not your fault." She sighs. "I need to pick better friends."

While Caroline's in the bathroom, Mom pops into my room and shuts the door. Here it goes. She's gonna let loose on me for lying to her for weeks about the tuition, working at El Lobo's and going on those errands with Olga. I brace myself.

"Look at this," Mom hands me the newspaper. "Look in the middle section."

It's an article about El Lobo's as a drug distribution center. And there are mug shots of Olga and Henry underneath the few paragraphs.

"Don't let the kids see this, Mom."

I want to put that mess behind me. Someday, Weasel will get out of jail and come looking for me or my family, if he puts two and two together. I told Uncle Mario I was worried about that, but he said for us not to worry about Weasel.

"That's why I decided not to send you all to school. Officer Palermo says they go to court tomorrow morning. I want to make sure they don't bail out. He'll let me know."

Mom takes the newspaper from me and points to a paragraph in the article. "Read this."

"Mrs. Bravo, age 37, attended the protest along with her four children. When asked why she marched, she replied that her husband died for his country and his children deserve equal treatment."

"Mom?" I gulp. "You really said that?"

"Not only did I say it, I believe it. And this morning, a veteran's group leader called me. He's going to help process the military benefits I filed for months ago."

She folds the paper in half and tucks it under her arm. "Petey called this morning."

My stomach jumps.

"I told him he could bring your homework to you tomorrow. If he wants to stay to help you study, that's okay."

She's actually letting a boy come over to the house?

"Wow, thanks." I hesitate, but I want to be truthful with her. "Mom, I'm paid up for March, but in April, another payment is due. After that, I have graduation gown rental and grad night in May, all of which take the money we don't have anymore."

Not to mention Lucy's party and Senior Prom, if Petey asks me. I'm really going to miss all of that, but I decided it's not worth going through the hassle of worrying about the tuition or watching Mom work herself to an early grave.

Her chest heaves. "I know times have been rough, but we're going to make it. I'm caught up with bills and rent. Hopefully, the military aid comes in, and we'll get by. I promise."

CHAPTER 42

Caroline's fourteenth birthday is in two days. I have exactly five dollars left to my name. I'm splurging on a *Tiger Beat* and a *Seventeen* magazines, plus a Yardley lip gloss, for her gifts. Mom has money to buy Caroline jeans.

"Jacqui, are you ready?" Mom asks. "Let's go."

For once, Caroline doesn't complain about watching the kids because she knows we're going out to buy her birthday presents. She asked me to make sure Mom picks out cool clothes from the thrift store, but we have a surprise I don't tell her about.

The station wagon rumbles to a start. "Sanders first, okay?" Mom says.

"That's cool that Margot offered a discount. I think she's trying to make up for the last time me and Lucy were followed at her store." I tell Mom all about it.

"If they keep that up, perhaps the CBC can meet with them?" she says.

"What? Yeah, definitely."

"Your dad always said you have to speak up. Before, I didn't really see the prejudice until I started working my office job. My female coworkers notice the difference in how we're treated. The men act like we're beneath them and make remarks."

"Like what kind of remarks?"

"One of the women said that they are sexist remarks. I think they're disgusting."

"You guys could organize."

Mom nods. "Yeah. I think we might."

We park at the department store and see Margot standing near the cash register. She waves. I introduce her to Mom, and she says, "*Encantada de conocerla*," in excellent Spanish. Mom's eyes grow larger than usual.

"Nice to meet you, too, but I do speak English," Mom says. "Your pronunciation is very good."

A red flush grows over Margot's face, and she smiles. "I've had two years of Spanish."

"Hey, where's the snobby saleslady?" I ask.

"We moved her to the stockroom. We had a couple of complaints before," Margot says, glancing down at her shoes. "Uh, we should have talked to her sooner."

"I didn't know you worked here part-time."

"This place will be mine someday. That's why I'm going to study business. There's only me and my sister in the family, and she doesn't want it."

Margot has the saleswoman put a satiny bow and silver sticker on top of the gift box that contains a pair of flare jeans and a sharp looking blouse. When Mom comes back to the counter, her eyes light up, she's so happy. Before we leave, she invites Margot to our house for dinner. Margot accepts. I don't know who to be more surprised at, Mom or Margot. We wave goodbye and leave with the prettiest gift box I've ever held.

"Let's go to lunch. The new Denny's."

"Why way over there?" I say. "Wimpy's is better."

"Officer Palermo wants to see how you're doing."

"I don't think I should see him without Rudy."

"He'll be there."

Palermo's in jeans and a T-shirt, wearing an Angels baseball cap this time. Next to him is Rudy, in a Beatles T-shirt and jeans. Palermo nods to me and smiles wide when he spots my mom behind me. She returns the smile, her eyes brightening up.

"Glad you could come," he says.

Rudy winks at me and says, "Hey, Jacqui. I'm here to make sure you're okay and answer any questions."

I understand he's really here to make sure I'm not pulled into anything else, like testifying in court.

Before we order, Palermo tells us the cops had their eye on El Lobo's ever since Barbie Ríos went missing. There was something she told one of her sisters that made the cops interested in Henry.

"We had an idea about El Lobo's but never enough evidence to do a search. We wouldn't have been able to do anything without your help. Barbie called her family after the bust and let them know she was safe."

"What about that man, Weasel?" Mom says.

"He's in jail on a parole hold. We put him there the day before we arrested Olga and Henry. I've said all I can say about the case, but he'll be gone for a very long time."

"Jerry's dad owns half of El Lobo's, and what if Jerry thinks I have something to do with his uncle's arrest?"

Palermo shrugs. "I don't think he'll pin that on you."

"How can you assure Jacqui that he won't?" Rudy says.

"We had a guy working on the inside. I can't say anymore."

Carlos. It had to be him. He always had his eye on Olga and asked so many questions. He was like my guardian angel at El Lobo's.

"But what if Jerry's father tries to bother my family?" Mom says.

"Not gonna happen. The owner will probably skate on any charges. Olga and Henry won't."

My stomach screws into knots. When is this going to be over? What if Jerry suspects me? What if it got around the neighborhood that I worked with the police?

"Mom, I'm not going to go back to St. Bernadette. The tuition is too expensive, and I'm tired of this whole thing. If I don't win the scholarship to UCLA, I just have to suck it up. I can attend another college."

Although her eyes flicker, she doesn't seem shocked or angry. She nods and reaches for my hand, pulls me toward her and hugs me. She understands what it's like to have a dream turn into a hallucination.

"But you only have two and a half months left," Mom says.

Palermo clears his throat. "I want to give you this," he says, tugging at his wallet. He draws out a folded envelope and pushes it over to me. "We had a reward out for information on Barbie Ríos. The way I figure, you helped us in finding her and locking up drug dealers. Here."

Rudy removes an envelope from his pocket. "We wanted to meet with you so I could give you this, too."

My hand is shaking so badly, I push it against my forehead. I stare at the envelopes sitting in front of my plate. "What's up with this?"

"Go on, open them," they say.

I reach inside the unsealed envelope from Palermo and pull out a long green check. "Pay to the Order of Jacqueline M. Bravo, one thousand dollars." My breath hitches in my throat. I grab the other one. To "Jacqueline Monsivais Bravo, One Thousand dollars from the Mexican American Legal Defense and Educational Fund."

"A few organizations pitched in. We give scholarships to students who achieve academic success and are committed to civil rights," Rudy says. "You're a prime candidate, and we're proud to support you if you go to a university. You'd make one heck of a lawyer."

CHAPTER 43

Two months ago, I thought I knew exactly what I wanted. Win the scholarship to UCLA, leave this town and live on my own. Those were the most important goals in my world, but the alumni application, Ms. Fine's resignation and the work of the CBC changed my ambitions.

Without the application questions, I never would have attended the Chicanos for a Better Community meetings, learned of my history or found out how to organize. The announcement for the alumni scholarship won't be made until May 1st, but I'm not sweating it anymore. I applied to three other colleges besides UCLA. I know I'll get in somewhere.

The reward money and the scholarship from MALDEF will take care of the rest of my school year, with enough left over for my first year's living expenses at whichever college I attend. Whichever one gives me the most financial aid is where I'll go, as long as the school is in California. As much as I want to leave here, I don't want to be too far away, either.

Lucy's birthday party was a bash. I wore a satiny dress that Caroline and my mom made. It came out fairly close to that magazine picture Lucy gave me months ago. They're working on the dress for prom, taking place two weeks from now. I can't believe it, but Petey asked me to prom last month.

Mr. Singh has offered me a stocking job at his store so that his father doesn't have to work full-time. I'll work there all summer while Petey works with Mr. Reyes at Los Hermanos Market.

There's so much ahead of me and Petey. Both of us decided not to worry about the draft lottery. Who knows, maybe by next February, the war will end. We're enjoying the days ahead before he finds out which college will give him an athletic scholarship, and I decide what university I'll choose.

After graduation, there are four years of college and three years of law school ahead of me, but like Ms. Fine and Mom once told me, I have to dream big and do a little bit at a time.

The protest didn't result in the immediate construction of another way in and out of our neighborhood, but the city and the CBC came up with a compromise in the meantime. A bond is needed to fund the construction of a bridge over the railroad tracks. Until it's built, a fire station has been relocated to our neighborhood from the other side of town, where it was originally planned. My brothers were super excited to hear about that plan.

The march gave the community a lot to think about, and more people joined in the meetings. CBC now stands for Citizens for a Better Community. We have several projects to tackle within our neighborhood.

Along the way to my goals, I discovered more important things: family, friends, community and the ability to make change happen, even if it's a little bit at a time. I spent so much time waiting to leave here as if it was the cause of my problems.

I believed being a success meant leaving the neighborhood. I didn't need to forget the barrio to succeed. The bridge became a way home. I'll always have my neighborhood and family in my heart wherever I go.

ACKNOWLEDGMENTS

With heartfelt thanks, I am grateful to my support system—my mother, Maria, my children, siblings, family and friends. Their steadfast encouragement has been the quiet force propelling my novels forward.

I owe a debt of gratitude to the Women Who Write (WoWW) tribe, a circle of inspiring women. Amada Irma Perez, Florencia Ramirez, Danielle P. Brown, Lori B. Anaya, Toni Guy, Melinda Palacio, Sheryl "Eddie" Leonard and Eva Gehn, your critiques, camaraderie and friendship have been my anchors in the unpredictable seas of writing.

The Macondo Writers Workshop served as the cradle for the inception of this novel. Their workshops and instructors provided the fertile soil where the seeds of this novel were planted. I'm grateful to Arte Público Press for believing in this work and providing the platform for its publication.

Acknowledgment is due to educators from the 1970s to the present who have encouraged the aspirations of students toward higher education and given them the guidance to nurture their dreams.

A salute to the civil rights activists of the 1970s, especially those within the Chicano Movement, who ardently championed education, equality and societal transformation. We, the torchbearers of words and dreams, stand on the foundation they built with unwavering resolve.

To the readers of my first novel, *The Garden of Second Chances*. You supported, reviewed and hosted book clubs and helped make my debut book successful. I'm grateful to each of you.

If you enjoyed this novel, I'd greatly appreciate a review or mention on your social media platforms, Amazon, indie bookstore sites or by telling a friend. Your feedback is important to me and helps others discover my work.

You can find me at www.alvaradofrazier.com, Instagram: m.alvaradofrazier, TikTok or my newsletter at monaalvaradofrazier.substack.com

Thank you.
Mona Alvarado Frazier
January 11, 2024